The Bandit King

Also by Lilith Saintcrow

As Lili St. Crow

The Bandit King

A Romance of Arquitaine

LILITH SAINTCROW

www.orbitbooks.net

Orbit
Hachette Book Group
237 Park Avenue
New York, NY 10017
www.orbitbooks.net

Originally published as an e-book by Orbit Books
First print on demand edition: January 2013

Orbit is an imprint of Hachette Book Group. The Orbit name and logo are trademarks of Little, Brown Book Group Limited.

ISBN: 978-0-316-25158-7

Printed in the United States of America

To Mel Sanders, because she knew I could do it

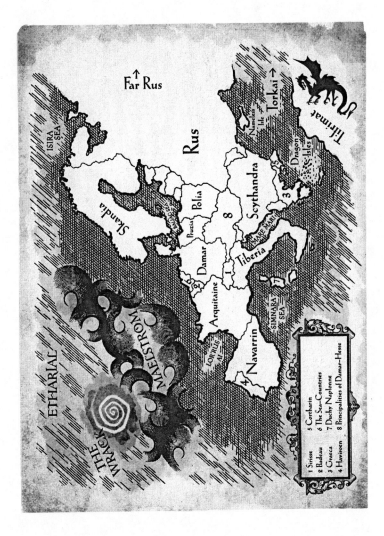

Far Rus

ISIRA SEA

Rus

Skandia

Pruzia

Polia

Damar

Arquitaine

Navarrin

Scythandra

Tiberia

MARE MARUM

SIMNARA SEA

Dragon Isles

Nameless Isle

Torkai →

Tifrimat

ETHARIAL

THE WRACK

MAELSTROM

LORAUS AI

1 Sirisse   5 Cortharin
2 Bodeau   6 The Sea-Countries
3 Craeca   7 Duchy Naplonne
4 Havroen   8 Principalities of Damar–Hesse

Contents

It is the Eighth Crossed Year of the Stag, or, more precisely, the Interregnum between the death of Henri di Tirecian-Trimestin (sixth of his name, thirty-one years reigned, and peace upon his shade) and the rise of the Bandit King (long may he reign, by the Blessed)…

Timrothe d'Orlaans, the surviving brother of King Henri, has taken to the throne. Yet the Blood Plague stalks Arquitaine, and her borders are menaced as always by the Damarsene shadow. The new King's touch does not cure the sickness, and the whispers from the far provinces are full of unrest.

A Queen, they say. A Queen who holds the Aryx, though the new King cannot have been crowned without it. Was he truly crowned? Is she merely a rumor, or is she flesh? What of the traitors who slew old King Henri VI and his daughter-Heir, the half-Damarsene Princesse who was to be our surety against Damar's aggression?

A Queen, they say. A Hedgewitch Queen, the common people add, for hedgewitchery is their purview, and such a Queen likely to gain their approval.

The Great Seal, the mark of the Blessed and their continuing favor of our land, is more active than it has been for many a year. It feeds Court sorcery, the mark of the nobles—and that noble magic has strengthened, but it behaves erratically, as a newborn colt will stagger.

What does it mean?

News is scarce, rumor rife, and winter approaches with the tramp of boots and hooves, the creaking of siege engines, and the coughing of the Blood Plague. Those who take ill rarely recover. First the fever, then the chills, then the blood from mouth and nose and every other orifice.

And then, the death.

The people cry out for their King to take the sickness from them, and there are those who whisper he cannot…

…but that a Queen will.

Chapter One

Thief, liar, assassin, whore. Tale-bearer, spy, extortionist, confidante, scandal-smoother. A knife in the dark, poison in a cup, a shield and a defense on the battlefield as well as in the glittering whirl of Court. Puppetmaster, spymaster, whoremaster, brutal thug, protocol handler, cat's-paw, pawn, troublemaker, cutthroat, fiend, pickpocket, swindler, brigand, pirate, kidnapper, alter ego, usurer, false witness…

This, then, is the Left Hand. And more.

The Hand does what must be done to cement the hold of the monarch on the realm, to protect the sovereign we swear fealty to—even at the cost of our own lives. Even at the cost of our honor.

There is only one word never applied to us, only one thing a Hand has never been.

Traitor.

To be the Left Hand is to be the most trusted of a monarch's subjects, a position of high honor, though very few will know the truth of your face or name. Most of a Hand's work is done in shadow, and well it should be. The Hand does those necessary things, by blood or by leverage, that a monarch cannot do. According to the secret Archives in the Palais d'Arquitaine, the first of us was Anton di Halier, who created the office in the time of Jeliane di Courcy-Trimestin—the Widowed Queen, history names her—who depended on Halier for her very life during the great wars, both internecine and foreign, of the Blood Years.

Those were winters when wolves both animal and Damarsene hunted in our land, and we have not forgotten. Nor have we forgotten the famine. *Thin as the Blood Years*, the proverb runs, and always accompanied by the avert-sign to ward off ill-luck.

I find it amusing the first Left Hand spent his service under a Queen. Sometimes.

We rode through the *Quartier Andienne* toward the white block of Arcenne's Temple glittering on the mountainside: three of my Guard, Adrien di Cinfiliet the bandit of the Shirlstrienne, and I.

And *her*, silent on my mother's most docile palfrey, hood drawn up over her dark head, moving like a slender, supple stem.

Hard campaigning, the cat and mouse of catching bandits or criminals, the melee of the battlefield, and the quick danger of Court-sorcery duels—all these I have endured, and I rarely think of fear. Rather, I think only on what must be done, and there is no room for terror. Yet Vianne di Rocancheil et Vintmorecy threatens to stop my idiot heart each time I glimpse her.

A long strand of dark hair had slipped from under her hood, and just the sight of that dark, curling thread made me long to tuck it away, perhaps brush her cheek while I did so. That, of course, led to the urge to take her in my arms. For so long I held myself in abeyance, barely daring even to glance at her. I was still in the habit of stealing sips of her face. That is what starvation will do, make you a thief even when you possess a table of your own.

Arran half-stepped restively, catching my tension. The King's Guard ride large grays, thoroughbred and battle-trained. Arran had been my companion for three years; he had borne both Vianne and myself away from the danger of the Citté.

She still had little idea how narrow our escape had been.

I could have lost everything. At least once a day, the cold consciousness of the almost-miss caused me to sweat. Another man might have soaked it in liquor or another form of oblivion. I kept it close. It sharpened me.

Muffled hoofbeats echoed against the shuttered houses on either side. This *Quartier* held the domiciles of merchants and some few petty officials and small nobles, pleasant villas of white stone snuggling against the lesser processional way to the Temple. Late-blooming nisteri showed blood-red in window boxes, their color faded under torch- and witchlight but still enough to warn of autumn's approach.

Then would come winter, and with it snow, rain, uncertain roads. An army would find it most difficult to assail Arcenne once the season turned.

But before? That was another tale, and one we were faced with now.

I had found her in the bailey with di Cinfiliet earlier that afternoon, pale but composed, stunned by the arrival of ill news. She had afterward told my father and her Cabinet to prepare the city for siege, as di Cinfiliet had arrived bloody and missing half his men, bearing news of impending doom. I had heard the report of her commands from my father, and right annoyed with her action instead of docility he was, too.

Chivalieri en sieurs, *I will decide tomorrow morning if I am to risk open war or if I will surrender myself to the Duc and hope for peace. I am loath to risk even a single life...Until I decide, I leave*

3

the preparations for this city's defense to you. I have another duty now. Sieur *di Cinfiliet, I will ask you for a few more moments of your time, tonight, in the Temple. Until then, rest and look to your men and horses.*

She was far too quiet. I have learned to mistrust such peace. When my *d'mselle* is so silent and grave, it means she is thinking on a riddle to which the answer is most likely dangerous. My *d'mselle* is of a quick mind, an understanding as surprising as it is deep; she had never been content to simply be an empty-headed Court dame. Studying Tiberian, hedgewitchery, playing riddle-sharp, her influence at Court was used for scholarly pursuits and decorum. Which the Princesse, truth be told, had sorely needed. Henri's daughter had been that most shallow of royal creatures, a spoiled pet I could not imagine ruling Arquitaine. The King had largely left Princesse Lisele to her own devices, perhaps thinking the Damarsene blood in the wench would make her cowlike and docile as her foreign mother. Henri had often contemplated another marriage while he was still fit enough to sire; Lisele had not known how slender her hold on the title of Heir truly was—nor had she known to be grateful to her mother's kin for their heavy insistence that she be accorded every honor.

For all that, Vianne had loved her, and still grieved her death.

Something no conspiracy had taken into account, my *d'mselle*'s fierce loyalty to those she cares for. It was a small mercy, and one with thorns, that her loyalty had included me when it mattered.

She had been so laughably oblivious to my presence at Court. And yet, her wits had kept her free enough to traverse the passages of the Palais, slip past a drunken Guard, and appear at my cell like a *demiange* of mercy, freeing me from a net my own folly had led me blindly into, seeking a prize I should not have reached for.

4

The prize that had fallen, all unknowing, into my cupped beggar's hands.

"A copper for your thinking, *m'chri*." My voice, pitched low, surprised even me.

Her shoulders stiffened. She turned, pushing her hood back a trifle. Her eyes, dark blue as the sky in the last stages of twilight, met mine, and I ached for the pain in her gaze.

"I have much to think upon." A soft noblewoman's murmur, accented sharply as the Court women spoke. "An army draws nigh, invasion threatens, and the Duc has outplayed me in this hand."

Was it bitterness in her tone? I would not blame her.

She must go north and east to the Spire di Chivalier while we hold this city against the approach of di Narborre. From there you may organize an army. My father's voice, as he stared into his winecup. *Above all, you must guard her with your life,* m'fils. *Or we shall all hang before this is finished.*

My own answer barely needed to be spoken, it was so laughably evident. What else could he expect me to say? *There is no risk I have not already taken for her,* Père. *I shall try to convince her.*

I did not think I could prevail upon her to leave Arcenne, though the need was dire. She did not wish war before winter. Yet if the Duc d'Orlaans had sent a collection of troops to lay siege to my father's city and Keep, the situation was graver than even my pessimistic *Père* had dreamed. That Timrothe d'Orlaans, the false King, was forced to allow Damarsene troops on Arquitaine soil was both balm to my soul and a deadly grievance.

How he must be cursing me, for not having the courtesy to die to ease his plans. And he must be mad, to purchase Damarsene aid within our borders. The dogs of Damar and Hesse both wish to bite at the rich softness of Arquitaine's vitals, and have since time immemorial.

Vianne's eyes were darker than usual in the uncertain torch-light. Her lovely face—winged eyebrows, the mouth most often serious and made to be kissed, the high planes of her cheekbones, the glow of her gaze—was thoughtful, a vertical line between her eyebrows. She studied me as if I were a puzzle of Tiberian verbs.

For all her loyalty and her quick wit, Vianne did not understand me at *all*. Which was a gift of the Blessed, for had she understood she may well have recoiled in disgust.

"We should remove to the Spire di Chivalier." I sought to sound thoughtful instead of persuasive. "Tis safer, and closer to the lowland provinces declared for you. I like not the thought of you trapped in Arcenne by d'Orlaans's dogs and foreign troops."

A shrug, under the cloak. "I will make no decision until the morrow." She pushed the hood back further, as if irritated at its covering. The single movement forced my idiot heart to leap.

By the Blessed, Vianne, why? "Tomorrow may be too late."

"Tis in the hands of the gods, Tristan." Quiet stubbornness lifted her chin slightly, sparked in her eyes, and fair threatened to rob me of breath. "I am *fully* acquainted with what your father thinks I should do. Do not press his suit."

I knew enough of her quicksilver moods to let the matter lie, for the moment at least. Humor, then, the kind of banter indulged in at Court. She had a reputation for a sharp, quiet wit; well-earned, too. And a gentle rebuke from her could sting more than the most furious scolding from another, because she so rarely uttered reproof. When she did, twas delivered with such earnest softness that a man might well fling himself into battle to win her approval.

So I attempted humor. "May I press my own suit, then, *d'mselle*?" I strove for a light tone and failed. It had been easier at Court, when I could not dare to speak to her, lest an enemy or even a gossip remark upon it.

Such a question usually calls forth a disbelieving half-smile that lights her eyes and turns her into one of Alisaar's maidens, those fair *demiange* who wait upon the goddess of love and comb her golden, scented hair. Now, however, she simply studied me, her hands on the reins and the line between her eyebrows deepening.

Before us rode my lieutenant Jierre, with a witchfire torch and his sword at the ready, behind us, Tinan di Rocham and Adersahl di Parmecy et Villeroche, both trustworthy men bearing torches glowing with crackling Court sorcery. With them, Adrien di Cinfiliet, the serpent in bandit's clothing. I would find an account to settle with him sooner or later, if only to make certain he did not seek to advance himself at the expense of my Queen.

"Tristan?" Such uncertainty I had not heard from her since our marriage-night. I wondered, to hear it now. "I have a question I would ask you."

I nodded, our horses matching pace if not stride. The thoroughbred's size meant I had to look down at her hood unless she tilted her head back to regard me as she did now, handling the reins with that pretty, useless Court-trained grace. And yet, on her, it looked so natural. "Ask what you will, Vianne. Whence comes this solemnity?"

She has a perfect right to be solemn; that quick understanding and loyalty will make her old before her time. Give her some small merriment, even if tis only that small laugh that sounds like weeping.

The street was dim with twilight; we would turn onto the greater processional way and start up toward the Temple soon. We had not come this way on our marriage-day, but I felt the same sharp pang I had then. A lance through the heart would hurt less.

Vianne pushed her hood fully back with a quick impatient movement. It fell free, braids in the style of di Rocancheil framing her face. I knew what it was to tangle my fingers in that hair, to taste her mouth; I knew what it was to sleep beside her. Now that I knew, was it worth the price I'd paid?

"Tell me what happened. After you left me, in the Palais. Retrace your steps."

My heart knocked against my ribs, settled back pounding. I tasted copper, but my face did not change, schooled to indifference. "I like not to think on it." *Do not ask me. It will not do you any good.*

"Please. For me." Pleading, delicate, and careful, as if she expected sharp refusal.

By the Blessed, why inquire now? But I sought to sound merely weary. "For you, then. I left you in the passage and reached the Rose Room in time to see Henri dying. His pettite-cakes had been poisoned. As his soul left, the Duc's guard burst into the room. I killed six of them before I was taken to that charming cell, where they beat me until the Duc paid me the honor of a visit. Then, I was left to contemplate my eventual beheading at the Bastillion until I heard your sweet voice through the bars." *There, does that satisfy you?* I heard my own harshness, bitter as the lie.

The sharpest sword, di Halier once wrote after his Queen took him to task over some trifle, *is directed at one's own soul. Yet what is murder, or worse, if it keeps Arquitaine safe?*

And yet. So easily, she reminded me of the man I should have been, instead of the one I was. When di Halier spoke of "Arquitaine," twas easy to see he sometimes merely meant the woman who embodied, for him, the country's rule.

Had Jeliane embodied far more to him, as my own Queen did to me?

Vianne examined my face as if I were a scroll or a dispatch. My heart mimicked a cobblestone caught in my windpipe. *Do not ask more. Let the matter remain there.*

"Nothing else?" Her eyes glittered, and she pulled her hood up with an expert movement of her fingers to settle the material just so over her beautiful bowed head. "Tis important, Tristan."

You have no idea how important it is. "Why? Is there a question of my movements? You are perhaps believing the Duc when he accuses me of regicide?" It fair threatened to choke me. *The truth will do so, when one least expects it. Di Halier never warned of that.*

She hesitated. "I simply…There is so much I do not understand of this, and I would understand all."

What more do you need to understand, m'chri? The King is dead, you are the Queen, I am the traitor who will keep you safe. If I must lie, and kill, and do the worst a man can do, I will.

I already have.

She said nothing else, her head bowed and her shoulders moving slightly.

We turned onto the processional way, hooves clopping on paving stones. Arcenne rose around us, the white stone quarried from the mountains the province is famous for glowing eggshell-delicate. There is very little as beautiful as my native city at dusk, as she gathers the last rays of the Sun's beneficence. Even the sinks and fleshpots of the *Quartier Gieron* are well-scrubbed, and the spires of the Keep above rival the peaks themselves for grace. Arcenne is cleaner than the Citté, more tantalizing than Orlaans, and smells far better than, say, Marrseize. In spring, the orchards are a froth of paleness on her white shoulders, and she is a lady of freshness and grace.

Another held my heart now, but a man never forgets his first. No matter how far he rides, his birthplace will always be at his shoulder.

"Vianne?" Her name, uttered so many times in the privacy of my room or the secret corridors of my brain. For so long I had kept it a secret pleasure, a fruit to be indulged in late at night.

She did not answer, but a slight movement told me she had tilted her head, the better to catch my words.

"I would have you know only this." I paused as Arran's ears flicked, noting some sound I could not. When they returned to pointing forward, I continued. "All I have done is for your safety. If you should find yourself in doubt—*any* doubt, for any reason—simply remember that."

The declaration earned me a startled glance. More tears, glimmering on her cheeks? In the uncertain light I could not be sure. "You were the King's Left Hand." Softly.

As if she thought I needed reminding.

"Now I am yours." *Even before Henri died choking on his own blood, I was yours.*

I was left with a suspicion of my own to keep me company on the remainder of our short journey. There was no reason for her to ask unless she thought something amiss. Which was not comforting. Nor was the thought that followed in its wake.

I did what I wished to do. It was worth the price.

Chapter Two

The Temple's courtyard echoed with hoof strikes and ran with ruddy lamplight; I caught Vianne's waist and lifted her down. Her hood fell back, revealing a glory of intricate braids held together with blue ribbon, and I took the chance to brush at a stray strand, tucking it behind her ear. She wore a pair of emerald ear-drops, longer threads of gem-weighted silver swinging heavy against her cheeks, that I did not recognize. They were not my mother's. *Mère* had all but fostered her, providing Vianne with dresses, hair-ribbons, jewelry—all the things a man would never think on, as well as sorely-needed gentle companionship. Vianne seemed easier with my mother than with most others, a smile blooming on her lately-solemn face whenever they met.

I took advantage of the momentary jostling to press a kiss to her forehead, a familiar rush of heat spilling through me as her skirts touched my breeches. I turned slightly, habitually, to keep my rapier-hilt free. She smelled of soap and heavy velvet, of sunlight and of *woman*, a peculiar aroma hers alone. At Court her hair-ribbons were imbued with bergaime and spice; it had taken a few gold coins to persuade the Court perfumier to blend me a tiny crystal bottle of the same mix commissioned by the Duchesse di Rocancheil. The vial had been lost in my room at the Guard barracks, along with all else—except the papers I had taken the precaution of burning the night before conspiracy broke loose.

I could not bring myself to destroy the tiny fluted crystal. The Princesse and her ladies favored lighter floral scents, but Vianne's aura of green hedgewitchery would have overpowered those blends. The two times I drank myself into a stupor, with the door securely locked and the window barricaded as well, I had held the crystal to my face and inhaled its bloom between draughts of *acquavit*.

If a man seeks to drink enough to blind his conscience, tis *acquavit* or nothing.

She could rest her head below my shoulder if she wished. Yet she did not, gazing past me to the milling horses and the Temple novitiates even now taking Jierre's mount. My lieutenant tucked his thumbs in his belt as I handed Arran's reins to a gray-robed novice, accepting the boy's bow with a slight nod. I had received my Coming-of-Age blessing in this Temple before going to Court, my birth had been registered here, and here I had held Vianne's hands in mine and pronounced my marriage vows.

Here, also, I had seen the statue of Jiserah the Gentle blaze with silver light, and my Queen's face also ablaze as she stared unblinking into that radiance, the Aryx's three metal serpents writhing madly on their slim silver chain against her breastbone. I had thought the gods were about to strike me down for my effrontery, kneeling at her side. Even now, I could not shake the feeling of being watched within the Temple's environs by eyes less human than a serpent's.

The gods take an interest in Arquitaine, of course. But theirs are not the petty concerns of smaller fleshly beings. They had let the Aryx—the Great Seal that even now hung at my *d'mselle*'s breast—sleep since the death of King Fairlaine and his beloved Queen, and hard-pressed every monarch and Left Hand since had been to hide that slumber.

Now the Aryx was awake, and the gods had taken an interest again. I will admit I was made uncomfortable by the thought, and by another: that they would not have made me what I was and given me Vianne if they did not expect I would set myself against even their fury to see her safe.

She slipped past, her cloak brushing me, and I had a moment to admire her grace as she stopped four paces away to tip her head back and look to the sky. A quick glance assured me there were naught but stars overhead, and a slender quarter-moon just beginning its long nightly walk. I moved to stand at her shoulder, my gaze meeting Jierre's as he exchanged a few quiet words with Adersahl and tilted his head in an unspoken question.

I replied with a fractional shake, *no*. And subtly, Jierre moved aside to let Adrien di Cinfiliet pass, the bandage glare-white against the bandit's head. He had finally changed out of his bloody, torn clothes, and he had eyes for none of us except Vianne. Even now, his storm-gray gaze rested on her as she drew in a deep breath, steeling herself. She lowered her chin, her eyes closed and her shoulders coming up under a heavy invisible weight.

It was my task to make that encumbrance lighter, or at least share its burden. I closed my hand over her shoulder as a priestess appeared in the Temple door at the north side of the courtyard. Twisted *jabak* trees framed the rectangle cut from white stone, and the white-and-green-robed woman of Jiserah's elect put up a hand to smooth her hair as she paused, looking out over this small courtyard used only by visiting nobility who did not wish to traverse the high stone steps of the front entrance. Twas Danae, the priestess who had heard our wedding vows—the *second* time, that is.

Slight blond Tinan di Rocham halted before Vianne. *"D'mselle?"* His dark gaze spoke too, worshipping her; the boy's open adoration earned him much jesting in the Guard barracks. For all that, the teasing was good-natured and gentle instead of ribald. We did not grudge him his blushes, though I think some of them envied his youth and the grace with which she accepted his sallies.

"Tinan. How is your wound, *chivalier*?" She favored the boy, taking comfort in his easy humor. For that, I allowed him familiarity.

"Well enough, *d'mselle*. Is there aught you require?" He cast a nervous glance at me; Vianne seemed not to notice.

"I am as any other supplicant here." Now she sounded sad, as the priestess approached, sandals *shush*ing on paving-stones. Jierre and Adersahl were deep in conference, Adersahl stroking the rebirth of his fine mustache as he glanced warily at di Cinfliet, whose own inspection of the courtyard paralleled mine. The bandit had not survived in the depths of the Shirlstrienne without wariness, and I had a healthy respect for that caution. It might make him difficult to…surprise.

But not impossible, should the situation require it.

The priestess reached us, her fair round face crinkling with merry lines around her eyes and mouth. "Your Majesty." A bow, a trifle lower than it should have been, and held a trifle longer. "You honor us."

Vianne's chin lifted fractionally, a queenly gesture. "I come not as royalty but as a pilgrim, Danae da'Jiserah," she said formally. Adrien di Cinfliet watched with narrowed eyes, stroking his swordhilt. My hand rested upon my own rapier. There has been royalty enough slain in Temples, whether the gods willed it or no. "Tis guidance I would ask. Is the penitent's cell ready?"

"Ready and waiting." The priestess straightened, her dark gaze touching me. We are a brunet people, the Arquitaine—not ill-favored as the Damarsene, though. Arquitaine breeds beauty, just as Pruzia breeds harshness and Rus cold, exotic cruelty. "*D'mselle,* your instructions—"

Vianne held up a hand; Danae's tongue halted. "Tinan, Jierre, accompany Tristan in seeing to the safety of the Temple. Adrien, I would speak to you privately; Adersahl shall attend me while I do so."

Adersahl saluted, as did Tinan. I felt the first faint stirrings of trouble. *I would not leave your side, even here. But neatly done, I cannot argue.* Ordering Adersahl to watch the door while she conferred with Adrien was a touch worthy of the lady who had caught many intrigues in the female world of Court, where the women played for privilege and position—and sometimes, the eye of a nobleman.

While Vianne di Rocancheil's sharp gaze was at Court, none dared offer her Princesse overt insult. Still, I had smoothed the way where I could, marveling at her loyalty to Henri's spoiled little half-Damarsene farrat of a daughter.

"If it please you," I said. "Though I like not leaving your side, *m'chri.*"

"It shall not be for long." She did not meet my gaze, and my unease sharpened. "It would please me to know I may sleep safely tonight."

If I am at your side, you will ever sleep safely. But she wished the penitent's cell, which meant she planned on a lonely slumber. "As you will it."

Danae visibly swallowed a question. I wondered what secrets my face was telling, smoothed my features. *As ever, Vianne. As you will it.*

"My thanks, *chivalier*." A small smile, as if she had to force her mouth to it, and she was gone, ushered away by the fluttering priestess.

I dreaded even her innocent questions; a guilty conscience leaps even at a pinprick. I nodded at Jierre, the command answered almost as soon as it was given, and he turned on his heel, a slight gesture bringing Tinan to his side. They would sweep the Temple and make a report later.

Adrien di Cinfiliet's gray gaze passed over me. If it were the first salute of a duel, I do not think I was the worse for it. He followed Adersahl. I watched as Vianne's slim shape silhouetted itself in the low door, her step light and graceful.

Before she entered the house of the gods, she did glance over her shoulder. Yet if her face held any expression other than resignation, I could not see it.

I was left to myself in the empty courtyard, but not for long. For the Left Hand, there is always a way, if there is a will.

And I had a will to hear what Adrien di Cinfiliet would tell my Queen.

Chapter Three

The penitent's cell is usually a bare stone room with a cot, a water-closet, and a gem-jeweled statue of Kimyan the Huntress. She is the Blessed who rules the Moon, and thus rules dreaming sleep. Brought from the Old Countries with the Angoulême, the first conqueror of Arquitaine, she was the goddess adopted most thoroughly in her new land. To receive instruction from her, the penitent swallows a draught meant to guarantee dreaming, and when morn comes they have their answer, for good or for ill.

What few know is that one of Kimyan's elect often secretes him or herself in a small closet, whose cunningly constructed wall is riddled with small eye-holes, and from whence could be heard the speech of the dreamer who had asked to receive guidance from the gods who steered the world's course. The closets are not visible from inside the cell, and few outside the priests and priestesses know of them.

The Hand is one of those few.

I took care to ease the door shut, soundless. Small swords of light crossed my path as I lowered myself silently to the padded bench, keeping my rapier well out of the way.

Danae was speaking. "—and there is a bell-rope, should you need immediate assistance. Is there aught I can bring you, before…?"

"Some light sup, for my *chivalieri*." Vianne, with the light, laughing accent of Court. "My thanks, Danae."

"I shall return in an hour's time to prepare you. An it please you, I take my leave." The priestess slid away on her sandaled feet. She would not interfere, should I wish to listen to my *d'mselle's* dreaming; my father's support of the Temple bought that much.

Even the elect of the gods are corruptible. Or, if not precisely corruptible, then merely amenable to the clink of hard coin accompanying a nobleman's polite request.

The door closed, and I heard velvet move. Her cloak, perhaps, falling to the floor. No, she was not so careless; she would drape it over the bed. A long, weary sigh.

"D'mselle?" Adersahl, uncertain. If there were a Guard most likely to aid her without question, it was he. "Shall I wait outside?"

"No, Adersahl. I would have you hear this. Di Cinfiliet? We have little time. Speak, I beg you. What proof do you bear?"

Of what? But my heart knew before the rest of me, and grew cold as the wastes of Far Rus.

"Proof not meant for gentle ears, *d'mselle*." Di Cinfiliet's boots clicked as he made a circuit of the room. A shadow slid across the thin spears of light bisecting the closet. I breathed quietly, falling into the peculiar state common to assassins and spies: listening so intensely every sound is magnified, every hair on the body erect and quivering to catch all nuance. "I beg your pardon for what I am about to tell you."

"I hardly think I shall shatter at shocking news, *chivalier*." Velvet moving again. Where was she? Abruptly, her tone changed. "Besides, you have already given me the worst news possible. I would hear the rest."

What has he said to her? And when? Silence. I barely breathed.

When she spoke again, it was very softly, and every nerve in my body leapt into singing alertness. "Adersahl bears witness of my recognition of you, *m'cousin*, and of your mother, who shall receive full honors in this very Temple." The last word broke, and the temptation to put my eye to a spyhole was nigh overwhelming. I denied it. "It grieves me that she was taken by di Narborre. She was the best hedgewitch I have ever known, and I mourn that I could not alter her fate. You are my cousin, and my Heir, should the worst befall me."

My brilliant darling. Of course she had guessed his parentage—or had the bandit told her outright? I would not put it past him.

Di Cinfiliet finally spoke, hoarsely. "It…it means much to me that you would acknowledge her."

A small sound. Was she weeping? When she spoke again it was without her usual lightness; twas the tone of brittle, impossible-to-refuse royalty she had so lately acquired. "Adersahl, please, come farther in so we may speak softly. Begin your tale, *sieur* di Cinfiliet, an it please you. We have little time."

Di Cinfiliet needed no prompting. "We came upon the Damarsene force bound for Arcenne from their rear, as we had turned aside to make a foray into the lands patrolled by the Tierrce-di-Valdale garrison. Consequently, we saw the dust they raised, and went cautiously. Then we happened upon a rare piece of luck: dispatches."

"A King's Messenger." The brushing of a woman's skirts. *She is pacing; I can hear her feet.* My back was alive with chill gooseflesh.

What mischief was he seeking to wreak upon her now? "Dead now, I presume."

"Of course." There was no pretense. "Most of the dispatches were useless, but there was this." Sound of paper rustling. I closed my eyes in the unforgiving dimness. "Twas in a sealed pouch for di Narborre's hand only. There are other papers of interest, which I have left at the Keep. But this, *m'cousine* Riddlesharp, you should see."

Heavy paper, by the sound of it. Unfolded and held. Silence ticked by; I could hear the flames of the lamps inside the penitent's cell burning, a dry hissing.

A squeak. She had sunk down upon the bed, perhaps.

"D'mselle?" Adersahl, alarmed.

"Chivalier." A colorless whisper of a word. Had she also gone pale? "Do you know what this is?"

"No, *d'mselle*." For the first time in a long while, I heard fear in Adersahl di Parmecy's tone.

"Tis a statement wherefore a man swears his loyalty to a certain cause. It is signed, witnessed by two others, and has a mark of blood upon it." Her throat must be half closed with tears to sound so. "The cause the man swears himself to is the murder of Henri di Tirecian-Trimestin, my half-uncle. The murdered King of Arquitaine." She took a deep breath. "Judge if this is not a familiar hand, though the paper reeks of some oddness, being far too cheap for such an important document."

The faint sound of paper changing hands. My heart lodged in my throat again, and I was cold. So cold.

"Dear gods." He was loyal to the last, Adersahl. "No, this cannot...this *cannot* be, Vianne. It *cannot*. He would not kill the King. He would *not*."

"D'Orlaans accused Tristan of regicide, yet untraditionally ordered his tongue torn out before his beheading in the Bastillion. There was *something* he did not wish the Captain of King Henri's Guard to say." Pitiless, she continued, each word a knife to the heart. "I was with Tristan that day, Adersahl, and something has oft crossed my mind since this afternoon. Tristan swears the King died of poison in pettite-cakes. I was there; I *saw* those sweets; I am not so bad a hedgewitch I would not have smelled a poison in them virulent enough to kill the King in scarce a quarter-candlemark. Once the alarums were rung to signal the start of the conspiracy, Tristan left my side. Some short time later I found my Princesse already dying and her ladies slain—work that would have taken some time. There is one other thing we must consider, Adersahl. Tristan was waiting in the passage I usually took from the kitchens to my quarters. So was the Minister Primus. Look at the second sheet of paper."

"I…" Adersahl was having difficulty speaking.

"'Tis a similar sheet, but on *far* better paper, detailing the Minister Primus's loyalty to the cause of regicide, and also to the removal of an inconvenient Captain of the Guard. Perhaps d'Orlaans thinks to convince me if I am given this…proof, in which case di Cinfiliet serves his purpose all-unwitting. Or di Narborre was to use this in some other fashion. The blood upon it would certainly make sorcery easier, would it not? Which might solve the riddle of how d'Orlaans and his dragoons tracked us so easily." Velvet rustled again, and I heard her footsteps, quick and light as she paced. Di Cinfiliet was silent. "Yet the paper is not of a fineness, many of the events I witnessed refuse to grant me some understanding of their true import, and no Court sorcerer of d'Orlaans's power and ability would let an opponent's willingly-shed blood leave his grasp. The question I am to ask myself becomes, did Tristan d'Arcenne, my Consort, conspire to kill King Henri? I cannot think d'Orlaans would have had him sign a sheet of common rag. If my Consort is a traitor, or merely gave a dance to the idea of treachery, then afterward, when he was betrayed so harshly, did he think to revenge himself on his fellow conspirators by setting forth a hedgewitch provincial as Queen—a *d'mselle* who would, perhaps, be so blinded by a crumb of affection she would not question him? It is no secret I have not had many suitors."

Rage tasted copper-bitter, the pulse in my throat and wrists pounding like maying-drums. I stayed perfectly still, red rising behind my eyes, my heart tearing itself in half. Hearing her so calmly, so *beautifully* string out a necklace of damning logic defied my self-control. It was the very softness, the sharply-accented Arquitaine singing in her beautiful mouth, that made the words cut so much more harshly.

Of course she doubted me. She would do well to listen to her instincts. And yet, a crumb of affection. Did she count me so small?

"Now I must beg you, Adersahl di Parmecy et Villeroche, Queen's Guard and my friend. Give me counsel, for I know neither which quarter to face nor quite what to believe. I wish you to tell me truly what you think of this." *Now* her voice broke, and she sounded perilously close to tears.

"*D'mselle—*" Di Cinfiliet. I wanted—oh, how I *longed*—to stride into the room, and…do what? What could I do?

At that moment, I did not know. And so I remained still and quiet, the trembling in me unmanly save for its source of pure white-hot rage.

"One moment, *sieur*, an it please you." A muffled sound—she was weeping. My Vianne, weeping.

Adersahl did not speak for a long moment. Vianne's weeping

was soft; she sought to conceal it. Tears that should have fallen on my shoulder were now uselessly being spent in the presence of fools. And here, I was the larger fool, for I could not even coldly plan how to salvage somewhat of this.

Di Parmecy finally finished weighing his response. "There is one question I would ask, *d'mselle*."

"Ask." She sounded marginally calmer.

"I have lived with Tristan d'Arcenne, I have fought at his side and under his command, I have seen him in nigh every situation that may befall a man. I tell you, I am not so blind as not to notice a murderous intent on his part. We must set our minds to *why* d'Orlaans would send this foulness to his own Captain at this particular time. *M'dama* Queen, I would stake my life on Tristan's loyalty, and this as some forged gambit of d'Orlaans."

Relief burst inside my chest, dueling with the cold fury. I let out a soft, noiseless breath. Perhaps I had a chance to explain, or even to keep the secret. But how?

More soft sounds, Vianne weeping without restraint. She would even do *that* prettily, and I could have held her during the storm.

"*D'mselle.*" Di Cinfiliet, now. His tone had softened, as if he took pity on her. Or as if he understood now was the time for gentleness if he sought to set her course. "'Tis a pretty tale, and it looks damning in many ways. But I've seen tales spun before, living at the dagger's edge in the Shirlstrienne, hunted like a dog by di Narborre's patrols. Now that I have had lee to think, I would say to let the man defend himself, for 'tis obvious he prizes you, and not just as a game piece or a broodmare. And yet…"

"And yet." More velvet rustling; she would be pacing furiously now, probably dashing at her cheeks as if the tears offended her. "*There was no poison*, and the murders of my Princesse and her

23

ladies took precious time. This bait must be salted with some truth, or it would not be even a half-effective lure for either Tristan *or* me. If I cannot trust my Consort, I cannot trust his father either. This fragile alliance will shatter, and the towns and provinces that have declared for me will be left without protection. Already civil war looks inevitable—or worse, a civil war with the Damarsene playing blind-hant in *quarto* to d'Orlaans. Blood will be shed, d'Arquitaine blood, and all those who depend on me for their lives—including you both—will meet worse fates than a Princesse's lady-in-waiting can easily imagine. It becomes a question of whether I trust a possible traitor and pray he will not turn on *me* when the time comes, or plunge my land into chaos. A pretty choice." The papers crinkled again. "Take these. Leave them where we spoke of, for I shall need them. Leave me the others as well, an it please you."

My eyes squeezed shut. Tears trickled out between my eyelids, traced hot down my cheeks. *Whether I trust a possible traitor and pray he will not turn on* me *when the time comes.*

I should have told her. But I could not have afforded more of her "gentle feelings," more of her naiveté. She had been all but dead of shock and grief, bearing each fresh indignity with numb, silent bravery heartbreaking to see in so fragile a body.

You did not tell her, for you feared the breaking of the image you saw in her eyes whenever she gazed at you. Be honest with yourself, at least, Left Hand. Else you will not lie so effectively to others.

"D'mselle…I truly do not think Tristan would…" Adersahl, almost knocked speechless. Of course, the sight of her weeping would astonish him.

"My thanks, Adersahl. I charge you with silence. Do not breathe a word of this. May I trust you?"

"I swore my service, *d'mselle.* I am a Queen's Guard." He was no longer young. I could almost see the stiff little bow he would perform.

"Go, and see to your sup, *chivalier*. It seems I am always leaning upon you."

"I am here to be leaned upon, Your Majesty. Your leave?"

"Of course."

He would bend over her hand—I heard the creak of leather, and his footsteps. The door, opening and closing. I scrubbed hot water from my cheeks with the bladed edges of my palms, taking care to do so silently. I kept my hand well away from my rapier-hilt.

I did not trust myself.

"So." Vianne, breaking the pregnant pause, her tone husky with weeping. "It would seem I owe you much, *m'cousin*."

"I count it an honor, *m'd'mselle* Riddlesharp." A flash of light humor, jarring after the tension. "I suspect you have aught else to discuss with me."

"It may not be…safe for you, here, if Tris suspects your parentage and di Narborre approaches. I would prefer to keep you near, yet I dare not." Her tone softened. "If I may…"

"*D'mselle*." The bandit sounded serious, now. "I may not have had the pretty training in bows and falconry, but I am still a nobleman. Blood must tell for something, must it not?" A faint whisper of steel leaving the sheath brought me to my feet, my hand suddenly clenched bruising-tight around my rapier-hilt. "I owe you service, *d'mselle*. Accept my oath."

Gods above. The filthy little tale-telling bastard. Calm restored itself, but only by an effort that left me sweating and shaking. I was again not merely a man, but a Left Hand.

It was a relief—at least it stopped the stupid, worthless tears.

"Accepted, *m'cousin*. Please, stand." Now twas the practical

Vianne, the one so sharp and rapier-quick it was a glad wonder she was rarely unsheathed. "Here is a purse, tis all I could safely beg and borrow. Take your men and flee over the border into Navarrin; there you will be safely out of d'Orlaans's reach. Here also is a formal introduction to the King of Navarrin; you will find some succor there. Above all, *keep yourself safe*. Take this as well. These are all I have left of my…of my other life, all I truly own. If I send a messenger for your return, I will send its mate as a token. Will you do this for me?"

A slight creaking movement. "And do you flee to Navarrin I will already be at the Court, to smooth *your* way. Well-played, lady Riddlesharp."

I could almost hear the slight, impatient toss of her head. Hers *was* a well-played hand, and di Cinfiliet for all his cunning was not her match. "I am not so concerned about my own health as yours. Whatever Tristan has done or not done, I do not think you are safe here. Not if he suspects what Risaine never bothered to hide overmuch from me." A slight, bitter laugh. "I find myself unable to trust the things I was most assured of."

"Tis life, *d'mselle*. Are you certain? I like not the idea of leaving you here. Come with us. My men are not so polished, perhaps, but they are loyal, and each one will fight to his last breath."

"*You* will need all their protection. Please, *sieur*. Keep yourself safe. Much now depends on you."

"Come with us." Still he persisted, his tone becoming far more serious than it should have been. "If it is right for me to flee, it cannot be right to leave you here."

"The Aryx chose me." The sadness was almost too much to bear. "Even now, you see, it will not move from my flesh. I am tied to this fate until I can find a way to slip its chain. If the gods speak to me tonight, I may even find a way to salvage something of my country." There was a soft sound, and when she spoke next her voice was muffled. "Go. Please. I feel the need to succumb afresh to a most ladylike crying-fit, and I would not have you watch. It disarranges me, you see."

"*D'mselle—*" He caught himself. "Vianne. My fair *cousine*. I would not leave you here, as a kit among wolves."

Worry not, di Cinfiliet. This wolf will not let his little kit receive the slightest harm, and his teeth are sharper than yours.

"Fear not. This kit will soon grow her teeth. Go, Adrien. Please." Velvet moved. Had she embraced him? It hurt to think of it, and hurt equally to think of her planning so quickly and thoroughly. How could she think herself in danger from *my* quarter?

Why had I said *poison*? A fool's move. I was accustomed to lying with far more aplomb. Now I was trapped by the story.

"Should you need me, send for me."

"Do *not* return unless I send the other half as a token. Go. Must I beg you?"

"No. *D'mselle?*"

"Oh, for the sake of the Blessed, *what?*" Irritation, wedded to sorrow and flashing witchlight-quick. I knew that tone of hers; my heart leapt to hear it. I wanted to take her in my arms, my bones aching with the need.

I could almost see the fey smile he practiced upon her. "My thanks." The sound of the door opening, his boots retreating.

I could not help myself. I dropped my hand from my rapier-hilt and edged closer to the wall, seeking one of the small holes glowing with lamplight. I peered through, almost holding my breath.

The room was not so severe as I had imagined. There was a bed, two chairs by the fireplace, a washstand in the corner, and a door slightly ajar to the watercloset. I could see a glitter that was the jeweled statue of the Huntress, her bow lowered. The lamps hissed, and it would be cold tonight; had they not thought to lay a fire for my Vianne?

She stood straight and slim, facing the bed. As I watched, she turned in a full circle, looking about the room, her skirts making a low sweet noise. I could not see her face; the angle was wrong.

"Tristan," she whispered, and I started guiltily, though I was well hidden. There was no way for her to know I watched. "What I would not give to be assured of..."

Twas not the words themselves. It was the tone, numb agony in her soft, cultured voice. Of all the people who should sound so hopeless, she was the last.

It fair threatened to tear my heart from my chest. *All I have done has been for you.* I longed to tell her so, put my mouth to the hole I watched through and whisper the words. Would she think it the gods speaking to her?

She took two halting steps toward the door; that removed her from my sight. Did she think to flee? No, for she immediately turned back and walked with quick, unsteady steps to the bed, flung herself down. She had not lied; she sobbed fit to break both her heart and mine.

Oh, Vianne. I should have been at her side, to hold her while she wept. I should have told her. I should have made her somehow understand.

At least you are forewarned. If I hewed to the tale of my innocence, would it satisfy? Why, in the name of the Blessed, had I told her Henri was *poisoned*? I had not been thinking clearly.

Now I was, and I had to move with some speed if I were to save myself.

Chapter Four

"Captain?" Jierre's lean, dark face greeted me as I stepped into the small room given over to our use, a pilgrim's cell in the heart of the Temple. Adrien was apparently deep in prayer before a statue of Danshar the Warrior in the central nave; Tinan stood guard at Vianne's door and it irked me to leave him there.

No matter. I would return soon enough.

They had dined, di Cinfiliet and the Guard; I did not. Time enough for that later. Now, as Danae the priestess prepared our *d'mselle* for her dreaming in the house of the Blessed, my expression brought Jierre to his feet. The remains of their dinner lay on the table, and there were four cots.

Adersahl did not look up. He sank into a chair by the fireplace, staring into the flames. His brow was thoughtful, but not troubled.

I led Jierre into the hall. "This goes to the Keep." I thrust the hastily penned letter into his hands. "Do what is necessary to delay di Cinfiliet's departure until my father reads it."

My lieutenant nodded. No shadow of doubt marred his clear, dark eyes; none ever had. "And should our bandit take umbrage…?"

"I trust your judgment."

He flashed me a wry smile. "A relief, I was beginning to think I had none left."

"Precious little, Jierre. After all, you are still following me." *Through even the gates of the underworld, you said once. You were drunk, and you thought I was, too.*

"That, my Captain, is a matter of taste. Not judgment. Look after the *d'mselle*."

"As always." *If only you knew how I look after her.* "Make haste."

He left with a spring in his step, a spare, sinewy man whose quick eyes and fine mind were worth far more than a King's Guard could ever be paid. He had held the last survivors of the Guard on the slopes of Mont di Cienne, waiting with unshaken faith for me to emerge from the bowels of the donjons. Which I had…but only because Vianne had trusted me.

Because I could not stand the thought of your beheading, Captain. Her chin lifting as she took me to task, a memory I did not have time to savor.

I stepped through the door again, bracing myself. Adersahl remained in the chair, staring into the fire. He did not stroke his mustache, and that spelled certain trouble.

I affected nonchalance, my thumbs in my belt. "*Sieur* di Parmecy et Villeroche."

He waved a languid hand. "Captain. Standing on ceremony?"

"No more than usual." *You defended me. Loyal as she is.* "How is she, Adersahl?"

He stared into the flames as if they held the Unanswerable Riddle's full solution. "I would be surprised if you did not know, Captain." It hurt, to hear him accord me the title with such brittle formality.

Are you feinting to draw me out? "I know far more than anyone credits, and far less than I like. For example, I think I know who is loyal to me. Strange, how rare such a quality is."

"Rare, yes. Very important in a King's Guard."

Ah. "Even more important in a Queen's."

He nodded. "Even so." He paused, as if he would speak. Settled for repeating himself. "Even so."

I drew my breath in softly; my hand curled around my rapier-hilt. All the Guard are trained in swordplay as well as Court sorcery; I had insisted upon as much when I took the reins of command. It had done little good for those taken by treachery. But those who had survived were the best of comrades—and the worst of enemies.

Let us see how well I cast my dice. I found my throat full of something, could not speak for a moment. My gaze dropped to his boot-toes.

My voice surprised me, rough as if I had been at ale or *acquavit*. "If I suspect di Cinfiliet of treachery, Adersahl di Parmecy, I will show no mercy."

A long pause, filled only with the snap and rush of flame. Would I have to be more explicit? I did not think so. What did he believe, if anything? There was a time when I would have been certain he would take my word as a writ from the Blessed themselves.

Adersahl sighed. It was a long, heavy exhale, full of weariness. "I know nothing of treachery from his quarter. What would you have of me, Captain?"

"You will remain with her when I cannot, and you will kill Adrien di Cinfiliet if he threatens her. And you will breathe no word of my orders." Even as I said it, I flinched inwardly. It was the first lesson a Left Hand learns: The only way to keep a secret is to consign the bearer of it to Death.

Including, sometimes, the Hand himself. That is the oath we take: *As one already dead, I swear myself to service.* I had often thought long and deep on the meaning of such a vow. If I was a dead man, did it matter who I killed or how I debased myself?

The problem was, I was still alive. *She* had resurrected me.

He still did not look at me. "You truly think di Cinfiliet so much of a danger?"

"His aunt raised him to hate the King." A world of meaning lived under those words.

"The King is dead," Adersahl murmured. "Long live the Queen."

Absolutely. "If I have aught to say of it, she will live to a ripe old age. No matter *what* I must do to ensure it. Do we understand each other, di Parmecy?"

That caused his gaze to swing through the darkness, but not to me. He looked up at the ceiling, closed his eyes. Was he even now expecting a knife to the throat? The garrote? "I thought I understood you, Captain."

"And do you?"

The weary old veteran examined the roof beams. "I am no fool." He settled himself further in the chair's embrace. "Loyal to a fault, but no fool."

"I am gladdened to hear it." I turned on my heel, gave him my back. "Go to your rest, *sieur.* Tomorrow may well bring surprises."

"Of what sort?"

"Of whatever sort Vianne will dream up next." The skin of my back tightened and tingled, expecting…what, a blade? No, twas not in Adersahl's nature. He had *defended* me to my *d'mselle.* My unease was the sort that had followed me since I arrived at Court, the expectation of danger such a constant refrain I could hear no other music.

He said nothing else, and I left the room dissatisfied. The conversation had gone as well as could be expected…but still, there was something amiss.

What bothered me—now that I had time to turn my attention to less pressing problems, as I closed the door and set off down a stone hall in the house of the Blessed—was what further use d'Orlaans and di Narborre had thought to gain from such a paper as the one my *d'mselle* now held.

For I could have sworn I burned the only copy of that distressing oath, on paper as fine as any the King's brother had access to, the night before the conspiracy broke loose.

Chapter Five

A priestess in green-and-white robes swayed gently out of sight down the hall as I relieved Tinan di Rocham of his vigil at my *d'mselle*'s door. The boy was pale, but he returned my salute and hurried away in the opposite direction, wincing as if pained. To be sent away from the lady's door was probably mortifying. And he had recently come close to death, gut-stabbed by a Pruzian assassin and healed by sorcery. Wounds closed in such a manner sometimes pain one more in the aftermath than in the receiving. The body knows it has been violated, and not even the grace of the Aryx can dissuade it from remembering. *Ghost-pain*, the healers call it, the same term for a limb lopped off and yet still felt.

Which led me to the Aryx, the Great Seal of Arquitaine, its triple serpents twined in an endless knot and its power singing through my *d'mselle*. The Seal had been asleep since King Fairlaine's time, true, but it was still a mark of the Blessed's favor for Arquitaine. And now it was awake. Plenty of the old accounts of its power were…thought-provoking. Did Vianne know what other Left Hands had written of the Seal's capabilities in the secret archives, she would no doubt seek to claw it from her flesh.

One more danger to guard her from.

I touched the door's surface, smooth wood-grain under my fingertips. No line of candle or witchlight showed under its edge. She must be in her bed, prepared for dreaming with a soporific draught and left to embark on the sea of sleep. Danae would have prayed over her, and I pondered what wonder, if any, the priestess would have witnessed. Would the Aryx respond to this ceremony as it had responded to the marriage-vows?

A chill walked up my back. The door smelled of hedgewitchery. A thread-thin tracery of green, visible to passive, sorcerous Sight, twined through the wood. Was it a defense, a hedgewitch charm meant to bar passage? Did she fear to sleep here, knowing I would be at her door?

Not that. Please do not let her think that.

I took up my position to one side, and listened. The temptation to enter the closet of Kimyan's elect and peer through the darkened eyeholes, to perhaps hear her breathing, ran through my body like fever, like ague.

Instead, I played the same game I have played through countless nights of watching and waiting. A Left Hand spends many nights in silence, like a viper under a rock, waiting in darkness for a victim to blunder past or an assignation to take place. Moreover, many a man has been proved unfit for the Guard, no matter how noble his blood, by the simple inability to *wait*.

To wait successfully, a man fills the time as best he may. My game runs thus: I think of Vianne. I consider her in different lights—under a flood of sunlight in her garden, on her knees and digging, sometimes cursing under her breath before she worked hedgewitchery, a green flame on her fingers threading through whatever herb or flower she sought to save or replant. I envision her under torch- and witchlight during the Court dances, in the slow stately measures of a pavane or during the wild whirl of the maying, her feet unseen under her skirts and her dark curls flying.

I think of her perched in a windowsill, bent over a book, the kiss of sun through glass bringing out threads of gold and darkness in her braided hair, gems winking against her throat and ears, sometimes with pearls threaded into the complex architecture of Court style.

I think of the moment Henri told me of his design to marry her to some Damarsene tradesman-turned-noble, if his plans came to fruition and the ruling house of Hese-Arburg suffered a setback. To a king, the female side of Court is a garden, some flowers culled for pleasure and others to be used as bargaining chits, played for alliance or to shift the balance of power.

That is a singularly unpleasant thought, though it arrives during any dark watch. So, I turn myself to remembering the grace of her wrist as she plucks at a harp, or of the grace of her wit when she and Princesse Lisele played riddlesharp and Vianne let the Princesse win, making a blunder too subtle to be anything but intentional.

I had sweeter remembrances to take the sting away. The moment she turned to me, in a bandit's hut in the Shirlstrienne, and told me her strength depended on mine. The moment I realized she was mine for the taking, that my patience had plucked the flower I had tended as carefully as she ever tended a bed of priest's-ease or finicky aurlaine.

The night wore on. That thin thread of green wedded to the wooden door mocked me. I longed to touch the knob, to steal on cat-feet into the *d'mselle*'s chamber and whisper the truth in her ear. Would she take it for a god's voice, and would I be struck down for blasphemy?

What further blasphemy could I commit? Lying to tell the

truth, lying to hide a truth, lying to cover my crimes, lying because I had lost the habit of truth itself—

You? Tristan d'Arcenne, worrying like an old provincial m'dama about blasphemy? What next? Spending all your time on your knees in black skirts, counting your prayers on your fingers?

I almost laughed at the vision. On a nightwatch, the mind does strange things.

Far away, reverberating through stone, the temple bells tolled. I counted the strokes. A carillon, then twelve. Midnight. After now would come the time of deepest darkness, the time when I most often lay awake, listening to Vianne's soft breathing next to me and cherishing each moment of her warmth. How long had we been married?

Not nearly long enough to cool the fever in a man's blood, when the only woman he wants is beside him and the world has spread itself at his feet. Or, at least, all of the world that matters.

The bells quieted, stone vibrating slightly against my back. I closed my eyes and touched the edge of her door, running my fingertips over the knob as if it were the sweet curve of her hip. So soft, and so—

I snapped into full alertness.

Boots. The jingle of spurs, metal clashing.

I hesitated. If twere merely news, there might be no need to disturb her. If twas something other…

They rounded the corner, torches spilling witchfire, almost the full half-dozen of the Queen's Guard. Jespre di Vidancourt, named for a stone; dark Jai di Montfort; Tinan di Rocham pale as death, swept along with them. At their head, Jierre, my lieutenant, with his countenance graven. He seemed to have aged ten years since I had commissioned him to my father's Keep.

I stepped forward, hand to hilt, and Jierre drew, steel singing from the sheath and his left hand lighting with venomous yellow witchfire, Court sorcery capable of blinding a man.

Treachery? Here?

"Hold!" Jai di Montfort yelled. His dark hair was disarranged, and he clasped Jierre's shoulder, his other hand occupied with a torch dripping orange witchfire. "You have your orders, di Yspres! Stay your hand!"

We faced each other, the Guard and I, and I shifted my balance a few crucial fractions. Did they come for my *d'mselle's* door, we would find whose steel rang truest. My fingers tightened, tendon-knots, on my hilt.

Six against one. I have taken worse odds, and Jierre will attack inquarto. *He always does.*

Did he come for Vianne, I would kill him, lieutenant or no.

Tinan di Rocham gasped for breath. "The order. Captain, the *order—*"

"Silence!" Jierre's tone cut harsh as a clothier's knife through silk. "Tristan d'Arcenne, you are under arrest."

What? "What madness are you about?" My forearm tensed. The first thing to do would be to douse the torches, a flashy bit of Court sorcery but one I had practiced well. Darkness is where a Hand does his best work. "I stand guard over the Queen of Arquitaine!"

Di Montfort's fingers dug into Jierre's shoulder, white-knuckled, holding my second-in-command back. "'Tis our *d'mselle* herself who commands it, Captain." Jai was ever the voice of reason, one of the most levelheaded of the Guard. Tinan held up a scroll, its heavy waxen seal visibly imprinted with the symbol of royalty—the three serpents of the Aryx, twisting about one another.

My left hand leapt, not for a charm or killspell, but for the doorknob. It yielded, unlocked, the thin thread of hedgewitch-illusion that had darkened it breaking, and the door swept open as Jierre and the others surged forward. I saw the penitent's cell, lit by a globe of glowrock and the low-burning lamps, guttering untended. The cot was smooth, unruffled, and I remembered the priestess swaying her way down the hall as I relieved Tinan of his guard duty. A priestess with a familiar gait, but I had seen the green-and-white robes and dismissed it.

Outplayed, Tristan, and by your very own d'mselle. I halted, and the killing rage sharpened under my breastbone, cracked against the chain of duty like a cur snapping at its leash.

"Captain." Tinan di Rocham, his young voice breaking. "Please. We know not what the Queen is thinking—"

"I know what she thinks, boy. Hold your tongue." Jierre shook free of di Montfort's restraint. "We have orders to bring you whole and hale, d'Arcenne, but do you resist and it shall go ill for all concerned."

The best of friends, the worst of enemies. I gathered myself, and tension sprang through them, as the springs and ropes of a siege engine will tauten when the engineers apply the levers.

I had subtly encouraged them to swear their fealty to her, had fostered their loyalty to her, had tied their fates to hers. A hedge of safety around my Vianne, and she had used it against me. Fair blond Luc di Chatillon had the chains, their rattle strangely subdued.

"I am to be arrested?" I made a show of slowly unbuckling my swordbelt, moving carefully. The angles of Jierre's face contorted, whether with agony or murder I could not tell. "On what charge?"

"Treason." Pillipe di Garfour said it like a curse, as a man would spit out sour wine. "Written in your own hand, Captain. You are to be tried."

Oh, Vianne. You were so careful with Adersahl. "Tried by whom?"

"Take his sword, Tinan." Jierre's stare was pitiless, and empty. Of all of them, he would feel the most betrayed. How had she reached him, to turn him thus?

I offered it with both hands. *Should I play the innocent?* "I insist on seeing the order, di Yspres. It is my right."

"You *dare*—" My lieutenant took a single step forward, and a shining inch of steel showed between hilt and scabbard. He was perilously close to murdering me where I stood—that is, if the knife in my boot did not find his heart when I killed the lights.

Jai di Montfort sank his calloused fingers into Jierre's shoulder again, drawing the man back. "Tis true. But I think it would not be wise of you to insist, d'Arcenne. Let us be calm, as befits the Queen's Guard."

"In the Queen's name." The words fair sounded to choke Jierre. His face shifted again, terribly, and shame suffused me.

I thought I had plumbed the depths of any shame I could feel the first time I killed an unarmed man in service of Henri di Tirecian-Trimestin.

I was wrong.

"For the Queen's honor." The words were ash on my tongue. My swordbelt was handed over. Luc di Chatillon did not clasp the irons overly tight, but he did make certain of them, and handed the key not to Jierre but to di Montfort. Jierre stood to one side, watching, hand on his rapier-hilt, and fury fair boiled the air around him.

When I was braceleted with iron and standing quiescent enough, Jai di Montfort let loose of my lieutenant's shoulder. "Come. We are due at the Keep."

Jierre appeared not to hear him. His gaze sought mine, and we weighed each other for a long, endless moment.

"I would have followed you even to the gates of the underworld, *Captain*," Jierre said quietly. "I would have wagered my life on your word. I *did* wager my life on it."

What could I say? He spoke truth. "You are still alive," I pointed out. "I trust Vianne to your care, if she is to be robbed of mine."

Even Jai di Montfort was not quick enough to stop him. He struck me across the face, a good blow with muscle hardened from campaigning and daily drill behind it, and I made no move to avoid it. It took Luc di Chatillon and di Montfort both to restrain him, and Pillipe di Garfour and Tinan brought me to my feet, near dragging me down the hall. My jaw had not broken, though I could feel the swelling in my cheek already. Twas not a love-tap, and yet my heart ached worse.

It is ever so, with men who are too loyal and too honest. Not even the thought of eventual revenge can restrain their rage when they find they have been used.

Twas why Jierre di Yspres would never have been a fit Left Hand.

Chapter Six

This cell did not stink, at least. I paced it—fourteen strides one way, eight another. There was a pallet, and no *oublietta*.

So I was not meant to be forgotten in a dark hole. At least, not yet.

The chains gave me lee to pace, fastened to a staple driven into the stone of the wall, and a witchlight torch outside the bars gave me no shortage of flat orange light. My face ached, dull pain spreading down my neck, and I winced every time I turned, chains rattling, measuring off each stride with a definite snick of my booted heel.

They had not searched me, and thus had overlooked the knife in my boot and the thin flexible stiletto in my sleeve. The lock on the cuffs would yield to some persistence, and there was no guard at the door. They had simply left me here, Jierre fiercely silent, Luc di Chatillon with an apologetic glance, and Tinan di Rocham looking halfway to tears.

I could expect visitors, but I could not know when. Would she not wish to measure my wounded countenance, see me in chains, present me with the proof?

What could I say?

He sought to take you from me, m'chri. *You were the lure that killed a King.*

One more reason not to tell her.

Arcenne throbbed above. An army drawing near with siege engines and some thousands, my *d'mselle* was probably still awake, planning feverishly with her nimble brain, seeking a way through the mire that did not mean shed blood. As dawn approached, the Keep would be readying itself, and the walls of the city would be alive with men, criers dispatched with orders to tell the common people their home was about to be flung into the maw of war.

You will fret yourself into a lather, d'Arcenne. You have waited in a prison cell before. Do so again.

The last time I had been trapped in a donjon, it was waiting for the Duc d'Orlaans to send a knife in the dark—because for all his bluster, he would not have had me publicly beheaded. It would have meant he feared me, did he put me before the crowd as meat.

Timrothe d'Orlaans flatters himself that he fears no man.

That waiting had ended with Vianne's voice in the darkness. *Captain? Are you there?*

Would this one end with her voice in the dark as well? My *d'mselle* was too soft to kill me—but someone else, perhaps di Cinfiliet, might not be.

The chains clashed. I had reached their limit and stood facing the bars. I heard footsteps, and the soft brush of a woman's skirts.

Vianne. Please. Come, hear my tale. I have woven tales for you before. Fine ones, simple ones, and ones to ease your pain.

Instead, appearing in the arc of witchlight, I beheld the worst that could befall me yet.

My father, Baron d'Arcenne himself, his blue eyes alight and his face set with particular displeasure. And beside him, her dark eyes grave, holding to my father's right arm with a hand whose knuckles had turned pale, was my mother.

More shame, hot and acrid, eating the last bit of hunger in my belly. I had not supped, and neither had Vianne before the ride to the temple.

My father stood, staring through the bars. Other footsteps halted—a Guard, of course, probably one of my men. As family to a traitor, and the hosts of the Keep where the Queen did reside, they would not be left here alone.

I could have laughed and told Vianne she need not have worried. The quality of my father's spine would not let him free a son from a prison cell, even an innocent one.

I learned as much when I was nine years old and accused of stealing apples.

My father, straight and unbending, gray feathering at his temples. I met his gaze with an unflinching stare of my own.

"Perseval," my mother said in her softest and most inflexible tone. "Greet our son."

The blue of his eyes was so like mine. I wondered, with the resemblance between us so marked, how I could have become what I did.

"That is no son of mine," my father replied. But quietly, to keep this a private matter.

My mother's hand tightened. She dug her fingers into his arm and pulled, leaning, her dark gaze fixed past me to the wall. Of course, she would not like the look of iron bars. "Perseval." A world of meaning in those three syllables, accented sharply at the beginning to make them not a question or a demand, but a simple reminder.

"M'fils." My father nodded, shortly, as someone stopped past my arc of vision. A gloved hand—a man's hand—presented a key to my father.

I retreated. The chains sang their unlovely music. *"Père,"* I greeted him in turn, without a nod. But it satisfied my mother, whose grasp on my father's arm eased slightly.

It was my mother who took the key and unlocked the barred door, and my mother who swept through, leaving it ajar. My father stayed outside, stiffly, his gaze turned flat and inward.

"Mère." I accorded her a nod, an approximation of a bow, accompanied by metal sliding and rubbing. *You should not leave the door so. You are careless as Vianne, ma Mère.*

"Oh, Tris." And she took me in her arms, ignoring my father's disapproval, expressed only in a clearing of his throat. He was right—she could have passed me the key, slipped something into my sherte, committed a treachery of her own. "My dear, my own. What *happened?"*

Of all the things that could disarm me… "Vianne," I said into my mother's hair. Her perfume was light, a mix of floral water and sunshine, a smell remembered from childhood as safety and softness. "Is she hale? Is she well-guarded?"

"Better guarded than ever." My father pushed the door open farther, took two steps into the cell. Now it was crowded, three bodies instead of one, and the chains a fourth body. And his rage, taking whatever space was left. "My own son. My *own son."*

"She says you must be called to account for the papers. That there must be an explanation, and you will be called to give it before the Cabinet." My mother pressed her soft cheek to my unshaven one, and kept herself between Perseval d'Arcenne and me.

I suddenly felt smaller than I was accustomed to, as if I were much younger. *But does she weep? Is she well?*

"Sílvie." My father made a restless movement. "I would speak with my son."

She let loose of me and half-turned, spreading her arms slightly to bar his passage. "*Your* son, now? Ah, yes. I carried him inside me, Perseval, and had the birthing of him as well. Until your suffering can match that, he is *our* son, and I shall thank you not to forget it. And I shall not let you speak until your tone takes on some kindness."

"The papers are *damning*," my father hissed, leaning forward with his hand to his rapier-hilt. "I read them myself. That woman wears the Aryx, it abides by her touch, she is the Queen, and her orders are *given*. I counted us lucky our family had remained untainted by treachery. What else did they teach him at Court, Sílvie? Beyond how to lie to his family, his Consort, his liege?"

I opened my mouth to reply, but my mother did before I could. I could never remember a time she took him to task without a laughing look or a simple grace that let him keep his pride, but now she turned on him with a ferocity I had scarce suspected in my gentle, ever-decorous dam.

"*You* said someone had to account for the provinces at Court, best it be us, and that he was seventeen and old enough to whore, hence old enough to catch the King's eye. Do you not recall it, sending my boy into that den of wolves they call Court?" Between us, the slim shape of my mother was a line too easily breached. She is a small woman, like Vianne, and barely reached my father's chin.

And yet my father retreated before her. I moved as if to put my mother aside, for it was not meet for a nobleman to hide behind a woman's skirts, but she merely slapped my hand gently away as if I had reached for one too many scones at the chai-table. Chains rattled, and her voice rose. "Henri di Tirecian-Trimestin used our son as he saw fit. And *you* colluded, Perseval d'Arcenne. You sent the boy I raised, the boy I labored fifteen hours to birth, the heir you were so set on that almost killed me—*you* sent him there, and now you would just as easily cast him from the battlements without listening to a single word in his favor?"

"Sílvie—" My father actually retreated again, and I could have sworn he looked ashamed.

"I held my peace for *thirteen years*, Perseval. Now I shall not. And as I live and breathe, if you do not keep a civil tongue in your head when addressing *our son*, I shall leave you with your pride to warm your bed at night and retreat myself to Kimyan's service, after I return your marriage-ring with a curse. Do I make myself clear?"

"*Mère—*" I had never heard her speak so, and a child's fear—that my father would strike her, though he never had in my memory—made me move restlessly, the chains rattling.

"As for *you*." She rounded on me, dark eyes flashing. "What have you to say for yourself, Tristan? Amazed you are not, and I see you have not been worrying at the cuffs to get them loose."

She was, as usual, correct. Had I been entirely innocent, I might have been working my wrists bloody under the cuffs, seeking to escape and return to Vianne's side. In one stroke, my mother disarmed me.

Silence ran through the cell like a dangerous river. What could I tell them? Whatever story I chose would have to be effective—and salted with the right leavening of truth. It would have to account for everything they had seen, and whatever Vianne suspected as well.

"Henri was about to marry her off." I heard the queer flatness of my tone, as if I spoke of another man's downfall. "To a Damarsene, if the proper assassin could be found for Corax Fang of Hese-Arburg; to marry *him* to a bastard royal would be too much. But to a younger Damarsene, a tradesman newly noble hungering for an aristocratic bride, a Damarsene family without a connexion to the Pruzians…for any number of reasons. To secure the alliance, and end the tribute payments. Then bastard scions of the Tirecian-Trimestin royal line began dying. Once was chance, twice was coincidence, thrice and fourth conspiracy—and always, I was a step too late. There are not many who can anticipate me, or could use Court influence to track my comings and goings more closely than was wonted."

"This explains nothing." But my father had folded his arms, and his wintry gaze had fastened on me at last. It was like being nine again, and about to receive the lashing.

Enough. Tell them what you can, what they will believe. "Twas necessary for me to enter the conspiracy to flush it out. It took time, and while that time ran, Vianne was kept at Court under close watch. *My* watch. I followed the conspiracy to its root, and that root was the heart of the royal House itself."

"D'Orlaans." My father nodded once, sharply. "You were playing the courser to flush the hare, and this is part of it?"

I can still salvage this. My heart gave a thin singing leap, was throttled back. *If I can make them believe, tis halfway to making Vianne believe as well.* "Tis. The King was dying when I arrived. I told Vianne twas poison, to ease her mind—what was I to do, describe the blood and bowel-loosening? I thought twas a gentler thing for her to think on, and well she needed it." It sounded so reasonable.

It *had* been so reasonable, so natural. *You should have let me have her, Henri. Safely wedded, I would have been your Hand until my death.*

And the final twist of the knife home, when he had winked broadly over my *d'mselle*'s head and said, *He must favor you, child.* Telling her a secret I had not confided, except in my one request, the only boon I begged after years of service. As a noblewoman of the sword on both sides of her family, she would have to seek Henri's blessing to wed. If he had given me permission, I would have courted her more openly.

My mother sighed, a sound of innocent relief more painful to me than her tears. "Then you can explain before the Council, and this will all be over."

"Not so quick, my dove." My father had not taken his gaze from my features, seeking to read the stamp of truth or falsehood. "There must be a deeper reason for him to be chained here. If anything, *she* trusts our son to a fault. Something else has happened, and it centers on this di Cinfiliet. What of him?"

If I could but catch him with a gallery and a sword, we would see. But it was enough to sow the seed of suspicion in my father's mind. "Probably already gone, that canny beast. Did Jierre arrive with my letter?"

"He did. Hard on his heels came our liege, and she took the missive from him. I was not allowed so much as a glance." My father's face twisted sourly.

How it must gall you, that a woman does not bend when you frown. She has shown herself not so amenable to your ideas.

But *damn* it. Had my father been able to detain di Cinfiliet, I might have been able to salvage somewhat more of this. As it stood…"He has reasons to make her doubt me." I let my tone darken, staring at the cuffs about my wrists as if they held the solution to every riddle.

I had not written aught incriminatory. Merely for my father to detain di Cinfiliet until I could question him, as I suspected. *What* I suspected I left unsaid, and my father would read it very differently than my *d'mselle*.

"Tristan." My mother searched my face. "There is summat more. There *has* to be. Vianne looks grave, and I would swear she has aged since you left for the Temple. She—"

"She is serious, as befits a liege." My father made a restless movement, reminding my mother of the guard just out of sight. It must be someone *Père* would at least suspect no mischief of, since he spoke so freely. But whom? "The charge is treason, the evidence is enough that I cannot protest, and your trial will be at the Queen's leisure. You are under *letire di cachet,* my son, and you will receive the treatment due your rank *and* the charges against you."

I cupped my palms and held them up, indicating the cuffs. "I will not be fleeing the nest anytime soon, *Père*." *Send Vianne to me, drag her here if you must. I* must *see her.* "Tell my Consort I miss her."

If I had known how long I was to be left, I might have said more. But my mother pressed her cheek to mine again. "Fear not," she whispered in my ear. "I have my ways."

Just as she always had, when as a child I feared some reprisal. My father gave me no comforting words, merely measured me again, shook his head, and left, his heels fair threatening to strike sparks. The door clanged to, and my mother trailed behind him, exchanging some low words with the guard, who paced away as well.

I was left to a torchlit cell, cold stone, and my own comfortless imaginings.

Time ceases to exist for a man imprisoned. Oh, at first one marks every breath, every swallow. One devises games to keep the mind from cutting itself into ever-smaller pieces. One counts every witchlight sputter of the torch, and looks forward to the moment a stone-faced guard will bring a meal.

At least I wasn't starved. The food was colorless, but there was enough of it. I merely checked it for poison as well as I could—not that I thought my *d'mselle* would poison me, but she was not the only player in this game—and bolted it to keep myself strong. After two days, or what I *thought* were two days, I exercised myself as well as I could while chained, too.

The guards were men I did not know even by sight, grim and silent in the uniform of Arcenne. I did not bother to question them. I merely counted myself lucky that the one holding their leash did not think to soften me with violence.

She would not do that. But then I remembered how I had tried to teach her the necessity of distasteful actions, and I wondered if she had another adviser willing to take on the duty.

Like my father. Or Jierre.

I kept track of time as well as I could, counting meals as the swelling in my jaw subsided bit by bit, covered over with stubble. I have seen the results of isolation and imprisonment, men forgetting their own names, reduced to groveling worms. There is only so much one can do.

On what I thought was the fourth day, a familiar face appeared at the bars.

Adersahl halted, touching the new growth of his mustache. Soon it would be its old, magnificently waxed self again. He looked into the cell, and his lip did not curl.

I had settled myself on the lone cot, where I lay when it seemed to me sleep was possible. The chains had rubbed weeping sores on my wrists, and a simple charm would rid me of the risk of infection.

It was not, however, a charm I possessed. What need, when there were hedgewitch healers in every town and army? What need, when my own sweet Vianne was a hedgewitch herself?

My magic was only of the sort that would kill a man, or conceal a death. The rest of Court sorcery is illusion made of light and air, beautiful and useless. Spectacles are wrought at Festivals and fêtes, and during a duel the birthright of nobles is used to dizzy, distract, steal the breath, cut as steel. But to heal requires peasant hedge-witchery or Tiberian physicker's training.

"Captain?" It was not like Adersahl to sound so uncertain.

Is it treason to name me thus? I decided against waving a languid hand and making the chains clash. Instead, I watched him through slitted eyelids, my jaw aching ever so slightly under the itch.

"I bethought myself that you would wish to know." The slight hissing of witchlight underscored his words. "The army has arrived. Damarsene troops, and Arquitaine units as well. Some thousands, all flying d'Orlaans's colors. With siege engines."

My helplessness caught in my throat.

"The *d'mselle* is well, though she is working herself to the bone and spending every night in the Temple praying. Your father has prepared a defense for the city."

I did not move. If he saw my face now, he might well regret carrying the tale.

"Di Narborre is at the gates. He is sending an emissary in the morning under a parlay flag." Adersahl paused. "The Queen intends something, but just what I cannot tell. She closeted herself with your father this morning, and even now rides to the Temple with Jierre and some few of the Guard. The city is in a ferment."

With an army at the walls? I should think so. I almost opened my mouth to ask questions, decided not to, again. *You are best served by muteness here, Left Hand. Silence unnerves.*

"I came to see if you needed aught." Adersahl paused. "Or if you wished me to take a message…"

What message could I send to her? She has not even come to my cell to spit upon me. I bit at the inside of my cheek to keep the words from spilling free. *No, I thank you, my loyal Guard, but it is best for you to hear no word of mine.*

I still had my stiletto. And there was the knife in my boot. Did I wish to kill the man who would bring me my supper?

Was it time yet?

"D'Arcenne." Adersahl hissed out the sibilant in the middle of my surname. *"Tristan."*

Here in the bowels of the Keep, there were none to hear a scream or a struggle. I knew this pile of stone well; I'd spent my boyhood hiding in its passages before I was sent to Court and learned the terrain of the Palais D'Arquitaine and the Citté's broad tangle.

Yet what would I do *after* I eased myself free of the cell?

You need a plan.

Had not all plans brought me here, no matter how well constructed?

Why had she not come? Did she think me so faithless? Was she afraid?

Adersahl sighed, the sound of a man with a heavy burden. He turned, the scrape of his heel punctuating the movement.

"Adersahl." My throat was so dry it turned the word into a harsh croak.

"Captain?" Damn the man; he sounded so hopeful.

"Tell her I long to see her." I sounded raw, unhappy. *No wonder.* I closed my eyes fully, the darkness spilling unkind into my brain.

"Is that all?" Softly, cajoling. Had he been sent to receive a confession? There was no confession I would give secondhand. If she wanted much else from me, she could come herself.

I did not reply. Let him make of it what he would. Let *her.*

"I shall, then." A slight creak—was he bowing? To me, as I took my ease on a prison cot? Wonders did not cease in the wide world.

He left me, his steps receding down the long hall under the hissing of witchlight torches, and I touched the stiletto's thin hilt. Escape was possible while I still had the strength.

I settled myself more comfortably. Or at least, I moved my arms so the chains did not weigh so heavily. The bracelets of raw flesh slid under the iron, and I was surprised into a quiet, humorless laugh. Not so long ago I ordered a Pruzian Knife beaten and tossed into an *oublietta*. She had taken me to task for it, sweet Vianne with the tender heart. And here I was, enchained and trusting that same tender heart for mercy.

If I am to get free of this, I must do so soon.

Chapter Seven

After the morning meal—or what I assumed was the morning meal—was brought, I fell into another uneasy sleep. An imprisoned man begins to slumber more and more, seeking to make the time pass quickly. There is also a manner of sleep where the mind slides the pieces of a conspiracy or plan together, then presents it whole to its owner when he awakens.

The wheels were turning and I slipped deeper, the borderland between waking and dreaming receding. Unfortunately, I was not left to find a solution to my predicament, for I heard the squeal of metal on metal and woke in a lunge, breathing in bergaime and spice as well as the peculiar greenness of hedgewitchery.

Perhaps my mother had found a perfumier. It was one of the little things a man would never think on, and twould perhaps soothe another woman's nerves.

The rustle of silk filled the cell. Chains clashed as I struggled to rise, and Vianne paused just inside the barred door.

She regarded me. The dress was dark green silk, holding her lovingly, her skirts whispering as she moved. Pearl ear-drops, pearls woven into her long dark hair, the complex braiding in the style of di Rocancheil carried with a particular tilt of her head on its slender neck. One of my mother's necklaces, an interweaving of thin strands of small freshwater pearls, dropped down to hold a large teardrop emerald just over her cleavage. Under it lay the silver chain holding the Aryx, its three serpents frozen in the act of writhing about one another, their gem-bright eyes winking. A ball of silvery witchlight hovered over her shoulder, casting her features into strange flat shadow.

The door stood open behind her, and I saw the edge of someone's shoulder—it seemed to be Jierre, but I could not be certain.

I moved slowly, curling up to sit on the bed, dropping my booted feet off the side. I filled my eyes with her, hungrily.

We regarded each other, my *d'mselle* and I, across stone flags and empty air. The witchlight at her shoulder, tinted with green threads of hedgewitchery, sizzled. I breathed in the same air she was breathing, I watched her face, and I discovered I still wanted her as much as ever.

It was little surprise. I did not think irons would cure me.

Was she waiting for me to speak? Her face changed, but it could have been the witchlight's treacherous shadows. She had saved my life with a witchlight once, one bright enough to tear the roof off a Shirlstrienne inn.

She folded her arms defensively, cupping her elbows in her palms. The copper marriage-ring glittered.

So she still wore it. She had not repudiated me yet.

"They should not have left you chained so long." A trifle defensively.

Still the same tender heart. I spread my hands loosely, listened to the metal rattle and clash, dropped my arms.

Did she wince? Perhaps slightly.

She looked away, and I caught a flash of expression. There were shadows under her eyes the witchlight did not disguise. And another shadow lay upon her—sleeplessness, and worry.

Had I been unchained, I could have shared the weight. I *ached* to share it.

She half-turned, as if leaving me.

"No!" The cry burst free. "Do not go, *m'chri*."

As soon as it was out I cursed myself. I should have held my peace to force her on the defensive. But I could not be so cold, so calculating. Not with her.

Not when she was about to leave me alone again in the dark.

She swung back to face me. And now I could see she had not meant to leave. An advantage, thrown away so needlessly. I did not begrudge it.

She regarded me again. Her hands dropped to her sides, curled into fists.

Will she fly at me? Strike me? The thought of it sent an oblique pang through me—her flesh against mine again, in whatever fashion.

"Why?" One short syllable, the word I dreaded. "Why, Tristan?"

When have I not told you why with every glance I gave you? Every time you allowed me to touch you I gave you my reasons. I swallowed, my heart a stone in my throat. And yet I could not let her take the field completely. A defeat at her hands I could stomach, but on my own terms. "Why *what*, Vianne?"

"I shall tell you a tale, Left Hand. Of a man who killed a king." Her chin up, no quarter asked or given.

I would grant her the quarter nonetheless. So I answered. "Perhaps I should tell you a tale in return, of a falcon at the wrist."

Her silence was grave, her face settling against itself. It only made her lovelier. "I am far more interested in your tale than you would be in mine."

No doubt, my love. "Then I shall sing you a harsh one." I gained my feet fully, the chains making their cruel music. "Do you know much of falconry? You train the bird with a lure, and you must reward it or it will cease to rise for you."

She made a restless movement. "I would have truth, Tristan. Not pretty Court-talk."

Ease yourself, m'chri. *There is a moral to this song.* "There was once a young boy sent to Court, and he fell in love." I could not help myself. It was like the lancing of a wound. "He beheld a girl dancing, and she stole his heart. And so he set himself to become *more*, so she would notice—but there was a barrier. She, a noblewoman of the first order, a noble of the sword, was not free to wed without a king's leave."

Did she start at that? No, she only became graver.

There was no retreat now. I pressed on. "The boy possessed ambition, and ambition is noted at Court. The boy was brought to wrist so easily, and with the lure sweet in front of him, he became something…"

I remembered, of a sudden, the first man I had killed at Henri's bidding, a troublesome minor noble knifed in a dark alley. How *easy* it had been, and the feeling of accomplishment afterward, as if I had proved something. And how that feeling had faded, because now I was set apart from my fellows. Now I was the keeper of secrets, and not merely that—now I was as far away from my father as it was possible to be.

"You have no idea, Vianne." Now I only sounded weary. "I became a thief, a murderer, the lowest of the low—and it was for *you*. You were the lure that kept the falcon hooded at the wrist, stooping only to the King's prey. Then Henri told me he intended to barter you, wed you to a petty Damarsene to stop the tribute payments. I could not brook that." The scalding flush went through me again at the thought of her under some filthy Damarsene, far from home and sold like a thoroughbred racer broken to a peasant's plow. My hands ached, and I could not stop their knotting into fists.

"You could not…" She ran out of breath halfway through, staring at me as if I were a new creature, neither fish nor fowl, found crawling in her chambers.

"I *could not*, Vianne. The King meant to sell you. Do not mourn his passage; the underworld has enough and to spare for *him*."

She wet her lips, and the flush that raced through me was of a different sort. "Lisele," she whispered.

Of course. Her Princesse, Henri's daughter. "I did not know they meant to kill her. Why would I have sent you to her chambers otherwise? You were my prize, my lure. Why would I have sent you into danger? I thought Lisele safe; I thought *you* safe at her side. Then, d'Orlaans—"

"There was no poison on the pettites, Tristan." Color rose high in her cheeks. "I would have smelled it. I am a passing-fair hedge-witch."

And so much more. "Oh, aye, passing fair." And then I cast my dice. "What was I to do, describe every moment of blood and bowel-cut to you? You were near to fainting with shock and grief, and carrying a burden far greater than mine. I misled you about the poison, yes. To ease your mind, and I would do it again."

"The papers. They involve you swearing yourself to the conspiracy." She did not look so certain now, my Queen. If I were to fan the flame of her suspicion, I could—and I could also, if luck let me, direct that suspicion's course away from my threshold.

"Of course I was involved with the conspiracy. I was *hunting* it. They thought me a prize too, and knew exactly the lure to cast. If you think I killed Henri, Vianne, you are correct. I killed him by being too late."

I almost expected the cell walls to shake with the enormity of the falsehood. Yet if you aim to cast your dice, to regain the only thing that matters, there is no use doing it by halves. It was salted with truth. Had I not stayed to gloat I would have been one leap ahead of pursuit.

Believe me, I prayed. And I had burned the only copy. Whatever paper she had seen, with a hand upon it similar to mine and its quality not enough to catch a nobleman's blood, it was not *mine*. D'Orlaans's lie would help me give an even greater falsehood the ring of truth.

"A pretty tale." Her shoulders slumped, came up again to bear that burden, one far too heavy for her. "Which presents a pretty choice indeed." Brittle, chill, and royal, the tone she had found so recently. A curl of dark hair feathered over her ear, loosening itself from the braids as if eager for my fingers. "Whatever alliance I have made will crumble, for I built it on the strength of my Consort and the loyalty of his father. If I cast aside the son, what will cement that loyalty?"

I could have laughed fit to wake the dead. My father's loyalty would never be in question.

"Or," she continued, "I could keep the son at my side, and wonder when the blade will find my own heart."

Is that what you think? The strength spilled out of me. I sat down hard in a clash of chains.

"I think we understand each other." Her chin was still tilted up. Still no quarter asked, and would I beg for respite? Her dark eyes were terribly sad, and determined. "What dagger do you have reserved for me, once I no longer fit your plans? Once I am no longer your lure?"

Dear gods. My mouth was dry as high summer in the Tifrimat wastes, where the sand burns itself to glass and sorcerous salamanders roam. Did she think I would strike at her? "Vianne—" A harsh croak, not even fit to be called her name.

"When, Tristan? When am *I* expendable?"

What? I would never...I could not. Was that what she expected? How could she misjudge me so?

Except it was not a misjudgment. She was right to accuse me thus, though she may not have known how right. My heart turned traitor to match the rest of me and cracked inside my chest. "No."

"That," she observed, "is not an answer." And with a swirl of her skirts, she turned as if truly meaning to leave me to the darkness.

She did not *believe* me.

"*Vianne*—" Her name almost choked me. "Vianne, no. *No.*"

She paused next to the door, and there was a faint fading hope that she was merely playing her hand again, feinting at her exit to force a cry from me. She had never been one for those games at Court, and was even less now.

Her head turned slightly, that was all, and she spoke over her slim shoulder with a noblewoman's air of dismissal. "I am reserving most of the papers di Narborre lost for another turn in the game. Sooner or later the Council will call for you, and I have no doubt you will be set free. I will not be able to avoid it." She took in a sharp, sipping breath. "So. Plan my death well, should it come to that pass. For I would wish it to mean something."

"Vianne—" The quick tongue I had never possessed when it came to her failed me utterly. "I—"

"I bid you farewell," she said formally, and swept from the cell. The door clanged shut, the lock catching itself. Her footsteps faltered as she reached the end of the hall. Mayhap her vision was blurred with tears, the same tears that would be uselessly spent on a pillow or a kerchief instead of on my shoulder.

Her guard, whoever it was, said something in a low, fierce tone. Twas Jierre, and he had heard it all.

Dear gods. I had never been one for prayer before, fashionably irreligious like most of the Court. Yet I found myself pleading, as if the Blessed were petty bureaucrats and I a supplicant for some sinecure or another.

The coldest part of me settled into its corner, the meat inside my skull nimbly running, running like a courser. *This is salvageable,* the cold part said. *She needs you. You will be free and able to prove yourself to her soon enough.*

How long was I to cling to salvageable before I turned loose of such wreckage, opened my veins or took a draught of poison? No, poison was woman's work, unfit for a nobleman. Falling on your sword was the accepted practice in Tiberian times.

The chains clattered like the cries of the Damarsene damned. There was no sword to fall on here. There was merely the ghost of her perfume, and something shifted inside me.

I was not ready to die just yet. I would cling to the wrack and ruin until until she sank the knife in my chest herself. There was nothing else.

Chapter Eight

The hour of dinner came and went. A long endless witchlit time, and I had lost all sense of hunger by what I judged to be morning. I lay on the cot, planning, the torch's sorcery-fueled flame a living breath in the silence.

There were other components to that silence, too. I do not know just when it began, but of a sudden I became aware of a vibration in the stone walls. Had I not grown up in this Keep I would not have noticed.

What is that? The instant I framed the question, I knew. A sick weakness filled my stomach.

It was the thunder of battle.

Dear gods.

Why had she not sent for me? Or had I been forgotten? It was not like Vianne to offer hope to a man, then snatch it away. She had said I would be freed.

Eventually.

If the city and the Keep fell before someone thought to come fetch my errant self, would I even be remembered? And my Vianne, alone in the midst of the fire and rapine of a citadel's fall.

The thought brought me up with a clash of metal. I worked the stiletto free and drew forth the pins from the small hollow in its slim hilt. The cuff-locks were easy enough to coax open, working the pins in and slipping tumbler by tumbler; this requires only a great deal of patience and time undisturbed by a guard.

I had the latter in abundance, but the former wore thin.

I remembered the thief who had shown me this trick. Driath, remanded to the King's justice for the murder of a drab, taught me much. As long as he had new skills to impart, he was safe from the noose.

But no man's skill is infinite.

The day he hanged, I was in the crowd, safe in a ragged cloak and a broad-brimmed, battered drover's hat. I do not think he re-marked me. I saw his mouth move before they hooded him, but I am fairly certain it was not to curse my name. He had far greater reasons to curse, and had never expected me to save him.

At least, I hoped he had not.

The memory of his close filthy cell and his nasal whisper as he coached me in the ways of lock-tickling and other useful things rose as I worked. He did not teach me how to knife a man quietly, for by the time I came under his tutelage I had already learned that skill. He *did* teach me small tricks to make the knifing easier, and a thief's way of hunting a victim, fat-pursed or not.

Of all my teachers, he was by far the calmest. Even then, I was cautious. I had learned, by then, not to turn my back on a man no matter how securely he was restrained.

Of such small habits and gentle lessons are a Left Hand made.

I was not *too* filthy. Unshaven, rank-smelling, yes. But at least I had possessed a slop-bucket. Once I freed myself of encum-brances, the next step was—

The cuffs parted and I hissed out through my teeth, rubbed-raw flesh underneath exposed to cruel air. Hedgewitchery may keep a body clean, but Court sorcery will not. It will not even mend the simplest of life's daily annoyances.

The vibration in the Keep's white stone walls, once attended to, was impossible to cease hearing. I eased the screeching door open and peered down the hall. The witchlight torches were sputtering; I had barely avoided being locked down here in the dark.

I did not take the route my parents and Vianne had, though the aching in my bones all but demanded I follow my Queen's steps. Yet I would not serve her best by being an idiot. When next I appeared to her, it would have to be in such a manner that my actions were unquestionably *loyal*.

So I turned, and plunged deeper into the Keep's recesses.

Chapter Nine

I do not think another living soul could tread the route I took from donjon-dark to the West Tower. I was somewhat taller and broader at the shoulder than I had been the last time I retreated in this manner—twelve, and fleeing *Père's* wrath. As usual.

My son must be above even the appearance of such things!

And my mother, in her gentle way: *Perseval, he is a boy.* Intercession I craved and was shamed of at once, for a man does not hide behind a woman's skirts.

That was something my father said often as well.

So it was a collection of dusty half-remembered passages, navigating by memory and touch in some dark places, until I found the spiraling, forgotten stone stairs rising through the disused part of the West Tower. There was precious little chance of attack from this quarter since the Keep's back was to the cliffs, but my father would have posted guard in the parts of the Tower still accessible from other areas of the Keep.

He believed in being thorough.

Three-quarters of the way up the Tower was a gallery where I could see the Keep and the city below. This would give me valuable information—and also, in that gallery, there would be water. At least, if the pipes had not been blocked in the intervening years.

Vianne.

I pushed up the trapdoor, wincing as it groaned. The gallery was empty, and my legs threatened to shake as I emerged into dusk. Time moves strangely to the imprisoned, and I was faintly shocked to find the sunlight dimming.

The roar of battle was much more pronounced. I hauled myself out and lay on the gallery's dust-choked floor, breathing heavily and staring at the lavender sky through tall narrow windows shielded by rotting wooden eaves.

When my lungs finally bore more resemblance to flesh than leather bellows, I dragged myself upright and crossed the gallery, shuffling through a thick carpet of dust. None of the windows were broken—this face of the tower was relatively sheltered—but a few were cracked, and all were dirty. It took much careful peering and polishing before I fully grasped what I saw.

Below, the other towers of the Keep jutted like white spears. The city of Arcenne huddled, a thicket of burning inside its confining walls. The *Quartier Gieron* blazed. The eastron half was all a-smolder, and the strip of di Roncail's Orchard—so it was called, though there had not been a Roncail alive for a good fifty years—along the wall was aflame with fire instead of blossom. The East Tower, its angle providing enfilade fire with the battlements and its back to a high-shouldered cliff, flew a tattered red flag proudly, the mountain-pard of Arcenne clawing defiantly as the pennant flapped. The West Tower, more vulnerable because of the fields at its foot and the wall connecting it to a similar rock-face rising to cradle the city, flew our colors as well. The siege engines were not so numerous there, because there was merely a postern instead of a great gate piercing the stone wall. Still, rick, cot, and tree between the westron wall and the edge of the Alpeis in the distance were ablaze. Their owners might be inside the walls, but the damage would be immense, and the winter a lean one.

A pall of smoke hung over the market district; I knew the wells were deep and the summer had not been dry, but a long, fiery siege would not help. Food would be the most acute concern, then disease.

All the more reason to find Vianne and take her from this place, no matter what she thought of my trustworthiness.

The attackers had not breached the city yet, but the siege engines—mangonels and the like—lobbed Graecan fire in high crimson-orange arcs. Sorcery sparked, rising from the walls in thin veils—Court sorcery and some leaf-green traceries of hedgewitchery, though most of the hedgewitches would be tending wounded and damping the fires inside the city.

There. On the walls over the main gate, a shifting globe of silvery witchlight, clearly visible even at this distance.

Of course she would be there. In absolutely the most vulnerable place in the entire gods-be-damned city. It was my father's place to be at the walls, but of *course* my *d'mselle* would not listen to reason.

I almost, *almost* sent my filthy fist through a pane of ancient, rippling, dusty glass. Control reasserted itself, and I took a deep breath.

Weapons. And a means of moving undetected. Though likely none will pay attention to you, not with an army at the gates and fire everywhere. Why not simply steal a horse and force your way to her side?

I considered this, my fevered forehead pressed against the

pane. Grit and the coolness of glass, and my pulse a frantic tattoo in my throat and wrists.

Why not indeed.

Night in a besieged city is rather like the Damarsene underworld, especially when the attackers possess sorcery. Flames rose, screams echoed, horses added their own cries, dogs howled. The men had been called to the walls; women, children, and old men either hid or were called to fire duty. Smoke and the reek of fear in every corner, but twas not as bad as I'd feared, seeing it from above.

The walls were holding. There was no chance to gather news; I was occupied enough in avoiding the fires and working my way toward the Gates. No street in Arcenne is straight; they are a jumbled patchwork, an additional defense for the Keep. Where Vianne *should* have been, watching the battle from afar. It should have been my father on the walls, braving death and rallying the defense.

The silvery shield-globe of witchfire was a thing spoken of in old scrolls and dusty books locked in secret archives—the Aryx, the great Seal of Arquitaine, protecting its chosen holder on a battlefield.

So she had discovered how to unlock that portion of the Seal's powers. Good.

Yet it was not a *guarantee* of safety. Chance could still kill her. Not only that, but each time she used the Seal, she surfaced terrified and disoriented. Who else knew what she faced as the Aryx worked through her? Who else had she turned to for comfort afterward?

I urged the gray gelding on. I had little compunction stealing a horse, and this sorry nag had been left a-stable. He had precious little life in him, and I spurred the beast unmercifully. Soot fell out of the sky, and the foulness of Graecan fire lay in a thick coat over Arcenne. It does not cease burning, that terrible flame, until a hedgewitch can deprive it of air and disrupt its grasping fingers. Still, the stink remains, burrowing under skin and clothes—and of all the things Graecan fire will attack, it loves to cling to hedge-witches most.

Looping trails of smeared orange in the sky—di Cinfiliet had reported at least five of the monstrous fire-flingers, one or two wallbreakers. And Damarsene troops flying their own colors, un-der the Duc's, on Arquitaine soil.

Oh, I will revenge this. I do not care how, I will revenge this.

Hooves clattering, iron shoes striking sparks from the cobbles, the weight of the foaming horse cutting a path through the crush at the edge of the Smallmarket, where healers' tents stood in neat rows instead of the smallholders' stalls. I wondered if my child-hood friend Bryony was about, organizing the tending of the wounded, or at the Keep. As the chief hedgewitch physicker of the Baron's household, his place would be with Vianne, but—

BOOM.

The horse foundered, queer weightlessness as I was flung from his back. A scorch-wash of liquid flame jetted past, and the geld-ing screamed as he became a torch. A horse made of fire, a crack-ing jolt all through me, and I picked myself up as avid little tongues of sorcery-fueled destruction spidered in all directions. The horse screamed afresh, a sound mercifully cut short as the flames crunched inward, *squeezing*.

I staggered. More cries, running feet, a clanging handheld alarum-bell.

Vianne.

Her name forced me into action, ducking into an alley as a fire brigade headed by a stolid peasant woman pelted by. The dame's skirts were hiked above her knees and her round, apple-cheeked face streaked with soot, the green scent of hedgewitchery hanging on her like a cloak. *"Invernus!"* she yelled, flinging out one work-roughened hand as the brigade behind her swelled forward, two junior hedgewitches adding their force to the charm and a Court sorcerer—the witchlight hanging above him spitting livid yellow sparks—making a complicated gesture, drawing air away from the borders of the fire. He was a young nobleman, the feather in his hat sadly draggled and soot-stained; the peasants and artisans behind him carried buckets of water and wet sheets, struggling with the weight.

The Graecan fire died with one last vicious burst. The horse was merely a charred lump. Bile filled my mouth. I spat and turned away, deeper into darkness, and fled.

Chapter Ten

I do not like to think on the remainder of that journey. Suffice to say there were death, and fire, and scenes of terror aplenty. Closer to the Gate, none paid me any heed—I was simply another soldier, their gazes passing over me like water. None could tell, or would care, that I was holding a dead man's sword.

I did not kill him—a falling chunk of masonry had. It would have been foolish to leave him the steel when I needed it so badly. Never mind that the sword was inferior, a chunk of potmetal. It had an edge and a hilt, and I have worked with worse. Before, and since.

The Gate was braced, Court sorcerers in a loose semicircle before the jumble of wood and stone. Here it was the hedge-witches who stood behind, two or three to each sorcerer, their charms tending the bodies of the noblemen and -women whose hands were outstretched, violent, showy streams of energy crackling over the pile of material bracing the Gate as they fought to keep it stable. On the other side would be a corresponding group of Court sorcerers or Damarsene *Hekzen*, battering at the Gate's sheer blank outer face, seeking entrance.

Archers atop the wall, more Court sorcerers and hedgewitches,

couriers dashing back and forth, and that silvery globe, fine crackling lightning-traceries describing a sphere in the darkness.

More Graecan fire, arcing and screeching overhead. The globe of
silver *flexed*, rippling with force, and the howling meteor of flame
was batted away. It was not hurled back at the engines that had flung
it into Arcenne. Rather, twas deflected to the side, as if she could
not bear to send it back on its makers and inflict yet more death.

She was not made for war, my hedgewitch darling.

Gaining the top of the Wall was no simple matter. Fortunately,
half-singed and covered in soot, I looked like any other courier, and
took care to move purposefully. My heart hammered, my legs threatening to give underneath me, hunger sour in my middle—once a
man sees death, he often wishes to remind himself of the business
of living, with food or other satiety. Cold fear at my nape, the idea
that I would be discovered at any moment making each step a pitfall.
Sweat greased me under the filth of donjon, dust, soot, and the
Blessed alone knew what else. I joined a flow of couriers scurrying
half-bent behind the archers, the man in front of me with laden
quivers he passed along to the archers, taking the empty ones in return. Every fifty paces an embrasure reared, with a slit for crossbow-
men; they worked in relays to load and shoot the mankillers, their
quarrels loaded with death-sorcery. Screams, the Wall rippling as
sorcery eddied and swirled, looking for an entrance. They did not
try the ladders yet, but sappers would be working busily below, in
trenches that would grow their fingers toward the city.

Sorcery was not the only way to bring a wall down.

She stood above the Gate, a moon in the smoky dark. Shadows
around her—there was Jierre, slim and dark, and Adersahl's
stocky figure. Other men, none of them giving a moment's attention to me. Were I an assassin, I could have—

A crashing impact. He hit me hard, driving me down, shouts

and curses. Yelling in an unlovely foreign language, he lifted a hand full of blade-blacked knife, and my own fist flashed out, crunching into his throat.

A lean face, dark hair clubbed at his nape with black ribbon, in night-melding clothing. A proud beak of a nose, spurting blood as I hammered at him again, I brought up a knee, striking true. It was sheer luck; I was weak from imprisonment and disuse.

It was the Pruzian Knife, the only surviving assassin of his trio. He had tried to kill me once before. What was he doing *here*, so close to Vianne?

More shouts, a sudden seething anthill with me at its center. The silvery radiance dimmed slightly, as if she was distracted, and I am certain I was wasting my breath on cursing. *No, protect her, do not pay any mind to me, brace her—*

The world turned white.

An immense globe of Graecan fire splashed against her shield of silver-threaded light, veins of green hedgewitchery spreading in complex knots as it sought to deflect. Vianne screamed, a sharp hawk-like cry, and I heaved the Pruzian away, striking him once more—again in the throat, to rob him of breath and fight—for good measure. Jierre was there, blade drawn, but I was on my feet and the knife from my boot was in my left hand as I gained my balance, the potmetal sword in my right flashing in the sudden livid glare, deflecting his strike. My knife sank into my lieutenant's right shoulder with the unheard sound of an ax biting dry wood, the shock rising all the way up my arm, twisting and wrenching the blade free.

He'll live. Vianne—

She staggered back, Adersahl's face a picture of dismay in the glare as he spun to face me. The Graecan fire looped forward, cracking the shield and hungrily arrowing for her, its sharp, rosy fingers brightening as they scented a hedgewitch.

The spell to snuff that hideous flame left me in a thunder of senseless effort, Court sorcery few know. I doubted it would have any teeth, for I was only one man. But the Aryx, fount of the light illusions and deadliness of Court sorcery, was close, and no doubt my effort tapped some of that wellspring.

That is the only explanation I can give.

No, that is a lie. I can give the truth, it will not harm.

Vianne's dark head had turned, and she stared at me, her countenance shining with the same radiance I had seen on a statue of Jiserah the Gentle on our wedding day. Under that gaze, I was stripped bare.

I did not care.

I reached her just as broken masonry showered around us, threads of Graecan fire eating into stone. The fireball had winked out of existence, leaving only its fringed edges, and my hand shot out, closed around her arm. I meant to pull her down, for in that one terrible moment I sensed how exhausted she was. Gaunt-thin under the quilted overjacket someone had bundled her into, her face pared down to bone and unutterably weary, her soot-laden skirts moving stiffly and her hair unraveling from its braids, she was still heart-stopping.

Still *mine*.

The Aryx shifted against her chest, a knot of unburning sorcerous fire writhing madly. I *felt* it each time she drew on the Seal's force, pulling on every secret fiber of me. Henri had never used the Aryx thus. Of course, it had slept until *she* took it. Why?

I did not know. I would have slept too, waiting for her.

The world went white again, and my battered body finally betrayed me. I fell into darkness, my mouth still seeking to shape her name.

Chapter Eleven

"The fires?" She sounded so weary.

"Largely contained." My father, grim and equally hoarse. The gravel of exhaustion in his throat, a sound I rarely heard. "They are licking their wounds outside the walls, my liege."

"I am *blind*. Stupid, and useless, and witless besides." Sharp frustration, a rustling of velvet. I smelled burning, the reek of Graecan, and spice-bergaime. Green hedgewitchery. Leather, and metal. "I should have *known*. I should have…*gods*."

My eyes flew open. Or rather, I struggled to open them, and succeeded with rather more effort than such an operation should have cost me. The room was dark, a fire in the grate, and I had, for once, absolutely no idea where I was.

A few moments of studying the ceiling gave me the answer. A stone cube—a room in the Keep's infirmary, one of the smaller corners for patients who required seclusion.

"Lie still." Bryony was beside me. His usually merry face was solemn, his mouth pulled tight against itself. He was bruised and scorched too, soot ground into his hair, and the dark smudges under his eyes were fatigue itself. "*M'dama, sieur* Baron, he's awake."

Savage aching in every part of me. I blinked, and over Bryony's shoulder, Vianne appeared. She bit her lip, her hair knocked free of its braids and spilling in a glory of dark curls. My body betrayed me as I sought to rise. I had not the strength, and fury at my own weakness rose sharp and iron-tasting in my throat.

"Be *still*." Bryony had my shoulders, pushed me back down. Vianne regarded me, solemn, small white teeth worrying at her lip as if she expected to tear a piece free. Soot grimed her, but she seemed otherwise hale. *"M'dama?"*

She laid her hand upon his shoulder. "Take what you need." The Aryx glinted at her chest, rills of light moving along the finely-scaled serpents.

I did not understand until Bryony nodded and Vianne's eyes closed. The hedgewitch charm burst over me, a tide of cool warmth, my wrists giving one last bruised flare of pain before subsiding.

Hedgewitchery takes its strength from free earth, sky or living things, or from the charmer him- or herself. Somehow, Vianne had found a way to make the Aryx fuel it through her own body.

But it cost her so much to wield the Seal, and even with the Aryx's help such a charm would take a toll on her physical frame. Vianne staggered as the hedgewitchery ceased, and I sought to rise to her aid. Bryony pushed me back down, and I swore at him with an inventiveness that surprised even myself.

He was unaffected. "Such language. And in a *d'mselle*'s presence, no less."

Vianne sighed. Her eyes opened, and she swallowed hard. She was paper-pale, and I did not like the way her gaze did not quite focus. Her pupils were huge in the dimness. "There is much work to be done," she murmured. "Baron?"

"My liege." My father, hushed for once. "It will do no good if you collapse during negotiations."

Negotiations? Did he mean to have her surrender? My hands turned to fists. Caught in the lassitude of a fresh charming, twas the only protest I could offer.

"It might almost be a relief to collapse." A momentary flash of tired, wry wit lit her face. She turned away, not even glancing at me. Her dress rustled stiffly, and she swept at curls falling in her face, irritated. "They cannot hold the Gate for long without me. And if di Narborre breaks in—"

"He will not. He can siege us, but he cannot overwhelm; they *can* and will hold the Gate without you for a time. You serve us better by regaining your strength, my liege. The only pressing matter at the moment is what to do with…my son."

Your son will do with himself, thank you, sieur. "Vianne." A husk of a word, my throat full of dry burning. "Are you hale?"

Her thin shoulders came up, as if she expected a blow. "Hale enough." Even such a gentle lie lay uncomfortably on her tongue. "Jierre will mend, too; he has already been charmed. His shoulder aches, but will be well enough."

Of course she would turn my concern aside and speak of another. "I did not seek to kill him." I pushed aside Bryony's hands, sought to rise. "I meant to—"

"I care little for what you *meant*. But at least we have acquired valuable information from that display of disobedience." She took a single step, faltered, and her chin came up. She looked to my father, who was straight-backed, imperturbable, and, now I could see, covered in a thick layer of grime and firebreath as well. The lines graven in his angular Arcenne face were a trifle deeper, and his blue gaze was shadowed. That was all. Had he been on the walls too? Perhaps at the westron walls, for they were the weakest. "Baron. Set a guard upon him, in a comfortable room. Send for me at dawn; that is the longest I may tarry."

"Vianne." She would not even *look* at me.

"Dawn, Baron." And she swept from the room. Bryony pushed me back, and for once, I could not simply shove him aside. I sagged back on the cot.

"My liege." My father bowed as she passed, the obeisance due to royalty. There was a murmur outside; I thought I heard Adersahl di Parmecy. My father watched the entrance for a short while, a muscle in his cheek flicking. "Bryony. Leave us."

The hedgewitch rose. His expression changed—a warning, perhaps. It was the same look he had worn when he was sent to find me and deliver the news that the Baron wished my presence for some punishment or another. He rose slowly, and in a few moments I was alone with my father.

I have always disliked such an event.

He stood, arms folded, by the grate, the low glow of the fire casting his face in sharp relief. How many times had I seen an echo of his features in the mirror, and been tempted to curse my own face as a traitor? To match the rest of me, I suppose.

"So." My father did not move. "And so."

I gathered myself. The best defense against him is often an attack. "A birch lashing? Or perhaps you're thinking of leaving me in the donjon again, until she can be induced to forget my existence?"

"You were not *left*. You were to be under guard. There have been other pressing matters to attend to." His arms loosened, and he dropped his hands. One tapped his swordhilt.

I lacked weapons, had not even the stolen potmetal blade. I read the consideration passing over his face—swift, a momentary thought, no more.

And yet. I began a consideration of my own, a faint sheen of copper laid against my palate. Twas not fear, simply the metallic taste of approaching action, the body readying itself to shake off lethargy and battle for its bare survival.

"Or even worse." I settled back on the cot, watchful. At least I was not chained—but a chain could be a weapon, especially against a blade. "Run me through? And be rid of the disappointment I have always been to you."

"Disappointment?" My father considered this, cocking his head. He held himself so stiffly, as if a momentary bending would shatter his very bones. "No." A long pause. The words came, very evenly spaced, each carrying a heavy load. "Your mother. She is of the opinion that we are too alike, you and I. That our...difficulties...spring from the fact that both of us are..."

I waited. There was no use in anything else.

"Stubborn." My father gazed steadily at me. "You left your cell, acquired a sword somehow, and almost killed two of her Guard."

Only Jierre. "Two?"

"The Pruzian Knife." His mouth pulled sharply against itself in distaste. "She insists."

"She allows the *Knife* to—" I levered myself up shakily. "Blessed save us! You *allowed* this? He was sent to kill her, or take her to d'Orlaans!"

"I am fully aware. However, she is my liege, and she is of the opinion that she is Fridrich van Harkke's client now. I cannot dissuade her." He sighed heavily, and his shoulders slumped. "Di Narborre is observing another parlay. Tomorrow. You will attend her."

In that you are absolutely correct. I will. "Will she have me?"

"She has no choice." He turned on his heel, as if he could not stand to be in the room one moment longer. I heartily agreed, but his next sally drove the breath from me as I set my burned boots on the floor and assayed rising once more. "The Aryx, you see. She has informed me she requires your presence to use it effectively."

The breath left me in a rush. *What?* I could not even frame the word, and struggled again to push myself upright. *There was no hint of that in the archives!*

"So, it seems, whatever cloud hangs over you, *m'fils*, you are necessary." His shoulders sagged briefly. On him, it was like a shout. "I tell you this as your father, and as I am very conscious of our...difficulties. *Take care.*"

"I—"

"Take better care, I mean. Of yourself." And with that, he was gone as well. I was left with an empty stone cube, legs that would not hold me, and a fire in a grate.

She requires your presence to use it effectively. Now there was a mystery. What message did it aim to convey? That she still trusted me? Was this an intrigue, one my *d'mselle* was playing? What was its endgame? Against me, or around me?

There was a movement at the door. I looked up, and Tinan di Rocham's dark, boyish face appeared atop a ragamuffin's collection of torn, ash-stained clothes. His swordhilt glinted, and his dusky eyes were ablaze with something other than his usual good humor. He studied me closely.

"Di Rocham." I gave up trying to make my legs work. Strength would return as my body realized I was still its master. "You look terrible."

His grin was a balm, and the shadow of manhood on him fled. "No more than you, Captain. I'm to guard you. But I would wager you'd take a bath and fresh clothes, and your word of honor you won't stray can be your surety."

You are too trusting, and if I meant harm you would be foolish to offer me an opening. "Straying is the last thing on my mind, di Rocham." I considered him, taking stock of my strength—or the lack of it—one final time. "But you will have to help me stand."

Chapter Twelve

Tis a wonder what a shave and fresh garments will do for a man. Still, it may have been the six hours or so of sleeping like the dead, while the gods spun all our fates on a wheel and decided what to do next with us. I was shaken into wakefulness by di Rocham, who also looked much better for the application of hot water and clean cloth.

The city was quiet, the streets cleared and the fires merely smoke now. Despite last night's chaos, the damage appeared moderate—as such things went. Di Rocham rode beside me, and any questioning produced the same piece of information: He had been told to take me to the stables, collect Arran and his own Guard gray, and convey me to the Main Gate. He must not have known more, and I saw Vianne's hand in this particular fillip.

The sun beat down, late afternoon turning the white stone of Arcenne to soft tawny and the red tiles to sienna both burnt and raw; the clopping of hooves almost soporific as Tinan took a wandering route designed to avoid damaged streets. The mince pies the boy had brought me, swallowed quickly just after waking, sat uneasily behind my breastbone.

I teased out the implications of what I knew. Di Narborre and a parlay, perhaps not the first of such. How would they bring him or his envoy inside the walls? Who would his envoy be? And what plan was lodged in my Queen's nimble brain?

She requires your presence to use it effectively.

There were stories of the Aryx, of course, but even in the secret archives the exact method of its usage was not put to paper. It was simply given from one monarch to the next—but the Seal had been sleeping since the time of Queen Toriane's death.

The archives had much to say about King Fairlaine's following madness and eventual suicide, but none of it concerned the Great Seal. Their son and Heir, Tiberius the Great, managed to keep the Seal's slumber from common knowledge. Tiberius's Left Hand was integral to that quasi-deception; it was his crafty assassinations of a few key Damarsene nobles that created enough confusion that Tiberius could wriggle out of war at the price of tribute paid to Damar. Which bled Arquitaine, true, but at least it kept her borders safe. Since the Angoulême had arrived with his army and the New Blessed to marry the Old, none had invaded.

At least, not with any success, the Blood Years notwithstanding. Those had been dark times, Damar and Hesse vying with the merchant princes of Tiberia's fracturing principalities *and* Navarre's glory-hungry Queen Ysabeau I and her cursed Consort to take bites from the apple of Arquitaine. Not to mention Arquitaine's own nobles seeking to displace or marry the widowed Queen Jeliane. Di Halier had shepherded his Queen through those dark times, and sometimes I suspected that her Heir, King Henri I, who my own dead King had been named for, was di Halier's instead of her Consort's.

Di Halier had never written as much overtly, but…

History did not matter. What mattered was that Vianne, somehow, had wakened the Seal from its slumber. I did not think even *she* knew what she had done. The Seal frightened her, and well it should—she remarked once or twice that *she* did not use it, it simply worked *through* her. Being so used did not strike me as a comfortable event, especially when I saw her afterward, blank-faced, pale, needing careful chivvying to wake and warm her.

And to remind her of who she was.

My head was down as we rode, peripheral vision serving to keep me aware while I thought as deeply as I dared. Tinan hummed a courtsong, taking at face value my promise not to stray. Of course, I was the Captain. His habit of treating me as such had not yet eroded. What did the Guard know, and how could I turn that knowledge to my favor? Jierre, of course, might be lost; Vianne had no doubt worked her will thoroughly there and meant to use him as a balance to my own influence. And yet—

The square behind the Main Gate opened around us, and I looked up.

"Dear gods," I breathed. *Is she mad?*

For the bracing behind the Gate had been cleared, and there was my Vianne, cloaked, on the same docile white palfrey. Adersahl di Parmecy beside her on his gray, and on a dark gelding to her right a familiar bruised face sat atop a stiff body. Fridrich van Harkke sat his horse like a nobleman and glowered at the Gate. Even a hedgewitch charming could not erase the damage I'd done to his face.

Serves you well. You were between me and my Queen, assassin. It was twice I had worsted him. The next time, gods willing, I would kill. He was far too dangerous to be allowed so close to her.

The other figure was a Messenger—Divris di Tatancourt, dark curls, a nobleman's carriage, and his uniform freshly laundered. The killspell laid on him had not found its target, thanks to my

Vianne, and he would no doubt be gratefully loyal. Or at least, so she obviously hoped.

My father was there too, on an ill-tempered black charger. The slim figure on my mother's horse bent toward him, a last-minute conference.

Garonne di Narborre would not be entering the city.

She intended to sally forth to meet him.

"Do not trouble yourself, Baron." Vianne's face was set and remote. She did not seem to have slept, if the bruised circles of flesh under her eyes were any indication. The blue silk she wore bore the marks of my mother's dressmaker, and her hair was braided simply.

Still, she was every inch the royal. Perhaps being locked underground had given me fresh eyes. Where had she acquired this look of brittle grace, this air of command? The woman I had married was an unwilling Queen at best. This *d'mselle*, her set, pale face as fine-carved as a classic Tiberian statue, was…something else.

My hands tightened on Arran's reins. He tensed before I could master myself, and I let out a long slow breath.

"The more I think on it, the more I think it unwise—" My father's objection was merely brushed aside. She raised one gloved hand, and the novel sight of Perseval d'Arcenne swallowing his words fair threatened to lay me flat with surprise.

"I told you not to trouble yourself, Baron. All will go well, especially if…" She broke off as we approached.

"I brought him!" Tinan di Rocham announced. Adersahl sighed, but twas the Pruzian I watched.

Fridrich van Harkke paid no attention to my presence. He gazed at the Gate with surpassing intensity, and with a jolt I realized he considered it the greater danger.

Though it rankled me to be counted less, it did not matter. A distracted man was easier to overpower. Let him, with a Pruzian's arrogance, think me soft.

Though I would have thought I had taught him the truth of the matter earlier, before tossing him in the *oublietta*.

Vianne's smile was a ghost of its old unworried self, but it held a depth of affection altogether too profound to be wasted on a mere boy. "So you did. My thanks, *chivalier*. Now, be so kind as to accompany the Baron and *Chivalier* di Tatancourt to the Keep. Watch over them well, Tinan, for I need their services. Baron, take care." She turned away, handling the palfrey's reins with Court grace. "Raise the Gate." Her tone sliced the honeyed afternoon glare.

"My liege—" My father made one faint attempt at dissuading her, but it came to naught. He retreated with Tinan and the Messenger as the levers and counterweights began to move, the Gate creaking and moaning heavily. Lifting, steam hissing up as layers of charm and countercharm spilled along its pitted, dark-oiled surface.

"Vianne." My gray nudged Adersahl's aside, and he allowed it. "This is madness. Why not let di Narborre come to you?"

"Because I do not wish it." Each word cut short, without the laughing accent of the Princesse's ladies. The Pruzian clicked at his horse, which ambled forward; Adersahl's stepped to the side. In short order Vianne rode through the still-opening Gate, Arran and I hastened after.

The wind rose, ruffling the edges of her cloak, swirling dust and soot in odd whorls. The white palfrey lifted her head, stepping very prettily, and the Road unreeled before her hooves. Vianne rode, straight-backed, the Pruzian Knife before her like a herald, into the jaws of Garonne di Narborre's army.

Chapter Thirteen

There was some faint courtesy, at least, though they sent no herald or honor-guard. The great half-fan siege-shields had been pulled aside from the Road's shattered surface, and we were not swarmed. Campfires burned, the besiegers at rest, the smell of men packed together too closely for too long, the foreignness of Damarsene cooking.

They bring their own spices, the hounds of Damar, when they come baying in a foreign land.

Infantry-heavy. Well, what else to siege with? And many engineers. Their flags are high, morale is good. All from border provinces; those are devices from the Reikmarken Charl. My belly was curiously cold. I had felt this chill before, riding into an armed camp, hoping my disguise would hold—but I wore no disguise here. And there was Vianne, slender and so vulnerable, the cloak and hood not masking her grace or her fragility. The Aryx on her chest sang, a thrill through the blood of every d'Arquitaine who could hear it—what did they think, those among di Narborre's dogs who watched her ride past?

Adersahl's horse moved beside hers, and he made a low remark.

Her answering laugh rang clear but false—it was the merry biting sound she used when she was not truly amused, but had to appear so. Others would think it lighthearted, but I had watched her too long to be misled. The breeze showered us with dust, and from the commander's tent in the distance came a commotion.

They know we have arrived.

My hands loosened on Arran's reins. He was taut with readiness, sensing my unease in the way my knees tightened, my palm aching for a swordhilt. I had not been given steel.

And why should I have been, if she expected me to slide it twixt her ribs? Who had my sword now? Jierre, most likely. I had stabbed him in the right shoulder, gauging the blow to leave him alive; it was not beyond Bryony's skill to mend such an injury. My lieutenant would ache in the winter there, did he grow much older.

Di Yspres would seek an accounting for that, one way or another. That was a problem for another day.

Wait. Watch.

The siege camp's layout was standard. No surprises. Guards and challenge-patterns, the Damarsene leaving their tents to see this tiny group come to treat with them, a murmur running through their ranks.

Vianne's head lifted. She looked about with interest, hopefully noting the mangonels, the machines capable of flinging the Grae-can fire. The vats of bubbling tarry stuff the fire would be made from, each with a hedgewitch or a Damarsene sorcerer—they, as the Pruzians, call them *Hekzmeizten*—standing watchful, to make certain it did not overheat and explode, doing the enemy's work. I saw only a flash of her chin, a slice of her cheek.

If they surround us, the only hope is to kill a few and drag her onto Arran's back. The Pruzian may hold some of them, but di Narborre was his client—or his client's lundsman—to begin with. Adersahl is a canny Court sorcerer, but against so many... Sickness took me by surprise, a wedge of bile rising to my throat.

The mince pies were sitting *most* uncomfortably. And the thought of Vianne before me in the saddle, as she had ridden through half of Arquitaine during our escape, did not help.

The commander's tent was a monstrosity of dark fabric, dust and smoke hazing its sides. It flew the new device of d'Orlaans—the crowned serpent over a rising sun. The swan of the Tirecian-Trimestin family, being his murdered brother's sign, perhaps gave him an uneasy conscience.

You know better. The man has no conscience. Be ready to exercise a similar lack.

The stamped-down space in front of the commander's tent was a strategic nightmare. It would take so little to make Vianne a prisoner, and then I would be faced with terrible choices.

Calm, Tristan. Watch. Wait, and plan.

It was Adersahl who lifted her down from the saddle, and though his hands did not linger at her waist a bolt of something hot and nasty speared me. Twas not the mince pies.

Van Harkke took her horse, murmured something to her. Another laugh, this one truly amused, from her throat as I dismounted, not liking to leave Arran behind but unwilling to let Vianne wander farther alone.

There was no party to meet us at the entrance to the tent—an insult, to be sure. Vianne did not seem to mind. She took a deep breath, shoulders squaring, and glanced once more at the Pruzian Knife.

He nodded slightly, and she looked to Adersahl next. He nodded as well, the crimson feather in his cap waving finely.

I waited for her gaze, but it did not turn to me. Instead, she arranged her skirts and stalked for the tent. The song of the Aryx rose, its melody developing a counterpoint, and familiar fire raced along my nerves. I did not wonder at it—the Aryx is the fount of Court sorcery and a mark of the ruler's legitimacy.

And also, twas *her*. I would be dead not to feel that pull. It is the Moon's longing for the Sun, chased across the sky night and day. Or the aching of a lock for a key, a gittern for the hand that makes it sing.

How could she think I meant *her* harm?

Smoke threaded up. The folds of hanging fabric before my Queen suddenly crawled with silvery witchflame, lapping tongues of it devouring the entrance-flaps. They ate the material in a spreading pattern, and by the time she reached the hole in the tent wall it was large enough for her to simply pass through, her head down and her hood pulled so close none of the falling ash would foul her.

As entrances go, twas a dramatic one.

Adersahl was slightly behind her, and I was at her heels. The Court-sorcery flames died, smelling of cinna and clovis. She pushed her hood back, and the men at the map-table all leapt to their feet.

I knew the d'Arquitaine among them, noblemen and d'Orlaans's creatures all. Simeon di Noreu, di Narborre's foppish little puppy, with his blond curls and his curled lip; portly dark Firin di Vantcris with his hand at his swordhilt, a duelist fond of cheating. Tathis d'Anselmethe, the pointed beard he affected dyed coal-black, a nobleman who stooped to collecting his own taxes. A few others who did not merit mention. The Damarsene commanders were unknown to me, but I stored their insignia in memory with a swift glance and began calculating how best to rid one of them of his weaponry.

Vianne stood, straight and slim on the costly carpets over hard-packed earth, her simply-braided hair a glory in the haziness, before Garonne di Narborre, d'Orlaans's Black Captain.

He was a gaunt man; food held little interest for him. Di Narborre glutted himself instead on violence, on misery, on the sheer joy of causing pain. It was the hands that gave him away—spidery, fingertips twitching as if they longed to roll slippery blood between them, the calluses blackened no matter how much he oiled and perfumed them.

His flat dark gaze dropped to Vianne's chest, where the Aryx hung. The avidity of his expression brought a rush of boiling to my head.

No man should look at her so.

"Garonne di Narborre." Clear and crisp, a carrying tone she must have learned at Court.

"As you see." He swept her a bow, but his gaze did not stray from her chest. I took a single step forward, but Adersahl's hand appeared around my elbow like a conjure-trick, and he squeezed.

Hard.

"*D'mselle* di Rocancheil—" di Narborre began, and the oily self-satisfaction in his tone alarmed me. The offal-eating pet of d'Orlaans *never* sounded so happy—unless the prey was fair caught, with no chance of escape.

"Silence." She made a slight movement, and the incredible happened.

Garonne di Narborre choked. The charm was a simple one—Court sorcery, to steal the breath from a man. Twas meant to be transient; it required far too much force and concentration to maintain for longer than a few moments.

Yet maintain it she did, the Aryx ringing and the rest of them curiously motionless, perhaps shocked. This was, no doubt, *not* the way they expected this interview to pass.

Di Narborre's knees folded. He clawed at his throat, and the Damarsene tensed to a man, sensing something amiss. The one closest to me—a stocky man with the red-raven hair common among them, his mustache waxed and his hand at his rapier's hilt—had far more presence of mind than most, and I lunged forward a split moment before he had committed himself. The knifehilt at his belt smacked into my palm, the blade serving me far better than him at this moment, and I had his belt slashed with a twist of my wrist. Shoved him, *hard*, and the rapier rang free—but in my hand, not his. Adersahl had drawn as well, and I was briefly both thankful and disappointed that Jierre was not at my side.

He would have enjoyed the challenge.

"Ah, no, *sieurs*." I showed my teeth as Vianne made another slight movement, di Narborre's knees hitting the carpeting as he began taking in great heaving gasps. "My Queen did not give you leave to move."

The substance of a threat must be such that the first among equals does not dare to test it. With di Narborre neatly immobilized, the rest were unsure. I marked di Vantcris as the one most likely to give us some trouble, and the Damarsene I had so neatly disarmed as the likeliest among his fellows as well. So I moved to the side, a light swordsman's shuffle, and Adersahl moved forward as if directed to do so.

It was gratifying to see he still followed my lead.

"Murderer." Vianne's right hand was half-lifted. Slender fingers held just *so*, threads of Court sorcery woven among them, ribbons sparking silvery as the Aryx flamed with light.

"No…more…than *him*," di Narborre choked, and he was staring at me instead of at my Queen. I did not seek to hold his gaze. "Orders. Given."

"Oh, I know your orders." Bitter as *kupri*-weed, she laughed. "*Make certain none still live.* Those were your orders for Arcenne too, I wager. And for Risaine. Is it so easy to kill, then, *sieur*?"

Risaine? Then I knew—the hedgewitch noblewoman in the Shirlstrienne, slain once di Narborre realized she was not Vianne. My Queen had taken her death hard, as hard as the Princesse's, though I wondered at why.

Di Narborre sucked in a whooping breath. The plummy shade of suffocation faded; more was the pity. "Ask d'Arcenne. Do you know what he did, *d'mselle*? He—"

I could have stood to see him choke for the rest of his life.

A single peremptory gesture, Vianne's fingers fluttering. "I know what you would have me *think* he did."

Di Narborre almost cowered. I will not lie—it gave me a great deal of pleasure to witness.

A very great deal indeed.

"Whatever he did, whatever you would have me think, matters little." The Aryx rang under her words, and that thrill along my nerves returned, stronger than wine or *acquavit*. "Return to your master. Inform him you have seen me, and that a few Damarsene and some Graecan witchery will not save him from my wrath. *I am the holder of the Aryx, I am the Queen, and you are forbidden my presence again, on pain of death*." She tilted her head. A pause stretched every nerve to breaking. "I will give you a gift to take back to Timrothe d'Orlaans, as well."

The noise was massive, a welter of melody from the Aryx, screams and shouts and the coughing roar of flame from outside. The tent's walls flapped, lines straining against a sudden wind. Heat roared through the hole behind us, and the rest of the tent burst into flame. The Damarsene shouted, wisely dropping to the ground; every d'Arquitaine, however, stayed bolt-upright, their knees locked.

Every one but Garonne di Narborre, who stared up at Vianne. The mocking smile was gone from his sharp hungry face, and he gaped as if he had never seen her before.

Like a man witnessing a miracle.

Flags of charred fabric flapped, lifting away, the heavily resined tent-lines sparking and fizzing as they burned. Vianne stood, straight as a sword in the midst of the chaos, and my heart lodged itself in my throat. It forgot to beat, that senseless organ; it forgot everything but her name.

A final lick of silvery witchflame, and the map-table went up in a burst of orange and yellow. Smoke lifted, a cleaner reek than the Graecan fire. A hush descended outside, and I did not dare to glance away from my Queen, who gazed down on the cringing di Narborre. Her curls lifted, stirred by the hot, playful breeze.

The flagrant power was almost as terrifying as the precision of her control. The sensation of her using the Aryx was a velvet rasp against every inch of me, reaching down to bone and spilling out through my fingertips. How could the rest of them seem so unaffected? Perhaps terror robbed them of the ability to react.

"This is the gift," she said clearly. "I allow you to live, Garonne di Narborre. Run back to your murdering master. Tell him *I am coming.*"

Her pale hands lifted; she settled the velvet hood over her hair and turned. Rich material fell forward, hiding her face, and her thin shoulders trembled.

Help her.

I dropped the sword, spun the knife to reverse it along my forearm, and reached her just as she swayed. The movement tipped her into my arms. I did my best to make it appear as if it were intentional, as if she had sought my presence, without making her appear weak. Still, di Narborre's close-set, red-tinted eyes lit, hungry as ever, as I took her under my wing.

So to speak.

He came up in a stumbling rush, but Adersahl di Parmecy was there before I could even cry warning. His rapier point dipped, resting at the hollow of di Narborre's throat.

"Do not," the Queen's Guard said, coolly. "Or another shall carry your message, and you shall dine with Death tonight."

Vianne almost staggered. I held her upright, glanced through the ruins of the tent.

The vats of Graecan fire had exploded. The siege engines lay twisted and useless, moans and shrieks rising in a chorus of the mad, horses screaming with fear. The half-fan siege-shields before Arcenne's Gate burned merrily, sending up plumes of black oily smoke.

Blessed save us. She did this?

"Tristan," she whispered, and leaned in to me. For a few moments I almost thought she had forgotten.

But no. She stiffened, the Aryx's melody receding, velvet turning to a scraping along my nerves. "Vianne," I answered, stupidly, pointlessly.

The Pruzian Knife appeared, wreathed in smoke, his gloved fists holding the reins. His eyes were round, and he was ashen.

I did not blame him.

Whatever she thought, whatever she suspected, for that moment Vianne clung to me. And it was enough.

Chapter Fourteen

"Decamped. In an unseemly haste, as well." My father sounded far more amused than the situation warranted. The decanter gurgled as he poured a measure of heavy red unwatered wine. He looked fair to bursting with satisfaction, and of a sudden, I longed to smash something.

Freshly bathed, freshly clothed as well, my sword returned by a blushing Tinan di Rocham, I stood at the casement, the window before me begging to have my fist put through it.

Vianne had retreated to the chambers we had shared—my own rooms, now hers. I did not grudge her the use of them, but I most certainly did grudge the way she freed herself of my hands with a decided moue of distaste once we had dismounted in the safety of the Keep, her eyes almost-closed and her mouth tight, as if one of the half-heads she was prone to had struck.

I had held her during one of the half-heads not so long ago, a bit of Court sorcery plunging the room into utter darkness while she wept with pain. I knew of the severe headaches, of course—twas gossip at Court that di Rocancheil suffered them and sometimes retreated to her bed for a day or so, blind with riven-skull agony.

Was she enduring one now? After single-handedly destroying every siege engine in di Narborre's invading force, and causing the vats of Graecan fire to explode straight up in pillars of flame? Or was it brought on by the battle at the Gate, or by any of a hundred things that could trigger such a condition? A bright light, tension, exhaustion—the list was long.

"The Council will meet as soon as the work of reordering the city is well enough underway." My father swept up the two goblets. "The signs are…well, they are not *bad*. Siguerre thinks it Timrothe d'Orlaans's clumsy attempt to drive a wedge between you and her. Di Falterne and d'Anton reserve their judgment—it is they you will have to sway. Di Dienjuste is rattling his rapier, ready to sally forth and slay them all. Di Rivieri and di Markui think this all a load of nonsense, and the Queen's attention better turned to other matters." He glided across the room, offered me wine.

Crusty ancient di Siguerre was my father's friend of old, and behind his craggy face lay a mind much sharper than a liege would find comfortable in a provincial lord. Di Falterne and d'Anton were normal enough noblemen except for their probity—always a quality in short supply among men. They were younger than di Siguerre by a good deal, though, and gave the Council forward momentum. Di Dienjuste was a young blood, and his attentions to Vianne approached the edge of the permissible. The remaining old men, di Rivieri and di Markui, were stolid weights to balance the young ones, and their provinces were necessary if we were to fight a war for Arquitaine's heart. I passed their faces through my memory, arriving at the same answer I usually did when weighing a group of men: Some were more likely to be troublesome, some were less, but on the whole they would be easy enough to manage.

At least, with my position as Vianne's Consort secure, they

would have been. As matters now stood, one or two of them, di Dienjuste in particular, might be disposed to be…difficult.

A fire snapped in the grate; though the afternoon was warm, the evening would turn chill. The wind always rose to welcome evening here in Arcenne.

Like a woman rising to meet her lover.

She will not see me alone, and the damnable Pruzian is at her door. "The Pruzian. How did she come to trust him?" I sounded harsher than I liked. The goblet's metal was cool against my fingers, charmed to the proper temperature for a red.

"She may or may not trust him." My father gave me a sharp, very blue glance. "She *relies* on you, *m'fils*. The Pruzian is a useful tool, no doubt. She has as good as forgiven our family—"

I turned back to the window. The urge to strike my own father had never been so marked. "He is dangerous. And he is at her very door, while I am sent away to cool my heels and be examined by a clutch of old men."

"You are lucky. The papers could be your death, no matter that Henri sent you into the lion's jaws. Not only that, but this clutch of *old men* is the power of—"

I surfaced from my thoughts with an unpleasant jolt. "Take care what you say next, *Père.*"

The words vibrated in the still air of my father's study, leather-bound books frowning from their shelves, the tasseled sling over the fireplace with its crust of ancient Torkaic blood still sharp and restless.

Silence enfolded us.

I decided to break it first, for once. "You were quick to cast me aside when Vianne doubted me. Now you are quick to have the Council do…*what*? While she lies abed, possibly in agony, after sending an army away with its tail between its legs?" I stared down at the stones of the bailey, my back tightening with instinctive gooseflesh. He was behind me, and armed.

He is my father.

And yet. "Let me be absolutely clear. Since we are men, and may speak freely." I set the goblet on the windowsill. "You are my father; I am your son. But I belong to the Queen of Arquitaine, and even if I am sentenced to the unthinkable at her pleasure, *I am loyal.*" The words burned my tongue. *Never too late, is that it? Or am I lying, as I lied to Henri?* "The Council may examine me, because *she* wishes it. Well and good. But no collection of old men will work against her will. She is the Queen, and as long as there is life granted me I will not hesitate to…*remind*…those who mistake her soft heart for weakness of the fact."

More silence. The shaking in me was Vianne's—the shudders as she stumbled for her horse, whispering my name as if 'twas a charm or a prayer, and my own soft replies. She had mounted with that same pretty, useless Court grace, and her horse had followed the lead of the Pruzian's. The silent ride back to Arcenne's Gate through the seething mass of confused, frightened, and wounded Damarsene had borne a distinct resemblance to a nightmare.

Adersahl had vanished to the barracks, and a great weariness swamped me. What would he tell the rest of the Guard? And how would they react? They were a fine defense for my darling, but I had not intended to be on the outside of that palisade.

"So," the Baron di Arcenne said quietly. "At last we find your measure, *m'fils.*"

Oh, you have not seen the half of my steel yet. "Do you remember when I was nine, *sieur*, and whipped for apples I did not steal?"

He was silent again, but I knew enough to abandon hope that it was from shame.

"I did not cry for mercy." *And I dare you to reply to this sally with any honesty, though I know you will not.*

A long pause. "So you did not."

"Did you ever wonder why?"

"Perhaps because you knew there was none to be had. You are d'Arcenne. There must not even be the *appearance* of—"

"Be *silent*!" I rounded on him. Sick fury struggled for an outlet. "The *appearance*. You provincial old *fool*. Appearance is *nothing*! Truth lies below it, behind it, above it—had you even a month at Court you would be taught as much!"

"Oh, *Court*. That nest of vipers. You rose high in Henri di Tirecian-Trimestin's service, *my son*, and what fueled that rise?"

I do not think even *he* quite believed he had said it. The old rumor, that I had been catamite for a King who preferred boyflesh—and who was I to dispel such a slur when it had proven so initially useful?

"That nest of vipers was where you sent me, *father mine*." Each word a knife-cut, shallow but telling. "And I rose in Henri's service by being willing to kill at his word. You wish the truth? There it is. I killed for the King. I whored for him. I poisoned and stole for him, I bore false witness for him, I did things no honorable man would stoop to. That is what you fathered. And I will do more, and worse; I will be as black as I must, for Vianne." *It was for her all along. But I do not expect you to understand.*

He was silent, examining me afresh. Now I felt the fool, showing my weakness so openly. That is the price of being an instrument of royalty; it means even your own flesh becomes suspect. There is no rest to be found, no safety, and even less softness.

And by the time you realize what you have cast aside, it is too late to seek a remedy. Had I not been such a sharpened instrument, my *d'mselle*, unshielded, might be dead.

Or worse.

Why am I even here? Weariness threatened to swallow me whole. *Because Vianne wishes it.* I strode for the door. Did I stay longer, there was no telling what idiocy I would give voice to next. Or what weapon I would give him to strike me later with.

"Tristan." For the first time, my father sounded old. "Tristan, *m'fils*, wait—"

I did not. I stalked into the hall, and Tinan di Rocham hurriedly scrambled to his feet from the padded bench across the hall. I dismissed him with a gesture, and such was his instinctive obedience that he froze long enough for me to disappear up a staircase and into the Keep's depths.

The familiar hall was empty, but I did not show myself. Instead, I waited, breathing lightly and silently, tucked into a shallow alcove behind a tapestry. The passage leading here was thick with dust, tickling my nose as I waited, my gaze sliding from near to far, alert to any slight movement.

It still took longer than I liked.

When I was certain I knew, I stepped lightly back and followed the hidden passage for a long fifteen steps, then slid out from behind another tapestry and a wooden stand holding slowly-rusting pikes from the di Roncail's time. Quietly, softly, I paced to the corner and peered down the hall once more.

There it was again, that same flicker of motion. I strolled around the corner as if I had not a care in the world, my hands aching for my rapier-hilt. But no—for this, twas knifework, and I could not draw yet.

I did not wish to be caught approaching her door blade-in-hand. Appearances lied, yes—and she did not need another reason to mistrust me.

I was almost past his hiding place when the Knife exploded

into motion, a flash I almost did not catch. Even though I was prepared, the bastard was *quick*.

I was down in a heartbeat, shoulder driven into his midriff and both of us flung on the stone floor with bruising force. He made no sound, the same black-bladed knife not lifted but held low and trapped between us, for I had taken the precaution of carrying a filched doublet over my arm. A knife is only as effective as the reach of its wielder. And cloth, any cloth, as a baffle is preferable to stopping a blade with one's flesh.

He heaved, boots scrabbling, seeking to free his arm, but I had him pinned. Taller and broader, my weight was an advantage, and he had no companions to help—the rest of his trio had been slain the night of their attack on the Keep.

"Cease!" I hissed in my heavily-accented Pruzian. For a moment I regretted not telling Vianne I was familiar with the tongues of Arquitaine's enemies; it could have been useful to hear what she would have had me translate into his native speech. *"I mean her no harm. Do not force me to kill you."*

I wrenched the knife free of his fingers, but I did not relax. No assassin worth the name carries only *one* weapon. The prick of the blade near his belly, where I only had to turn my wrist to drive it home and gut-cut him, calmed the situation somewhat.

He went limp, breath coming in harsh gasps. Both of us sweated, a rankness of fear and violence filling the hall.

"I understand your tongue," I told him in Arquitaine. "And you understand mine."

A nod, his clubbed hair moving against dusty stone. The glaring damage to his face, though charmed and healing, was unpretty in the extreme. Though he would never win prizes even at the best of times. Pruzians are an unlovely race, ill-favored, even though the ruddy-blond Damar—who they claim kinship and share some language with—are sometimes passing fair.

"Now." I thought it likely I had his attention. "What are we to do with each other, Pruzian? I do not like how close you are to my *d'mselle*."

"*I am to protect her,*" he hissed in grinding Pruzian. "*From you.*"

Hardly unexpected, but it still scored me. No trace showed; at least, I hoped it did not. "She needs no protection from me, *friend*." Heavy sarcasm on the last word. "In fact, she is safer with me than without. I do not trust a Knife whose *aufsbar* is still alive."

"*He is not my client now, dogfaced minstrel.*" The insult sounds truly hideous in Pruzian. "*My client is behind that door.*"

"You are a whoreson, and a liar, friend." Insults in Arquitaine have their own rhythm. "Your client is here with a knife to your belly. Three times I could have killed you now, and I've refrained. You work for *me*."

He thought this over. "*You cannot pay me eno—*"

My wrist tensed. The knifepoint slid through a layer of fabric, and he went very still. Cold sweat lay against his cheeks and brow; I found myself hoping nobody would appear at the far end of the hall. "I do not need to pay you." I changed to Pruzian. "*For the black bird rises…*"

"*And the dead tree blooms,*" he answered automatically, then realized what a weapon he had handed me. "*No. No—*"

I took that passphrase from a man much harder to trap than you will ever be. "Oh, yes. I am much more than I appear, Knife. I am your brother now, and if you deal fairly with me, I may let you live." *And he was brave even as the blade was in his belly.* My skin crawled at the memory. I had not dealt fairly with the last Knife I had held at bladepoint. But it had been necessary.

Just as this was.

"You are none of ours." He did not sound happy.

"You are bound to brotherhood now that you have answered, Knife. Now, will you be reasonable, or do we learn the look of your guts?"

I have seen defeat in faces of every shape and station, and his was no different than any other's. *"You are my master,* mil'Hier. *What shall I do?"*

I eased aside, gained my feet. Extended my free hand carefully, the knife ready. "Wait, and watch. Keep *m'd'mselle* safe when I am called away. And be ready."

"For what?" He lunged upright, using my hand, and did not seek to pull me off-balance. Well enough. We would see if the passphrase I had tortured out of another Pruzian Knife held good.

I had gained the knowledge—the phrase, and how to use it—during Henri's long-ago royal visit to the border province of Mietsiere, to negotiate an extended trade agreement. The Pruzians had brought not only their diplomats but a few trios of Knives as well, but after the first trio vanished and the third's lone limping survivor expired broken and bleeding on the steps of the temporary residence of the Damarsene ambassador, negotiations became much less…complex.

"You shall see." Enigmatic enough, I decided. "When is your duty at her door done?"

"Four hours." Grudging, the man examined me.

"And who comes to relieve you?" I could still feel the pleasure of ordering him shoved into an *oublietta*. Vianne had rescued him, and I found myself almost grateful to her soft heart. Had it been one of the Guard at her door, I might have had a harder time of it. He was, after all, only a Pruzian. No match for a nobleman, and his blood would carry precious little guilt.

He shrugged, spreading his hands.

"Very well. Is the door locked?"

Another shrug.

I gave a soft token rap, tried the knob carefully. It was not locked. The Knife stiffened, and I could see the hole in his doublet. I had been very close to eviscerating him.

"Easy, *mil'Brödenr*," I told him. "She is in no danger." *Unless it is from you.*

I twisted the knob, and stepped through.

Chapter Fifteen

The cup on the night-table held the remains of a thick, sticky-red hedgewitch brew. A bitter tinge to its odor warned me, and when I touched the residue with a cautious fingertip, numbness slid up my finger. I hurriedly wiped my hand clean on my breeches.

Bell's-ease, bleeding mallow, and ghostberry. A powerful draught, one capable of drugging even a sedative-resistant hedgewitch into insensibility. A dangerous mix, as well—too much ghostberry and the heart pounds itself to pieces, too much bell's-ease and the languor ceases the circulation instead of merely inducing restorative sleep. Bleeding mallow was for the grievously wounded, or those whose ills could not be cured and whose passage needed easing.

Despite the strength of the draught, she moved uneasily as my shadow fell over the bed. Her arms were up, cradling her head, and the sound she made—a slow, terrible moan of pain—tore something inside my chest.

The half-head. She had kicked free one soft velvet slipper, meant to keep a woman's feet from the chill of stone floors; her small feet worked uselessly, seeking an escape from the pain. The

Aryx shivered, a thick note of distress not heard by the ears, but thudding through the bones.

Dear gods. I dropped the knife onto the night-table, almost touched her hair. Caught myself. *The light is painful for her. So is sound. Well, then.*

Court sorcery is not very practical unless one wishes a duel or a delicate illusion. But there are things that can be done with light and air—a simple bit of work to plunge the room into utter darkness, a muffling-charm to deaden noise. Blackness lay against my eyes, and I found the edge of the bed by touch. My swordbelt fell to the ground, useless against this foe.

Slowly, carefully, I sank down, wincing each time she moved.

She sighed. Her hair was loose and tangled. Her brow was fever-damp; I pressed my fingers against her lips and felt the passage of her breath.

All is well, I wanted to whisper. *I am here.*

And now that I was, layers of cloth between us but the shape of her underneath remembered with fierce exactness, the familiar urge to touch what I could all but shook me.

There is a blind part in any man, who thinks it perhaps easier to take than to ask. If he denies it, he is lying. He who does admit it is a liar as well, for a man will never admit to the full depths of what he is tempted to commit when a woman is that close, and that helpless, and so achingly sweet.

Even after she had me clapped in chains and turned from me in disgust, even after she unwittingly caused my downfall, even as she drove me past every shred of honor or decency, she was still…

She is not to blame. You are the criminal here.

And what did it say of me, that even as she writhed with pain, my thoughts turned in such a direction?

My hands tensed, to keep them from roaming. She gasped,

stiffening, and struggled. "Be still," I whispered in her ear, stroking sweat-damp curls back. The sound-deadening charm held us in a bubble of stillness, absolute blackness pressing fiery phantom images against my eyelids. "Shhh, *m'chri*. Let the draught work."

"T-T-Tr—" The sedation betrayed her, made the attempt slow and slurred. "*Tris*. Is…it…time?"

Time for what? I did not care to guess. "Sleep." She was in too much agony to note the effect she had on me; I am no more than flesh, after all. "I would take the pain for you." My whisper was a bare mouthing of the words, but it still hurt her. She moved, restless. The half-head makes every murmur a gouging inside the skull; any light is a spear of misery. I sought to say no more, simply pressed my lips against her temple and held her. Clumsy, I had not removed my boots, but she did not move again when I wrapped my leg over hers, the irritating fabric between us a bar against the animal in my flesh, and I did my best to hold her so tightly the pain could not slip between us.

A cold, sharp point touched my throat.

I half-opened my eyes, lunging into wakefulness though my body did not dare move. On my back, arms spread wide, I was seemingly helpless—and Vianne stood at the bedside, one knee braced near my hip, the black-bladed knife to my throat, her hair a tangled mess and bright fever-spots on her gaunt cheeks. She was shaking; her half-unlaced dress had slid aside to expose a slice of her pale, perfect shoulder, and I realized the light through the window was morning.

I felt more clear-headed than I had in a very long while.

"How did you—" She halted, perhaps aware of the uselessness of the question. "What are you *doing*?"

I barely even dared swallow, the point at my throat was so keen. I took refuge in levity. "Hoping your temper improves?"

"My temp—" she began, but I had her wrist locked and surged up from the bed. She stumbled back, . I kept pressing her, and her shoulders hit the wall near a low bookcase, next to the watercloset door. Her wrists were so thin; she struggled uselessly. Even fresh from the donjon I was more than a match for her slightness. She did not let go of the knife, though I kept it well away, her arm stretched overhead.

"You were saying." I pressed against her. "About your temper."

She heaved against me, achieved nothing. The fine down at her temple was edged with gold; gold threaded through the dark honey of her tangled curls as well. The urge to lean a little closer and bury my face in her hair all but made me sweat.

"*Sieur.*" Brittle and haughty, she lapsed into stillness. "What must I do to free myself of you? Take your hands from me."

"Oh, I don't think so, *m'chri.*" She was so *thin*, I felt her ribs as I leaned against her. I eased my grip on her wrists slightly. She might well snap in half, did I press too harshly. "Not until you *listen.*"

"Listen to *what*? You were to be examined in Council, you—"

"I did not care to have a clutch of old men wasting my time while you were abed with a half-head." I noted the shadows under her eyes had eased somewhat, and was grateful for that, at least. "My place is with you, Vianne. *At your side*, so the foolishness you fling yourself into does not kill you. I will not have that."

It was not what I had intended to say.

"You did kill the King." She all but choked on the words. "You *did*. Get *away* from me!"

A lie trembled on my lips. I had it prepared, the words that would make this salvageable. To soothe her, to lead her away. To repair what I could, to build on the foundation I had laid last time she was this close to me. She had not believed then, but now, perhaps, I had a moment's worth of her weakness to use.

Instead, I heard myself say dully, "Yes."

What am I doing?

"Yes," I repeated, a trifle louder. "Very well, *yes.* It was a choice. Between Henri, and you. I would do it again, did the gods grant me another chance." *As many times as necessary.*

She hung in my grasp. Her eyes were so dark, I had not found their true color until our wedding-night. Indigo, the deepest summersky evening shade before night truly falls. And now I wondered at her expression, for she seemed as amazed as I was by the admission.

Every lie I had thought to hide behind broke inside me.

"Tristan…"

"Tis very simple, Vianne." My fingers eased, slid up her hand. I did not take the knife from her. I lowered it, the point trembling, and it touched my cheek. Cold metal, and the Pruzian would no doubt be happy to see my blood on it. "I am a traitor; make me bleed for it. I am more useful alive, though. You need me for the Aryx, you need me for protection, you simply need *me.* But do it, if you like. I am at your service."

In every way.

The relief was immense, as if I had just spent myself in her. I had not realized the constant draining tension of examining her face, guessing if she knew or did not, if she suspected, what she would think of my actions. Instead, she knew, and I was exposed to her in a way I never had been.

"I did not truly believe…" She stared as if seeing me for the first time, or as if I had suddenly melted into a loathsome monster, a *demieri di sorce* with claws and fangs ready to rend and eat human flesh. "I thought to shelter you from whatever game the Duc had planned. I thought to *protect* you."

By throwing me in a donjon? But, of course. It made a great deal of sense now—she had perhaps thought to draw out whatever traitors lurked in the shadows by allowing them to think me disgraced and thus, of little value as a means to wound her.

And possibly, amenable to treachery. Which, after all, she had not believed me capable of.

Why had I not thought of it? *Too clever by half, d'Arcenne.* The pain behind my ribs mounted another notch, and despite it, I felt a curious comfort. There was no way to salvage *this*. I had become my own undoing.

"If this is *protection*, Vianne, I should hate to see its opposite."

I did not mean it cruelly. And yet, as soon as the words escaped, they sounded brutally ill-mannered, and much too sharp. I meant only to provoke her into an explosion, for after a woman rages she is usually amenable to reason. Or, at least, to smooth words. I have used such a strategy once or twice.

I should have known it would not work on *her*.

Utterly still, those fever-spots in her cheeks glaring at me, the pulse beating in her throat. "Lisele," she whispered, her lips shaping the sibilant most fetchingly.

It took me a moment to decipher the sudden turn of her thoughts. Her Princesse, Henri's half-Damarsene daughter. "I did not know they were to kill the Princesse." It was my turn to swallow dryly. "She was to be married. To the Damarsene. In your stead."

If I thought her pale before, she was ashen now. "In my…"

"Yes." Was this what the saying *truth is its own reward* meant? The feeling of exquisite nakedness, the idea that she, at last, was truly seeing *me*?

Her eyes narrowed, as a mountain-pard's the moment before it strikes.

A lick of fire tore down my cheek. The knife plunged, its tip glancing along my chest and tearing through shirt and skin both. Blood flew, and Vianne let out a despairing sound. I twisted her wrist, bruising-hard, and my mouth caught her cry as the knife chimed on stone, flung free. Kisses between us were often shy, tentative; this one was not. Copper and spice filled my mouth, she bit my lip hard enough to add to the bleeding, and I held her pinned as she writhed and fought.

For once, I did not ask. I *took* what I wanted from her. What she had, what she could give, what I would die without. I kissed her even as the blood welled and the wounds burned, the Aryx between us shifting against cloth and skin, metal scorch-hot and her fingers tangled in my hair, wrenching hard enough to add more fury to the explosion between us.

It was not Graecan fire, but it burned nonetheless. Across the room in a tangle of hot blood and her fevered mouth, tipped onto the bed's sinking depth, and it was Vianne in my arms again, her softness and the marks of her nails in my back. The hot tight core of her, desperation shaking her limbs and her teeth driven into my shoulder—twas deadly-silent as a back-alley assassination, neither of us weakening enough to give so much as a moan. Tears welling from her closed eyelids, the blood smeared between us, and when at last I let myself career over the edge, helplessly shaking in her arms, the Aryx burning between us like a star, she wept as if her heart would break.

I should have hated myself. But it was worth it. It *was*.

I would do it again, as well.

Chapter Sixteen

The knife was, of course, bastard-sharp. It had not cut deep enough to endanger me, but I would scar.

I cared little. Drying blood stung as I moved slightly, brushing her hair back. I had torn her dress, my boots still on, clothing and bedding tangled around us, thrashed and beaten into a mess. I kissed her cheek, the corner of her mouth. Tears welled between her eyelids, vanishing past her temples into her hair. Her mouth, smeared with crimson, was still the sum of most desires, so I kissed her again. Greedy, as if she were an exotic fruit, our tongues sliding, and the thirst in me was not slaked.

The woman was *dangerous*. What would I not do, for her?

I found myself murmuring endearments against her skin, leaving bloody prints as I kissed every part of her I could reach. She lay very still, trembling slightly as she wept. I tried to press the tears away with my lips, over and over again.

You are not meant for this. Let me take the pain away. "Shh, all's well. All's well—"

"It is *not* well!" she finally choked. "It is *not* well! You…I…*you*—"

"I am not a gentle man." I had told her as much before. I felt the need to repeat it, and immediately gave myself the lie by kissing her again. "But now you know. I am sorry for it, I can explain—"

She struggled uselessly. "Stop. Let *go*."

The first thread of unease touched me. This should be so *simple* now. Had I not just proven…

Well, what had I proven? That I was a *vilhain*? I already knew as much.

"Not until you see." The man using my voice sounded far harsher than I liked. "I am *not your enemy*, Vianne. Everything I have done is for *you*, for your safety, for you to—"

"Left Hand," she spat, going limp and glaring at me, drying blood streaking her face. "You betrayed the King, Tristan. You *swore* to him, just as you swore to me—how can you say you are not my enemy?"

"I swore to *you* before I ever did to the King. The first moment I saw you, everything afterward was part of it. I had to find a way." I stumbled over the words—after love a man is stupid, and I was doubly foolish to be seeking to explain this now. "One thing led to the next, but it was all in service to a single end."

"This?" She struggled again, seeking to free herself of my hands. "All this *death*? You *intended* this?"

I pushed her deeper into the bed's embrace. At least she could not run away; she *had* to listen to me. Dried blood flaked over us both. "I intended to be *with* you!" The force of the cry made her flinch. I sought to contain myself, failed miserably. My fingers bit her wrists, she flinched again. "I intended us to escape through Marrseize, taking ship to Tiberia. I intended for Timrothe d'Orlaans to have what he wished and much joy of it. I intended for you to be safe; I *intended* so much. Everything turned to ash, Vianne. They caught me, and of a sudden I was not only without you, I had *nothing*. Not even my honor. And you…You were *de-pending* on me. And the damnable Aryx, making it even more…I could not forsake you." I ran out of words. Struggled blindly with all I wished to say. How could the truth turn into such a complex mess?

"Lisele married off to a Damarsene, the King dead, d'Orlaans pillaging Arquitaine—all because of me? Because you…" She closed her eyes, as if she could not bear to look at me.

Of course she cannot. You cannot even stand to look at yourself, d'Arcenne. What makes you think she can? "D'Orlaans wanted Henri's throne for decades, Vianne. If he had not succeeded at this toss of the dice, there would have been another. Twas only a matter of time; I have known as much for years. I saw my chance and took it. The King had made the arrangements, Vianne. You were to be shipped to Damar, forced into—"

"A marriage? With a man I did not care for?" She laughed, a tiny, bitter sound. "Too late to save me from *that*."

It cut unexpectedly deep. I loosened my grasp on her wrists and slid from the bed. At least I had not torn my breeches as well, in the madness. She lay as if broken, her throat moving as she swallowed.

"You do not have to love me," I lied.

"Oh, if I do not, you will kill me as you killed the King? Or marry me off? What will you do to me? What could be worse than *this*?"

"I am your Consort," I reminded her. "Until you repudiate me in a Temple. I am your Left Hand, and you shall not be free of *that* as long as I breathe. As one already dead, I swore myself to your service."

"You swore to the *King*." A glimmer of eyes under her lashes. Was she examining me? She held herself so still, as if faced with a wild, unpredictable animal.

115

I was an animal, certainly. Look at what I had done to her. Shame bit me, hot and rank.

But I was exceedingly predictable once she knew where to apply the pressure. Once she knew that the sum of my desires lay in the form of one shivering, frightened, beautiful hedgewitch. What would I *not* do, to bring her where I needed her to stand? "He may have thought so. The world may have thought so. But in the end, Vianne, it was to *you*."

She finally moved, curling on her side, away from me. I had not just torn her dress, I had savaged it. I hoped I had not bruised her. Or…hurt her.

You have, I realized. *Of all the things you swore you would never do, and now you have. You did not ask her leave, you merely took.*

"Go away," she whispered. "Leave me be."

"You still do not understand." I stood, the light of morning drenching the bedroom, and loathed myself even more completely. "I cannot. You would have to kill me." I swallowed, my throat moving. "Until you do, *m'chri*, my darling hedgewitch, my Queen, you have a hawk at the wrist. Set me after prey or hood me, Vianne. But you cannot rid yourself of me."

I backed away from the bed, step by step. My face ached, and the wound on my chest stung. I found a chair by backing into it, and dropped down. I gripped the arms, but not in fear.

No, I held to them splintering-hard. Dear gods.

Loathing turned inside me, married to frustrated tenderness. She was deathly silent, and I cursed myself. Not for the first time.

And most certainly not for the last.

Chapter Seventeen

She did not look at me, and the new dress—rich crimson this time, its lacings loose because she had lost weight—rustled as she moved. Her hair was braided back; I had watched her trembling fingers perform the job. She did not wince as she settled into the hard chair at the head of the table, and the small fresh mark on her shoulder, where I had suckled hard enough to bruise, was covered by the red velvet.

What did it cost her, to look so calm? Her eyes were red with weeping, but none remarked upon it.

The Council, a collection of noblemen, took their seats silently once she had settled. My hands, crossed before me in a traditional posture, ached for my rapier-hilt. Outside the door was a fuming Jierre and a bruised Pruzian Knife; seeing the look that passed between my lieutenant and Vianne when she opened the door and he realized I was behind her had been…uncomfortable.

"You are called to order, *chivalieri et sieurs.*" Very quiet, very contained, she sounded every inch the Queen. Paper littered the table, and the Aryx gleamed. My gaze riveted itself to Vianne's expression, seeking to decode every nuance. "Before we examine…my Consort, I will hear reports. Conte di Siguerre? Your preparations?"

"Complete." The cranky old turtle hunched his shoulders and blinked. He was strangely subdued. Normally he was a whistling cantankerous rattle of a man. "All is in readiness."

"Thank you. Conte di Dienjuste?"

He was a young blond *chivalier*, his excitability muted as well. He stole a glance at me, sidelong. "Avicial has declared for you, Your Majesty. Between a third and a half of Arquitaine, now. I've sent the proclamations; we should start seeing the results soon."

Proclamations? She's raising an army. Hm. I caught Siguerre glancing at me as well. I stood before the fireplace, its warmth a balm and penance all at once. At least she had not ordered me clapped in chains again.

She had been seeking to protect me. I should have *known*. I had thrown away every advantage, and I had perhaps lost her. Who knows what a woman can forgive, much less a Queen?

Gnarled old Irion di Markui's fist crashed on the tabletop. "I see not why we must waste our time on this. Is the man a traitor or not? If he is, let us have him beheaded and done with!"

"If you speak out of turn again, *sieur*, you shall feel my displeasure." Vianne gazed coldly at him. "Marquis?"

Di Falterne, a stolid dark man with his hair long as a *chivalier*'s, his face seamed as a mended kettle's, nodded. "Our supply situation is…adequate. Trade with Navarrin is the deciding factor, of course, but they are continuing to uphold their bargain. A missive arrived not two hours ago…" He glanced at the window, as if wishing himself far away.

Interesting.

"And?"

"It did, my liege. It bore the mark you instructed to be watched for."

Vianne sighed. Her head dropped forward for a moment, but she squared her shoulders and lifted her chin. "Baron d'Arcenne."

My father, seated next to Markui, had not ceased to stare, his bright blue eyes seeking to drill through me and into the wall. His displeasure was obvious, but muted. "The Damarsene, with di Narborre, continue to retreat. They are still in disarray; the entire province is harrying them forth." My father paused, steepling his fingers before his face—a movement I recognized. "It will be difficult to keep control of the peasants, do they taste much more uncertainty."

"Theirs is the blood that is shed," Vianne murmured. "Advise me, Minister Primus. Can we win a war before winter?"

I could have answered, but I held my peace.

"Most likely...not. D'Orlaans will now know you have the Seal and the will to use it. Perhaps he will seek to treat with you. In any case, he will have many very distressed Damarsene to deal with, and the small matter of paying the army that is tramping back to the Citté to meet him."

"Tribute. And whatever he has promised them." Vianne sat bolt-upright, staring unseeing at the table. "I would give much to know..."

But she did not speak further. Instead, she sank into silence, and the entire room held its breath. My heart ached. She had dressed as a *chivalier* prepares for battle, doing her best to ignore my presence. I had cleaned off the blood as well as possible, and my face itched and burned. What did they think of the fresh slice down my cheek?

Did it matter? All that mattered was what she would do now.

The quiet stretched, an unsound fit to scrape nerves raw.

Finally, Vianne sighed again. She looked up, and her dark eyes were clear and steady. "*Sieurs et chivalieri*," she said formally, "my Consort stands accused of treason to Henri di Tirecian-Trimestin, the former King of Arquitaine. I wish you to advise me on the matter of his innocence, his trustworthiness, and his fitness to continue as my Consort. You are to examine him. He is to answer every question thoroughly and to your satisfaction. When you are finished, you may set him free or attend to the details of his execution." A heavy pause, and she rose with a slight soft sound of velvet moving. "I leave the matter to you."

Every one of them leapt to his feet. She swept down the fireside length of the table, and she did not glance at me. The pulse beat frantically in her throat, and moving air brought me a breath of bergaime and spice, green hedgewitchery and the indefinable note of her skin. I could still feel her under me, the marks of her nails in my back and a slight pleasant lassitude.

I swallowed the stone in my throat.

She paused at the door. "And..." Her head turned, I saw the curve of her cheek, the shape of her chin, and a glitter of swinging ruby ear-drops. "Should you judge him guilty, *sieurs*, tis not necessary for him to leave this room alive."

And then she was gone, the door closing with a quiet, definite *snick*.

They questioned me. Not ruthlessly, and I could sense my father's hand as if behind a screen.

Of course. She is not as tractable as they thought. I am a way to keep hold on her, and most of them are his friends of old. They attend the provincial Assizes together. I forced myself to concentrate, spinning my story. To Vianne I would admit my guilt. Not to these men.

Of them all, it was di Rivieri and d'Anton who gave me the most trouble. Over and over they asked small questions, manifestly not believing my answers. In their insistence I saw Vianne's influence—she had laid her ground well, perhaps hoping their calm thoughtfulness would sway the others. But di Markui still fumed over her taking him to task, di Siguerre thought it a load of nonsense and foppery intrigue, di Falterne simply listened, and di Dienjuste took up my cause with almost courtsong fervor. I had often noticed di Dienjuste seemed half in love with Vianne himself, and he seemed to consider me a proxy for his own suit. It was odd that he would defend me so strongly…so odd I wished I had the opportunity to sit and quietly think until I could wily-farrat out why.

But I needed all my wit to face them, and to keep my lies in proper order.

My father, after noting that he could not very well be expected to judge his son dispassionately, leaned back in his chair and folded his arms, his gaze an uncomfortable weight. I had thought I had outgrown such discomfort.

I was wrong.

"And you bear her no ill will for clapping you in chains?" di Rivieri persisted. "For if a woman had done so to me—"

"She is not merely a woman." Immediate disagreement leapt from me. *She is Vianne, she is mine, and you shall watch your words.* "She is the *Queen.* She could not take the chance of leaving such an allegation unexamined. And I did lie—to ease her mind, I told her of poison, not of a bloody murder. She did not know what to trust." *And I am pinning the blame for the King's murder on di Narborre's men. Some of who are most likely dead now. Others are no doubt reserved to speak against me, if d'Orlaans ever finds the chance. We shall see what can be done about that later, though.*

Much later, when all is settled. "I have oft chided her for having a soft heart." I looked down at my clasped hands. Modesty was called for now, the right note of male chagrin. "I did not expect her to listen so closely to my advice."

A ripple of unwilling amusement went through them.

"By Danshar!" di Markui snapped. "Why do we waste more time on this? He was Captain of the Guard. Henri *trusted* him enough to set him to barking at his brother's heels. D'Orlaans—we know him of old, do we not? We have had his boot on our necks, whether his brother was alive or not, for a very long while. And if d'Arcenne's son wished to harm the Queen, he would have during their escape. He could have snapped her neck and left her in the Shirlstrienne."

I tensed. So did Dienjuste, and my father wore a very slight smile.

"Besides, the woman is mad," he grumbled. "Aryx or not, she is *mad*."

I took two steps forward, my face burning afresh. "I will pretend," I said softly, "that I did not hear that. Examine me all you like, *sieur*, but if you speak against the Queen I will call you to account."

"See?" Di Markui beamed, his salt-and-pepper mane glowing in the afternoon sunlight through the rippling windows. I heard hooves in the bailey below, decided it must be a dispatch, and kept myself tense, staring at him. "He will not hear a word against her. Arcenne is always loyal to the Aryx, my friends. This is all a load of nonsense, and the sooner we finish it the sooner we can return to guiding the Aryx—ah, the *Queen*—through the current unpleasantness." He settled back in his creaking chair, and the longing to strangle him even though he was useful rose under my skin.

Calm yourself, Tristan. This is going well.

"Very well." Di Dienjuste stood. "I pronounce the man innocent."

Markui lumbered to his feet. "Innocent."

Di Rivieri was silent. So was d'Anton.

"Innocent," Siguerre rumbled as he rose. "Gods above. Let us
be done with it."

D'Anton glanced at my father. "Perseval?"

"He is my son." My father's jaw set, a muscle ticking in his
cheek.

The *chivalier* considered this, then slowly stood. "Innocent."

Di Falterne and di Rivieri remained seated. Finally, both stood,
but they did not speak. They were unwilling to pronounce me
guilty, they would countenance the others calling me innocent,
but they would not add their voices to the chorus.

My father pushed his chair back. "Are we agreed, then?"

"We may as well be." Di Rivieri folded his arms, a lean, dark
man with a peasant's breadth of shoulder.

"Very well. Halis?"

Di Siguerre coughed. "Tristan d'Arcenne, you are ajudged innocent by peers. Be on your way."

Not one of you is my peer, sieurs, *but at least this gives me room
to maneuver. Which is a boon in any battle.* "My thanks, *sieurs et
chivalieri.*"

The feeling of liberation lasted only until I opened the door
and found the hall deserted. I set off to find Vianne and begin, in
whatever way I could, to repair the damage, but she was not to be
found.

For while I had been examined so thoroughly, the Queen of
Arquitaine had ridden forth from Arcenne's still-smoking Gate
with her Guard and a Pruzian Knife. Her instructions, handed
to my father on a sheaf of parchment bearing the impress of the

Great Seal, were explicit. We were to stay at Arcenne until she gave us leave to move, under pain of her displeasure.

We sent out riders to comb the province, but she had evaporated into Arquitaine.

Well-played, my love. Well-played indeed.

Chapter Eighteen

My mother poured chai, her dark hair glowing. She smiled pensively, her primrose silk rustling as she leaned forward. "A little less like a caged beast, and a little more like a *chivalier, m'fils.*" A breeze from the garden filtered through the open windows, and the harp in the corner mocked me with its gleaming. Vianne had once touched its golden curve, running her fingers along the pegs lightly, during a laughing conversation about the perils of fashion.

I swallowed my pride and my temper, tried again. "She is *in danger*," I repeated, through gritted teeth. "Where has she gone? She would not leave without some word to you. Why will you not tell me?"

"She left with some very fine Court sorcerers and handy blades. It is no less dangerous for her than it was here, between assassins and armies and what-have-you. She has her reasons."

"Which would be?"

"My dear, *I* am not privy to the Queen of Arquitaine's—"

I swore. Vilely.

My decorous dam set the silver chai-pot down and glared at me. The basket of bandages she had been sewing stood carefully aside, and the entire room made me nervous. It was so…soft.

"*Tristan.*" As if I were a boy again. She had not mentioned the wound to my face, but then again, twould be impolite. Especially if she gathered the provenance of the cut.

"Your pardon, *Mère.*" Grudgingly. "I must know. It is *dangerous* for her without me. Who will she look to for aid?"

"I believe Vianne di Rocancheil et Vintmorecy is capable of caring for herself in some small ways, *m'fils.* She is doing what she must for the good of Arquitaine." My mother's chin lifted. "Now come and sit, and have some chai."

I had thought Vianne would not have disappeared without taking leave of my mother, and I further thought my mother would be easily blandished into telling me more of my darling's plans.

My father was of the opinion that questioning servants would give us a direction, so we would at least know whither she was bound. I hoped he was having better luck.

It was odd—he and I did not speak of anything other than the task to be done, and we seemed easier with each other now than we ever had. At least he understood that to *find* her was paramount.

If he cursed me for whatever had caused her to take this course, it did not matter. I was already busy cursing myself. The fact that Vianne must have been planning this before I proved myself such a beast—perhaps even before Adrien di Cinfiliet whispered his poison in her ear—did not alter my self-loathing.

She is afraid. And she was the lady for catching intrigues at Court. She is playing for her life now; that sharpens her wits still further. And it makes her likely to act instead of waiting.

"*Père* told me she requires my presence to use the Aryx." I dropped down in the chair opposite my mother and examined her face. *Do not force me to use a Left Hand's methods, mother mine. Not against my own blood.*

She nodded, slowly. "Vianne...did mention summat of that."

I took the cup she had poured for me. *Enough.* I risked a raid against her borders. "My presence, or a man's presence, or...?"

I watched my mother struggle, her calm cracking slightly. *You wish to help Vianne, you want to help me. You know how much I love her; you are a gentle creature.* Another hot bolt of self-loathing speared me.

A Left Hand knows how to let silence work upon the holders of secrets. In the absence of rougher methods, it is surprisingly effective. Those who do not bend under the weight of a conscience must be approached with other methods.

But my mother was not a difficult castle to siege.

"*Your* presence," she said finally, picking up the chai-pot again. A cool afternoon breeze from the garden drifted through the filmy curtains, and I thought of Vianne in this chair, as the Baroness sallied to ease her. I had watched my mother draw a shy smile from my darling, again and again. "Tris..."

I dropped my gaze to my cup.

She poured her own chai, silently arranged a plate of dainties—of course, my father would see to it that my mother had those little things she loved. The things that made her so gentle, and so unlike him.

She set the plate between us, with her usual well-bred precision. Finally, she spoke again. "She did not say much."

I kept staring as if the spiced liquid in my cup held the solution to the Unanswerable Riddle. My face was frozen into a mask of quiet suffering, and I hoped its expression was even now wringing her heart.

"Only that the Aryx must be used to protect, and that she

could not fully make it do as she wished without you. Since you are her Consort. She said it was the Blessed's idea of a jest, perhaps."

She must have trusted you, to speak so freely. And I wonder how bitterly she laughed, thinking of a gods' jest. I still held my tongue. If there was aught more, she was approaching the edge of telling it.

"*M'fils*...you are not angry, are you? At your father?"

Of all the questions I expected, that was the last. A sigh took me by surprise, tension unstringing. My shoulders dropped. "Would it do any good? I am a disappointment, *Mère*. I always have been."

"No. Never." She moved the plate slightly, her slim fingers so soft.

Like Vianne's. Not for them the rasp of swordhilt, or the cold and hunger of uncertainty, or the screaming chaos of battle. They were not fit for it, and without their small rooms and bright chai-pots, their gloves and curls and soft brushing skirts, what was all the rest of the unpleasantness *for*? Useless and worthless, unless it set a hedge around this, my mother's sunlit room smelling of fresh air, sunshine, and a faint ghost of perfume and pastries.

My father would have preferred a different son. One more like Jierre, perhaps. One who would have never been a Left Hand. Would you, too?

His disappointment was at least expected. Hers would be more difficult to endure.

"You are so *like* him!" my mother finally burst out, with a toss of her head. Her peridot ear-drops swung. "I wish I'd warned her. Stubborn, both of you. It takes a light touch to manage a d'Arcenne; at least I told her that much before she went haring off—" She clapped her hand over her mouth. "Oh, *hellfire*," she muttered through her fingers. "Hell*fire* and damnation."

My eyebrows raised to hear such language from her. It took all my control to keep my face down and my tone soft. "A light touch? She does not even need that, *m'Mère*. She only needs to wish for it, to set me at it, and I will—"

"Do whatever it is you *think* she wants, or what you have convinced yourself she needs." My mother sighed. "You are so young. And so is she. Tristan, she has taken on a burden. It is one you cannot share, no matter what you would wish. The gods chose her for this."

Now that was surprising. "I had no idea you were religious."

"I am not overly religious, no. But it would take a fool not to see the hands of the Blessed in this."

Oh, the gods. They make trained farrats and apes of us all. Or perhaps life merely does so for them. Yet I could not discount the Blessed. I had seen them at work in the Temple. On my wedding day, the face of Jiserah the Gentle blazing no less than my Queen's—now *there* was a memory not likely to ease my mood.

Jiserah was the Blessed responsible for marital harmony. I wondered if her grace on my wedding day would do me much good now, did I make an offering a-Temple. "Gods or no gods, *Mère*, she needs me."

"I do not think she trusts the Council."

I went utterly still. The chair under me was far too finely carved for my comfort; it could tip me at any moment. "What?"

"Before she left, she told me in confidence…" My mother glanced at the open window. She leaned forward, the struggle she waged with herself clearly visible. "Tristan, she told me she suspects one or more of the Council are d'Orlaans's creatures. That was why she had to leave. There was…an attempt. To kidnap her, to take her outside the walls."

The cold was all through me. This was the missing piece of the puzzle. "When?"

"Just before the Damarsene arrived. She…the Pruzian, he fought them off. They were d'Arquitaine. Lowlanders, not mountainfolk. One said a name, but she would not tell me." My mother's soft cheeks were now damp, and another tear turned crystalline on her lashes, touching the fine lines at the corners of her eyes made by smiling. "The Pruzian was wounded, and Vianne…she sought to use the Aryx. It worked, but not well, and she was hard-pressed. Twas when she suspected she needed you to wield it properly."

Dear gods. Why did she not tell me? It had to have been after she left me in the donjon. "Why did—"

"She swore me to secrecy." My mother bit her lip. "Even your father does not know of this. She thought to protect you, *m'fils*, that her seeming disregard for you would ensure those who sought to harm her would attack more directly, instead of using *you*."

My mother needs reassurance, to retain her as an asset for later. She will hear things I do not, and now that she has broken a confidence once, she will do so more easily again. "You have done right, *m'Mère*." Slowly, to drive home that we were in unwilling league now. "A name on the Council. Did she say aught else? Anything?"

For now I would be doubly watchful of those old men. An attempt to take her person from Arcenne, and her only defense the Pruzian Knife. Perhaps he was trustworthy after all—or perhaps he saw someone else seeking to collect his eventual reward, and so interrupted the event.

"No." My mother shook her head. "Afterward, there was the battle. She was at the walls, struggling with the Aryx."

And now she is in the wilderness, with only a few men to protect her, and the Aryx unreliable. I forced myself to sip at my chai. It might as well have been mud, for all I tasted. *Think. What concerns me most, now?*

The most pressing problem was, of course, finding her. She did not wish to be found, and I was better placed to find the direction she had taken flight while here in Arcenne rather than haring about the countryside. And here, I could perhaps bait a trap for whatever treachery lurked on her Council. It would fill the time, no matter how I longed to saddle my horse, take up my sword, and go a-questing like a *chivalier* in the aftermath of the Blood Years.

Another thought struck me, almost violently.

She had used the Seal during our flight from the Citté, but I had not been her Consort then. A Consort, once taken, was necessary for the Aryx? Well, that was a problem easily solved, was it not?

There was no shortage of Temples within a few days' riding. Our marriage vows were the old ones, archaic and bloodthirsty in their phrasing, from the Angoulême's time. She could repudiate me in a Temple, but I could not divorce myself of *her*. I had wished it thus, so she could trust me.

You cannot be trusted, Tristan. You know as much.

And once she was at a Temple, another Consort would be easy to contract as well.

Who would she choose? And would the Blessed grant their blessing to another man, one more fit than a filthy traitor who had proven himself a beast?

Perhaps Jierre? He respected her wit and bravery. Adersahl? An older man, but steady and resourceful. Tinan di Rocham? He outright worshipped her. Jai di Montfort? He was whip-thin and handsome, and had an easy smile. Or Jespre di Vidancourt, or perhaps di Chatillon? She could have her pick. They were half in love with her already.

Who would not be?

I rocked to my feet. The chai-cup fell, splashing its contents onto a thick blue-patterned rug. My face burned, and the wound upon it twitched. My mother let out a small hurt sound, but I strode from the room.

If I stayed there longer, I would smash something.

Chapter Nineteen

The weeks that followed were stark with rage and fear. There was no word of her. The searchers failed to find any trace. Now I knew some little of what d'Orlaans must have felt when he found her missing. Except she was merely a foundation-stone for his plans, while to me, she was simply, merely, everything.

A small distinction, perhaps.

There was work to be done. The proclamations to raise an army had gone forth, and the effects began to be felt. Arcenne swelled near to bursting in the month that followed. To my father fell the task of turning the disgruntled peasants, fire-tempered noblemen, and mercenary adventure-seekers, not to mention the criminals and opportunists, into an army. The rest of the Council sought to keep themselves from boredom, and the swelling crowd soon gave them plenty of opportunity.

The only peace I found was during drill. I had been a Captain; I could have trained men to warfare in my sleep.

It takes time to make a man into a reasonable soldier, especially a peasant—time, attention, and a measure of careful brutality. You must break and rebuild a man before he will obey during the chaos of a battle, and you must train him if you expect him to wield his weapon with anything approaching minimum facility. The end of summer ripened into harvest-season, and every commander's eye was turned nervously to the mountains. The clouds held on their peaks dropped a little farther each day. The storms of winter's approach would mean feeding the men and their followers until spring, and even with trade through Navarre that was a daunting proposition.

No word from our Queen. Precious little news from the rest of Arquitaine. My father's nerves stretched almost to the breaking point, and my mother grew restless and worried, organizing the stockpiling of stores in case we were attacked again—and to prepare for winter's white siege.

I? I prowled the halls of the Keep, unable to sleep, and loosed my temper on those noblemen unfortunate enough to come seeking adventure and finding themselves under my heel as a cadre eventually meant for the protection of the Queen of Arquitaine.

Yes, I was training a new Guard. They did not measure to the task.

Then again, I had failed ignobly, too. If I pushed them ruthlessly, I pushed myself harder.

So it was after a long drill session, wet with sweat and with my fury a dim ember, that I dismissed them one long late-summer evening. The nights were growing chill, and the first etching of frost had appeared in the early mornings. It was already late, and the provinces that had declared for Vianne were busy bringing in the crops. The flood of recruits had slowed, but it would become a torrent once harvest was done.

Or so my father hoped.

I was in the dusty, stone-floored drillyard, giving one of the horse troughs a longing look, when a flicker of motion caught my attention. I flattened myself in a convenient shadow, saltwater growing chill on my skin. I wore darker cloth than a nobleman's linen, and my doublet was merely functional—what use in destroying something fine, when all I did was sweat and curse? Every inch of fineness had left me.

He caught my attention with a furtive movement, hugging the wall on the other side of the yard's stone-floored expanse. I went still, instinct nailing me in place.

The idiot was not paying heed, and had perhaps not even seen me in the gathering dusk. Instead, he hurried, casting a quick glance over his shoulder at the door the new Guard had disappeared through. I was normally at their heels, chivvying them along, but had turned that duty over to the quickest-witted among them—Siguerre's grandson Tieris, a muscle-shouldered oaf who might, with years of practice, eventually be able to swing a rapier without hurting himself. I did not know quite why I had lingered in the yard, unless I had caught a breath of wrongness without being consciously attuned to it.

Once a man has trained himself to look for the wrong note in a courtsong, he can hear little else. And a Left Hand is always on the alert for that single wrong note.

So I stayed, and watched, my hand loose at my dagger's hilt. The scar on my face twitched, an odd feeling indeed.

Interesting.

Divris di Tatancourt, former King's Messenger, skirted the edge of the drillyard with long strides. He was cloaked, and as he melded with the long shadows on the opposite end he pulled his hood up. Swathed in anonymous fabric, he was almost out of sight by the time I decided to drift after him.

One cannot follow a man too closely, especially if he is nervous. Sometimes nerves can make him blind to pursuit, but the chance of it heightening his senses and his caution is too large. Besides, I knew the city far better than he did.

Shadows gathered deeper as he hurried down twisting cobbled lanes, his cloak disappearing into failing light. My pulse beat thinly in my throat. I followed, every nerve suddenly strained and awake as it had not been for a long while.

The last time I had felt this alive, Vianne had been in my arms.

I winced internally at the thought, chose a small street that would cut farther to the west. He was bound for the *Quartier Gieron*, the siege-burned district that had been abandoned before refugees and soldiers swarmed into Arcenne. I did not know what I expected—this was a long way to walk for a man intent on whoring, which left skullduggery or intrigue as his possible reasons. Or, who knew? But I was curious, and so I followed.

And when he reached his goal, I was rewarded.

Laughter and cries, and crackling fires. I halted, amid the reek of their odd spices and meat stews, their odor of smithery and dry oil. Woodsmoke, horses, the scent of tinkerfolk.

R'mini.

They are dark, and fierce, and their hedgewitchery is not like ours. Furthermore, the R'mini do not settle in one place—they travel, in their brightly-painted wagons, oxen and horses pulling them step by slow step through the world. They are fine menders and blacksmiths, carriers of tales and sometimes disease, though the plague ravaging other parts of Arquitaine had not touched any province declaring for Vianne as Queen.

And you still do not believe in gods, Tristan?

They do not take to outsiders, the R'mini. But they had brought Vianne safely through the Alpeis forest and to Arcenne, and when she spoke of them her face softened. It was the only time I saw her...well, at peace.

Or, perhaps, happy.

Divris di Tatancourt was d'Arquitaine, a foreigner, and a nobleman to boot. But he was welcomed at the R'mini fire. Their women, shy and sloe-eyed, hung back, clicking their tongues. The men crowded him, and one heavyset older fellow with a red sash, a gold earring, and a dagger at his ample waist clapped di Tatancourt on the shoulder and offered him a tankard of something. Twas probably *rhuma*, their fiery liquor, and the Messenger took a draught with good grace. They engaged in close conversation while the rest of the company went about the evening business of dinner and tending to the camp and livestock.

Among them, I was…myself, Vianne whispered in my memory. We had been together in the dark, my hand on her hip and her breath soft at my shoulder. *They did not care for the Aryx, or d'Orlaans, or anything else. I was simply V'na. And right glad of it I was, too.*

I cast about for a better place to observe them from. Though the Gieron was filling as the army arrived, plenty of the buildings were unfit for habitation—so the unoccupied cottage I made my way into was a perfect vantage point. I watched through the slats nailed over a rotting, cavernous window, exhaling softly to remind myself to keep calm. It could mean nothing.

Of course it means something. Vianne traveled with the R'mini. And di Tatancourt owes her his life; else d'Orlaans's killspell would have taken him to the afterworld in short order.

Considering that the killspell had been intended for me, there was a certain symmetry to events. I spared a grim smile at the thought.

Di Tatancourt was taken into a red and blue-painted wagon, the headman followed. The rest of the R'mini, chattering and laughing in their strange spiked language, were a whirl of color and firelight. They favor dark reds and bright blues, greens and splashes of charm-cleaned white, gold at neck and throat and ears, and the women sometimes sport thin golden rings at the nose. The gold flashed against dark skin and dark hair—their coloring has an undertone of red instead of the d'Arquitaine blue. An old word for them was *noiruse*, the Black-Red. For all that, they treat their children well. Any youngling is prized among them. There are stories of orphans taken into their wagons, but I do not know the truth of such.

I waited, and watched.

When di Tatancourt reappeared, he was pale and shaken. He stepped heavily down from the wagon, and the headman—for such, I had deduced, he absolutely was, the leader of their little company—leaned out, cupped his hand near his mouth, and continued speaking in a low, fierce tone.

The Messenger shook his head. He had a leather satchel. He was even paler, too, and almost staggered.

I do not know enough about what would frighten this man.

Vianne had spent hours closeted with him, questioning him of Court. Some of her questions I could see the logic behind; others, not so much. And after I had been dragged off a-donjon, no doubt she had spent much time with him as well, laying her plans.

My hands shook.

Calm yourself. Anger serves nothing.

I wanted to burst forth from my lair and catch him, beat every living shred of information out of his quivering body, and finish by sliding a knife between his ribs. My savagery did not shock me.

The fact that my self-control was so thin did. So I breathed, soft and slow. Would I turn into *Chivalier* di Kassath in the old court-songs, so jealous of his *d'mselle* he slew a man for simply sighing as she passed?

The songs never said what the *d'mselle* thought of this, beyond one very pretty refrain—*oh, my love, give me room to breathe.*

I winced inwardly. Watched the headman of the R'mini land on solid earth, clapping di Tatancourt on the shoulder again. As he might brace up one of his compatriots who had suffered a misfortune. He said something else, and the Messenger made a wry face, hitching the leather dispatch bag higher on his other shoulder. He answered in Arquitaine, and I caught the words *the Queen.*

The headman laughed, kissed his fingertips, and Divris di Tatancourt swept him a bow. Then, his shoulders no less hunched and his step no less hurried and nervous, the Messenger left the circle of R'mini firelight, plunging back into the dark.

And I followed.

I chose the place with care—dark alley mouths, a ramshackle narrow street at the edge of the Gieron, very few avenues of escape. My doublet looped over my arm and my dagger ready, I waited for him—this was the best approach to the Keep if he wished to pass unremarked. Of course, he could be an idiot, and take another route.

I did not think him quite an idiot. Merely unpracticed. It takes a certain skill to move about a city at night without drawing attention. The trick is not to act with confidence, but with the correct amount of furtiveness for the street or alley in which you find yourself.

His step echoed against the brick paving. A crowd would have meant I had to kill him—I would have had to work close, slip the knife into a kidney, and take the bag while he fell. It was the tenebrous time just on the edge of full night, where dusk fills every corner with far more shadow than midnight. It is a golden time for secret meetings, assassinations, thievery, rifling a corpse's pockets.

The doublet was intended as a baffle against knifeplay, but di Tatancourt, with a nobleman's instinct, reached for his rapier instead of the far-more-practical dagger. So it was over his head with the doublet, the rapier singing as it was struck from his hand and hit brick paving, a ringing blow to maze his wits, and the dispatch bag's strap cut. It was in my possession in a trice, and I kicked him twice while he was on the ground, simply to disorient him and keep him down. Snatching the doublet up, avoiding his thrashing, I was tempted to say summat but quelled the urge.

I stepped back, and it was only the long habit of watching one's enemy even while he is aground and helpless that saved me. For I saw him lift the diabolical thing, and dove aside before it spoke with a *demieri di sorce*'s belching roar. The ball went wide, I vanished into the alley, and Divris di Tatancourt was left with his rapier, his Navarrin *pistolerro*, and his wounded pride.

Whatever was in the bag would tell me much. But however he explained his bruises would tell me even more.

Chapter Twenty

I burst into my father's study, and Irion di Markui half-rose, his hand to his rapier-hilt. My father outright bolted to his feet, his hair ruffled, and di Dienjuste, by the window-casement, whirled and actually half-drew. A curious expression crossed his flushed features, but I was in too much a hurry to grant it much thought.

"War is upon us." I tossed the dispatch bag onto a table choked with other paper. "The Damarsene have invaded; the next few dispatches will be full of their thundering. *She* is bound for the Field d'Or, to treat with d'Orlaans. We must move. Tonight. *Now.*"

"How did you—" di Dienjuste began, and for a moment his knees actually loosened. I did not blame him; the news was dire.

Irion di Markui, his seamed face grave, scooped up the dispatch bag with the speed of a man half his age. He had beaten my father to the table by at least a swordlength. He noted the slit in the tough leather strap with a raised eyebrow, opened it with gnarled fingers, and pulled forth a handful of papers.

Of course I had kept some few of them in reserve. Of the ones I left, their seals—each bearing the imprint of the Aryx—were broken. I had not time or patience for delicate measures.

"These just arrived?" My father leaned over di Markui's shoulder. I saw the gray in his hair had gathered strength, and the lines on his face had whittled themselves deeper.

For the first time in my memory, my father looked old.

"After a fashion." *Do not ask me such things now.* "The Damarsene have officially invaded. Sieging us was merely a feint—no wonder they only sent some thousands from border provinces to aid d'Orlaans. They have taken the *Dispuriee*, all the way to Diljonne and Reimelles. The Citté is preparing for siege. D'Orlaans is holding them, but not for long. He wishes the Aryx, and *m'd'mselle* the Queen wishes Arquitaine freed of invaders."

"Her will alone should have held the borders for a time," Markui muttered. "The Aryx—"

Perhaps she has not taken another Consort. It matters little. I have not hopped from foot to foot with impatience since I was eleven years old, but I was near to it now. "There is no time to waste. Every man we have gathered must march to Arquitaine's defense." *And it will strengthen her hand immeasurably to have an army of her own.*

My father glanced at di Markui. A long, considering look, two old campaigners hearing the trumpet again, speaking without words.

If Jierre had been here, and not likely to run me through, I could have had the small sour comfort of the same wordless communication. Or if Vianne had not hied herself forth to do Blessed only knew what.

Impatience rose hot and deadly under my breastbone. "Have you not *heard* me? The Damarsene are serious this time. No more tribute, no more being fobbed off by alliance or promises of marriage between Houses. They seek to swallow us whole, for Arquitaine's strength is occupied with civil war. Whether d'Orlaans seeks to kill us or *they* do, we will be just as dead. We can fight him, or we can fight the Damarsene—we cannot fight both, and we cannot afford to let them ravage each other on Arquitaine soil. Not while the Queen is bound for d'Orlaans. She has decided; we are to execute."

My father sighed. He rubbed at the bridge of his nose, his shoulders sagging for a brief moment. "Yes. Blessed guard us. What times to live in."

"*Sieurs.*" Di Dienjuste, flushed with excitement, approached the table. "There is much to be done. We should perhaps summon the others? I think di Falterne and di Rivieri went a-taverning..."

"A-whoring, you mean," di Markui rumbled. "Siguerre's asleep. D'Anton is probably dicing with the Guards."

"Wake them, fetch them, drag them from a doxy's bed if you must." My father's shoulders snapped back into their usual rigidity. "Di Dienjuste, fetch the commanders. Tristan, come make some sense of this with me. Irion, old friend, do you wake Siguerre—"

"One last ride for tired horses." Irion di Markui's dark eyes flashed. For a bare few moments he seemed younger than all of us. "Blessed guide us."

My heart hammered. I sought to calm myself. Vianne, stepping into d'Orlaans's clutches with only a bare half-dozen of her Guard to protect her. Too soft to do what must be done, faced with utter ruthlessness, playing for her life but hobbled by her very decency. The false King would eat her alive, or the Damarsene would kill her to put an end to the threat she posed them.

Not if I reach her in time. The urge to be gone, riding a horse to ribbons, boiled in me.

Di Dienjuste skidded from the room, di Markui hard on his heels. The fire crackled and snapped, and a slight breeze came in through the open window, ruffling the papers on the table.

"Gather your Guard," my father said, gathering the papers and beginning to organize them, glancing briefly at each one. "I will arrange matters here. You ride for the Field d'Or, and for the sake of the Blessed, ride hard. Tell none in Arcenne where you are bound."

The words opened a Tiberian mirror-box inside my head, light flashing through its interior and illuminating several things at once.

Had I misjudged him? Did he know of the treason breathing among his friends? "*Père.*" Perhaps I sounded strange, for he paused, examining me. "There is treachery even here in Arcenne. I have been told—"

He waved one sword-callused hand, and the spots of age on the back of it were suddenly apparent. "Did you think I did not know? Patience is often the better bait to root out such things, but we no longer have time. I have my own methods, and shall use them." A single lift of his graying eyebrow. "I shall give your farewell to your mother. Go now, and go with my blessing."

My jaw fair threatened to drop. Even when I had gone to Court, he had never unbent so much as to grant me a *blessing*.

He must have seen my surprise, for he laughed. It was a small, bitter sound. "I have not dealt well with you, Tristan. It does not matter. Attend the Queen, and do take care. I like not the thought of your mother's grief, should you…should anything happen. To my…my son."

Should I have stayed? Sometimes I think so. Yet at that moment I was simply glad to be set free, and to have a direction, a road that would lead me to my Vianne. I saluted him, one Captain to another, and was in the hall before I realized I was running.

The large grays the Guard rides are precious. Their fields are near Tiberius's palace at Vienciai, south and west of the Citté and under d'Orlaans's control. So Arran was the only one of their proud number to ride out; the nascent Guard rode their own beasts. Most were of high quality, since a nobleman should know to take care with his horseflesh. But they were motley, and we had no uniforms. I would be hard-pressed to remember a sorrier-looking group of noble younglings, sober with the import of their mission and frightened to death of failure or dishonor.

Sieurs et chivalieri, *we ride to the aid of the Queen of Arquitaine*, I had informed them in the barracks, a few of them retrieved bleary-eyed from the fleshpots of the *Quartier Salieu*.

If you have any doubt of your desire to be of Her Majesty's Guard, now is the time to express it. Any man may stay behind—there is no shame in deciding, now, that you would rather not hurry toward death. From the moment we ride forth, you are expected to comport yourself as a nobleman and a Queen's Guard, and any man who does not will feel my wrath.

I was slightly gratified to see no few of them blanch openly at the prospect.

We left Arcenne three hours after I stole Divris di Tatancourt's dispatch bag; I had no lee to worry of the Messenger and his fate. No doubt he would return to the Keep bearing interesting bruises.

The dark was still summer-soft, but with an edge of chill; the Road was cracked and broken from the siege. For the first hour it was a steady jogtrot, the horses warming themselves. Then I murmured to the lieutenants I had chosen—Tieris di Siguerre, the Conte's grandson, and Antolan di Sarciere et Vantroche—and the ride began in earnest.

There are songs written about the Ride of the New Guard.

None of them come close. I will say this for those younger sons of the Angoulême: Once they passed the gates of Arcenne, they rode uncomplaining, at a pace that punished mere flesh and bone, and they deserve every burst of melodic effort a minstrel can scrape together.

Two Arcenne hedgewitches rode with us, both broad peasant men unused to the saddle. To them fell the task of charming injuries and stretching the endurance of both man and beast. They started the ride with wide shoulders and bellies straining at their shirts; they ended it gaunt as the sleepless noblemen, their belts taken in notch by notch as we passed over Road and countryside as a burning dream through the mind of a fevered woman.

We did not gallop, though the temptation to do so beat in my chest like a Sea Countries clock-tower. Jogtrot and canter, cooling and resting the horses just enough, husbanding our strength as much as we dared. Fifty men and two hedgewitches—a pittance of a Guard. Henri's had been three hundred strong, and I their leader. Now a bare half-dozen of *them* were left, a frail fence around my Vianne, and they would likely try to separate me from my liver on sight.

We requisitioned what we needed from large holdings or towns on our way, meeting little resistance, as we largely paid in good coin for what we took—when necessary, that is. Rumor ran rife, and I am certain no few of those who provisioned us thought us a troupe of bandits fleeing d'Orlaans's dragoons. Haggard men with Court sorcery and finemetal blades are not to be trifled with, in any circumstance, and I was not overgracious.

Those days are burned into my dreams. Jingle of tack, the rhythm of hooves, creak of saddle, exhausted breathing of man and horse alike, Arran's back like a coracle on an unsteady sea, and the rasping. Rasp of stubble, rasp of leather, rasp of exhaustion against the nerves. The peasant men chanting, their throats dry and their eyes rheumy, one of them passing his hands over a horse's swollen leg, the injury retreating from a burst of green-scented hedgewitchery. Clerion di Hanvrault asleep in the saddle, swaying dangerously before Tieris di Siguerre woke him with a curse and a clout, Tespre and Luc d'Archim, brothers, sometimes singing snatches of courtsong when they had the breath. Antolan di Sarciere reporting on our supplies in a monotone, half-asleep on his feet but still sharp-eyed, his cheeks rough and thinning almost as one watched.

And I? I rode. That was all.

We took the north and eastron route past Bourdanneau, a city and region famed for its bright garnet wine and loyal to Irion di Markui. I had decided not to press too close to the middle of Arcenne held by d'Orlaans, and I deemed it the route with the best Roads; also, I thought it likely we might catch Vianne and her small group. For the R'mini who had brought the dispatches had recently come from very near Santie-di-Sorce, where the sea breathes inland and the famous cheeses are ripened in salt-crusted caves.

We struck inland on the great curve to Doitiers, and there the Roads became clogged with refugees. The Damarsene pressed hard, held at Diljonne and Reimelles at great cost. They burned as they came, and the border provinces, already ravaged by plague, were now scarred by rapine and fire. Citte d'Arquitaine was choked with those fleeing, d'Orlaans and his dragoons turning from the work of tax collection and squeezing every drop of the harvest to the more pressing problem of holding a line against the wolves of Damar. Reimelles had not yet fallen, but twas only a matter of time. An amnesty had been declared—any bandit or rebel, no matter how shameful, was offered a clean escutcheon if he came to the aid of d'Orlaans's army, and the Hedgewitch Queen, as she was called, had been seen riding hither and yon, rallying the fainthearted.

I worried much on this account, until we reached the warren of Chauvignienne and I heard she was said to have flax-golden hair, instead of Vianne's dark curls. Rumor, the false mistress, was merely working her mischief.

Peasants fleeing, their carts piled high and creaking; also, bloody and bandaged men, having had their fill of war already, trudging for the south and west with no real thought but to escape. The Damarsene's reputation—and the fact that their army contained several Pruzian companies with their fire-breathing siege engines, their high horsehair-crested helms, their black armor and their refusal to retreat—only added to the general terror. There were even wild tales of Far Rus mercenaries, Polis and Hese-Arburg vassal companies come to feast on the bones their lords threw.

Our passage slowed on the choked Road between Chauvignienne and Chetenerault, impatience bursting from me at almost every stop, halting only to water our glaze-eyed horses.

One must be careful with charmed beasts; after a while their submission becomes complete and they will run until their hearts burst. It falls to the rider to conserve their strength, to ask just short of the ultimate from them. It falls to a lieutenant to ask just short of the ultimate from his *peloton*, and the captain from his lieutenants. We had to arrive quickly, yes—but also with enough strength to fight.

Though the question of whether we would be given a chance to fight or be simply mown down as we sought to come to Vianne's aid was an open one.

It takes three weeks or so in good weather to ride from Arcenne to Orlaans—for yes, that is where we were bound. The Field d'Or is very near the city given to the younger sibling of the Heir to the Throne of Arquitaine, Timrothe d'Orlaans's pride and the fount of his power, from which he rode to Court and engaged in his dances of intrigue, duel, and debauchery.

Vianne—and the men I had commanded as well as the ones I commanded now—were riding into the jaws of a dragon.

It took us six days.

Chapter Twenty-One

Night, soft and prickling as the straw-yellow wine of Anjerou. Full of the rustling crispness of harvest season, a chill sparking in the blood of every creature. Sleek fat coneys gleaning the leavings, market-squares a-chaos in every town we rode through, peasants begging us for news as we passed with haggard faces and globes of witchlight spelled in relays among the men to light our way. From Tourleon to the outskirts of Orlaans we rode against the tide, but word of our passage seemed to have spread like wildfire. I did not know whom to thank for that—perhaps my father, or merely the chain of rumor written on air that tugs on every peasant ear. In any case, the refugees sought to scatter as we passed, some cursing, shaken fists, children crying in fear. Our pace quickened, though the horses were almost reduced to bone. Arran hung his head at every stop, barely flicking an ear as I muttered to him, apologizing for this treatment and yet, never ceasing to demand.

In the distance, Orlaans lit with torches and witchfire, and the faint carillon of its towers pealing to mark the watch wafted to us on the breeze. We breasted a short rise, as a bloody, not-quite-full harvest moon heaved its bloated self over the horizon, and the

Field d'Or glittered below us. Torch and witchlight, smoke from the cookfires, horses neighing in greeting and our own mounts too exhausted to reply. None of them lame or stumbled, one of the hedgewitches riding double with a Guard, the twain belted together so the peasant could sleep without fear of falling.

"Halt! Who goes there?" they challenged through the moonlit dimness, and I found myself forced to use my voice.

"In the Queen's name!" My shout, gravel from a long-abused and dust-scorched throat, surprised even me.

But what surprised me more was the answering bellow from fifty scarecrow-gaunt young noblemen, witchlights fizzing and sparking into being as they answered. *"For the Queen's honor!"*

Perhaps twas enough of an answer. In any event, there was some to-ing and fro-ing. Our horses stamped, the hedgewitches waking and tending to them automatically, several of the Guard dismounting to save their mounts' strength. Hands rested on rapiers, and there was precious little talk. We were too tired, too nerve-strung. And too conscious of the crossbows leveled at us, not to mention the size of the breathing animal that an army becomes while it sleeps.

"Dear gods." A familiar voice, shaking me from my torpor as I forced myself to perch, spine straight and knees tight, on Arran's bony back. "As I live and breathe, *Tristan!*"

It was Adersahl di Parmecy et Villeroche, in the familiar crimson-sashed uniform of a Guard—black doublet, white shirt underneath, black breeches, boots that had seen hard use and fresh polish. I finally dismounted, and he approached at the head of a dragoon of hard-faced lowlanders, their pikes held high and their mustaches waxed—though none so fine as Adersahl's.

He was freshly shaven, except for said mustache, and looked as fit as hard drilling can make a man. I offered my hand and we clasped forearms. To his credit, he did not flinch at my appearance. "You look terrible," he muttered in my ear, and relief threatened to unloose my knees.

"Where is she?" I rasped. "Is she safe? Is she well?"

"Oh, aye, well enough. Let us tend to your *peloton*; they look ready to drop. How did you come to be *here*?"

"Six days ago we were in Arcenne." I coughed, clearing the dust from my throat. "See to them, Adersahl; they are good men and well worth it. And tell me where to find my Queen."

"Six days?" He sounded baffled, a thing I had rarely heard. "But she only sent for you three—"

"I do not *care*." Why could he not grasp that essential fact? Behind him, the pikesmen eyed us with no little trepidation. "Where is she?"

"Abed, Captain, and we are loath to disturb her. Tis late. We'll see to your comfort—such as it is. You've arrived just in time." Adersahl was pale, and his smile, now that I looked more closely, was more stretched-thin than I liked. "Tomorrow she treats with d'Orlaans. It is well you've arrived."

I swallowed a venomous curse, made a sign to my lieutenants, and we followed him into the encampment.

To wake in the middle of an unfriendly army camp after a ride such as that is to truly understand *discomfort*.

In the moment before I lunged upright, the camp-cot almost collapsing under me—they are not made for violent movement—I thought I heard a muffled cry, or the sound of a blade drawn from its sheath. Cold sweat greased me, and I found myself with every bone aching, in a rude tent that barely kept the chill of a late harvest-season morning outside its flapping door and thin walls.

I was alone.

The wind moaned. Clashing metal, woodsmoke, nothing amiss. The sound was any army's rising-song, made up of cursing, the sizzle of cooking, horses stamping and speaking in their own fashion, and the regimented cries and clashes of drill. *One two three, get your arms up, you maggots; polearms come forward; march in time; swing it like you mean it, one two three—death doesn't wait for chai-time, you* saufe-tets, *move! Move! Move!*

The tent was small, no carpet but bare-beaten ground, my saddle and saddlebags on a rickety frame, my swordbelt and the cot. I rubbed sleep from my eyes, yawned, and pulled the doorflap aside to behold the familiarity of an Arquitaine army going about its dawn-waking business. My neck was stiff as bridge stanchions, my back a solid bar of muscle-locked pain, my legs numb. The rest of me did not bear mentioning. Suffice to say no part of my body was happy with the abuse it had endured.

But I forgot it all.

There was another tent, indigo-dyed and beautifully draped, its lines taut and its breadth proclaiming importance. Silver *fleurs-di-lisse* etched over its deep midnight, and the sight whipped bile into the back of my throat. Royal, certainly—the *fleurs* were the emblem of the Angoulême—but it was also too small to be a commander's tent. It was meant for a King's Consort, and by the Blessed, d'Orlaans had gone too far in forcing *my* Queen to sleep in its embrace.

Who else could it be for?

One of the flaps was pulled aside, and a nobleman emerged. It was Jierre, and he swept a bow as he retreated. Some things can be told at a distance—and I could tell, just by watching, that di Yspres was amused, a sally leaving his lips as the feather of his hat swept near the ground.

So. Is it thus? Every part of me turned scalding-cold.

My lieutenant straightened, returning his hat to its wonted, jaunty angle, and let the flap fall in heavy folds of costly fabric. Inside would be braziers to take the morning chill away, and soft rugs.

"Captain!" Tinan di Rocham cried, and I almost flinched. For Jierre di Yspres's head came up, and the di Rocham boy, obviously hailing him, darted out of a lane of beaten earth between faceless rows of other tents.

And Jierre is Captain now, is he. Well. My hands were fists.

I retreated into the shelter of my own thin cloth walls. Stared about me, unseeing, waves of hot and cold alternating through me as if I had taken the ague. Vianne had shaken thus, when she was fevered during the long ride from the Citté.

She needs you. *Jierre is too dull an instrument for what she must accomplish.*

So she needed me, yes.

But what if she *preferred*…somewhat else?

It was then, staring at my worn saddle and feeling the itch of road-dust all over me, that I understood who I had robbed, and of what.

And I could not even blame the Blessed. I had done it without their help.

Chapter Twenty-Two

Young Siguerre was sharp-shaven, bright-eyed, and fresh as a dandille flower. Of course, he was ten years my junior, and the subtraction of those years make it easy to shake off even a ride through the underworld.

"Here," he said, holding up a crimson sash. The weathering of our journey had been kind to him, erasing his usual pallor and the shadow of a double chin he had possessed before we started. He was lean and keen as a courser now. "I do not know where di Parmecy found these, but find them he did. At least we shall all match about the waist."

I flicked the razor, a tingle of Court sorcery cleaning the blade. I would be haggard, no doubt, never pretty even at the best of times. But at least I would be fresh-scraped, and that gives a man a certain confidence. "Well. And enough for all?"

"Except the hedgewitches. Though I might recommend settling an annuity on both of them; I have never seen peasants behave so nobly." A stubborn dark forelock fell over his eyes; he tossed it aside with a sharp movement that reminded me just how young he was.

Noble is rarely in the blood, chivalier. *Why, look at me.* "A fine idea." *If we survive the winter, I shall make certain of it.* "Any further injuries?"

"No. The horses are at their feed with a vengeance, the hedgewitches standing by to make certain they do not sicken themselves. Other than di Crifort's ankle and those cases of saddlerash, we are none the worse for wear. They are feeding us, at least." His eyebrows rose slightly. "Though I like not the looks that accompany the meal."

"What is the army's mood?"

"Mood?"

I strangled a brief flare of frustration. Jierre would have understood instantly. "D'Orlaans's men. How do they seem to you? Willing to fight? Beaten already? Under orders to feed us before they slay us all, including our Queen? Their *mood,* chivalier. Have you observed it?"

"Ah." He absorbed this. "I would say...confused. I have heard rumor among them—the coming of the Hedgewitch Queen has given them heart. *No plague in her provinces,* some say. Others reply, *The King was crowned in the Ladytemple.* Whispers of two Aryxes. One must be false, but which one? And the Damarsene." Another pause. "If there is a pitched battle in the next week, Captain, I do not like our chances."

I stowed the razor, wiped at my face with a silken flannel. He was slow, of course—but careful. Not much escaped the mouthful he set himself to chew.

I had not much time to teach him which bites were the most useful.

The rinsed flannel snapped, another bit of Court sorcery drying it in a moment. I could have finished this operation in my sleep. I took the sash, my hands remembering what to do with it, and looked up to find Tieris di Siguerre studying me.

"What happens now?" he asked, and I nodded as if the question was profound.

My swordbelt buckled itself on, the familiar weight of rapier and dagger comforting. At least now I was armed, and I intended to be so for the rest of this affair, however it ended.

"Now we attend the Queen." My throat was dry, despite morning chai. I was growing to hate mince pies, but I needed the heavy fuel. *And if d'Orlaans so much as twitches in her direction, my blade shall take the life of another royal.*

"My father says she is a beauty." Carefully, his tone light and nonchalant. "He says she has an effect on men."

He does not know the half of it. "She is our Queen."

"And you her Consort."

"Is there a purpose to this conversation, Lieutenant?"

"Merely passing the time, *sieur*. You seem on-edge. More than usual, that is."

I suppose I deserve that. "We are in the midst of an army loyal to a man who killed his own brother. Of course I am on-edge." *And my Vianne is in a tent a few paces from here, visited by Jierre early in the morn.*

"We rode from Arcenne six days ago," young Siguerre pointed out. "An army is of little consequence compared to *that*."

I wish I had your faith. "Indeed. Go make everyone as presentable as possible. The Queen shall need us soon."

"Aye." He snapped me a salute and was gone into the morning glare. Fog hung over the army camp, the exhalation of morning and man-breath, hazed with cooking smoke.

I braced myself, put the shaving-mirror away, and sallied forth to see the woman I had married.

Chapter Twenty-Three

Fair blond Luc di Chatillon tilted his head as I approached. I caught a low murmur, which must have been answered from the other side of the flap. He straightened and greeted me with a smile that did not look forced. "Captain!"

Am I still to be addressed as such? "How fares the Queen?"

"Relieved, I am certain. You are well-come indeed." He was always too cheerful by half, and the more unsteady the situation, the more his eyes twinkled. It was his shield, that good humor, and di Chatillon was not often seen without it.

The last time you greeted me, twas to clap me in chains. "How dire is it?"

That caused the smile to falter slightly. "Dire enough. D'Orlaans presses his suit, our *d'mselle* is ambivalent, and the army…well."

"The Damarsene?"

"Still held at Diljonne. Reimelles holds, too. D'Orlaans has been pressing to see her for a full day now, but she pleads exhaustion from travel. There are other events afoot."

No doubt. "Will she see me?" I did not like the supplicant tone I sported. Was she listening?

He reached for the flap, pulling it aside. "Of course. Pass, Captain. Thank the Blessed you're here."

"Aye to that." I had not expected so warm a reception. Of course, I was prepared for a chill inside, but I nodded and passed him by.

Inside, twas dim and scented with incense. Braziers simmered, taking away the chill. A slight movement, and I found the Pruzian Knife before me, his half-ugly face set. He was in the costume of his native land, his dark quilted doublet side-slit and his dark shirt and breeches button-laced. His boots were of a kind not oft seen in Arquitaine, soft-soled for walking catfoot or stealing through windows. Hatless, with his hair oiled and clubbed, he was a figure of exotic disdain.

He examined me from top to toe, slowly insouciant, then stepped aside. The hangings in the tent fluttered lazily—to one side, a sable curtain hiding where she had slept. The rest was an open space, surprisingly airy for all its dimness, with glowrock globes on stands providing light that would not set the fabric afire.

At a map-table, her dark head bent and her supple back to me, Vianne. She reached for a winecup and took a long draught, a quill scratching as she wrote upon a sheet of thick linen paper. A candle in a filigreed glassglobe burned, shedding a circle of golden glow on the table.

"A moment, an it please you," Vianne said softly, setting the winecup down with a click. She wore dark blue silk, and the same *fleurs-di-lisse* pattern was embroidered upon it with silver-spun thread. I had to work to unclench my fists—had d'Orlaans commissioned the dress for her? Could she understand what an advantage she would give him by wearing it?

I could not help myself. "A pleasure to wait for you, *m'chri*."

Did she stiffen? Perhaps. Silk rustled. A wooden rack to her left held an overdress, heavy sky-blue velvet worked with the flowers of the Angoulême. She would need someone to hold it as it slipped over her shoulders; it was a robe of state, and this touch also bore d'Orlaans's stamp.

The man wanted her. For pride, of course—Timrothe d'Orlaans ever had a taste for the chase. And for position; she was integral to his plans, and perhaps even more so now that he knew beyond a doubt that she held the Seal.

Had she met with her living half-uncle yet? Had they fenced with words? Vianne against *him*. My hands ached with the urge to close them around the Duc's throat.

The quill dipped, she scratched something that might have been her signature or perhaps a hurried postscript. The paper ruffled as she blew upon it, a trace of hedgewitchery drying the ink, then her quick fingers folded it beautifully, something enclosed with the words jingling. A wafer of deep crimson sealing-wax, applied with a deft hand, and she passed her palm over the letter. The Aryx sparked, a faint pleasant thrill along my nerves, and the impress of the Seal would appear of itself on the wax.

She half-turned. Her profile was not nearly the hammerblow I expected. Instead of turning me to a faint-kneed schoolboy, it simply sent an ache all through my sore muscles and bruised bones.

"Fridrich." Her expression was cool and remote.

"*Ja?*" Tense, keeping me well in his sight.

"Fetch me Tinan di Rocham. He is expecting this summons; tell him 'tis time." Enunciating each word crisply, in case the foreigner had trouble deciphering them.

"Fralein." A short bow, his heels touching—were he wearing a Pruzian nobleman's boots, the click would have resounded. He gave me one more long, considering look, and Vianne actually smiled.

There was a trace of sardonic amusement to the curve of her lips, one that had never been there before. "I shall be well enough, Fridrich. Go."

Another bow and he left, sliding through a second tent-flap on the other side. He did it without a breath of sound, and I had little doubt that d'Orlaans had not caught sight of *him* yet.

She sat, straight-backed, still presenting me only with her profile. Aristocratic nose, the faint steely curve to her soft mouth. "Captain."

I searched for an answer. "Do I still hold that title?"

Cool and calm, no breath of displeasure. Every inch the royal, now. "Unless you wish to be relieved of its burden. Is it time?"

The reel of my attention snagged. *She asked me this before.* "Time for what, Vianne?"

She had gained some little weight. Not much; her neck was too thin, her collarbones standing out starkly. The curve of her cheek was still beauty itself. Her braids were piled elaborately, her ear-drops swinging sapphires with pearls depending from them. A wash of her old perfume, bergaime and spice and hedgewitchery, reached me.

Had d'Orlaans brought her a fresh bottle? Had she taken the one from Arcenne?

She turned still further, bringing her knees from under the table with a graceful movement. Her hands arranged her skirts, a peculiarly feminine movement, and I found out that even miserable as my body was from a hellish ride through half of Arquitaine, I still wanted her badly as ever.

We matched each other, gaze for gaze, and it was the first time such a glance was a challenge. If it was the first touch of a duel, it was already lost on my part. I would not fight her.

Vianne's tone turned thoughtful. "No, I suppose not. I am still useful at this juncture. Tell me, how did you come to answer my call so quickly?"

"Your instructions to Divris di Tatancourt fell into improper hands." I hooked my thumbs in my belt, to disguise how my own hands wished to shake.

"Whose hands would those be?" As if she did not know.

Mine, of course. "I found it interesting who you addressed your missives to, *m'chri*. Who among your Council sought to kidnap you?" *And you fled Arcenne both to put an end to the attempts and to move against d'Orlaans. Did you foresee this?*

It was an uncomfortable thought. For if she were able to see the future so clearly, what need had she of me?

There is a need, Left Hand. However much she can see, she cannot bring herself to kill. That is your function.

She faced me fully now, her chin lifted, but she still did not rise. Instead, she folded her slim fingers together. The Aryx glowed against her skin, the dress's neckline low enough to make a man sweat. She nodded, as if she had expected me to ask. But she did not answer.

It rankled.

"Very well." I dismissed the questions she would not answer with a shake of my head. My hair had grown long as a *chivalier's* fashion again, and it whispered against my collar. "What would you have of me, Vianne?"

The dark circles under her eyes spoke as she did not—of weariness, of worry, of the weight on her. Finally, she moved slightly, as if to ease her steel-straight spine. "I have a task to set you, Left Hand."

"Say it, and tis done." The traditional response, did she but know it. Had it ever tasted this bitter, any of the times I uttered it in Henri's hearing?

She swallowed, her throat moving. I did not look at her mouth. "I am to meet d'Orlaans after the nooning."

I nodded, slowly.

Then she told me, very softly, what she required of me.

What did I feel?

Regret. Relief. My heart leapt, settled into a high hammering rhythm. *This* was what she would ask?

She waited, as if expecting me to disagree. I nodded again. "Tis done," I repeated. "Is that all?"

"Is it not enough?" She reclasped her hands, very prettily, as if she were on a divan at Court. "Tristan—"

So now I was *Tristan* instead of *Captain* or *d'Arcenne*. "Was my reply too complex, Vianne? *Yes.* There is my answer, and it is the only one you shall hear from me." *Unless you ask me to abandon you.*

The candle fluttered inside its spun-glass holder. It touched the gold in her hair. "Even though I am asking you to—"

"Oh, you knew there would be little trouble in inducing me to this." Did I say it to wound her? Perhaps. Her flinch scored me to the quick, and I instantly sought to reverse the damage. "*M'chri*—"

She recovered quickly. Far too quickly, and far too thoroughly. "It should please you that I am finally ordering such things."

Yes, she had changed. What had she been about these past few weeks, to emerge so altered?

I finally managed to catch a glimpse of the copper marriage-ring. It glowed on the traditional finger, mellow in the dimness, and a spike of something hot and complex speared me. "What pleases me is that you are alive. Is there aught else you would have of me, *m'dama* Queen?"

"Not until afterward." She tensed again, as if she expected me to cross the remaining distance and strike her. "You are dismissed until the nooning."

I bowed. No hat, but there was no polish lacking in the courtesy I did her. "It surprises me, Vianne, that you would trust me in this matter."

"It surprises me as well," she returned, brittle and quick, and I retreated.

If I tarried any longer in that tent, I would have tried to touch her.

Tried? No. I would have added to the list of my crimes, and torn d'Orlaans's gift-dress from her in ribbons. So, she had changed.

Or had I? If someone had told me that I would do half of what I had to her, I would have called him to a dueling-circle as a liar. I was not the man she thought I was.

I did not know whether to be grateful...or to curse who I had become.

A curious quiet hung over d'Orlaans's army. It was a hush not of stasis but of anticipation and preparation. The false King wished to ride to Arquitaine's defense—as soon as matters were settled with the Hedgewitch Queen.

Did it not occur to him that she would settle matters to suit herself? Or did he think her merely a catspaw?

The Field d'Or holds a stone Pavilion, gold leaf gleaming on its ornamental cupola and pillars of fluid sorcery-carved blue stone. That stone is not found anywhere inside our borders. Some say it is from the Angoulême's home, the blessed Isle riven to splinters by the Maelstrom off our westron shores. Others hold that it was transported from Rus, a gift from their Zar to a new conqueror in the days when Far Rus's borders lapped against the hedge of Badeau's boundaries, before the bull-headed god of Damar awoke, before Polia slipped the yoke and became a blood-soaked, obstinate collection of proud rebels preferring death to slavery. Even Sirisse, safe behind their mountains, had been watchful of Rus's power then.

In any case, the Pavilion d'Or is bluestone and gold leaf, kept safe from thieves by its air of sacredness. A round dais under its stem-legged dome, two wings curving forth and a gathering-ground of that same blue stone held in its arms, it was a ceremony-theater soaked in Arquitaine history.

Vianne approached it that day on my mother's white palfrey, her hair lifted on a crisp wind smelling of approaching winter. Any summer-heat remaining had broken, coolness soughing across the fertile cup of Arquitaine, and in the Citté there would be relief from the oppressive clinging breath from the shores of the River Airenne.

But we were not at the Citté or the Palais. Instead, we—the fifty gaunt noblemen of the New Guard and the half-dozen or so of the Old, lacking only Tinan di Rocham—paced in honor-guard behind our Queen. Dust whirled, the Aryx's song muted as Court sorcery threaded down our ranks, repelling the fine penetrating grit.

I did not walk with them. Instead, I held the palfrey's reins, leading *m'dmselle's* horse. The mare was sleek and glossy, and looked near to bursting with satisfaction at bearing such an august personage. She seemed to find my shoulder fascinating as well, and I held her to a stately pace.

There was not room for the entire army to see, despite the

Pavilion's crowning the highest point of the Field. There were nobles gathered, though, and the officers, lining the ribboning processional way.

It should have been Vianne on the dais, waiting for the conquered to kneel before her. Or d'Orlaans doing whatever he pleased, as long as my *d'mselle* and I were safe in Tiberia, beyond his murderous reach.

I took careful note of faces I recognized along our route. The closer to d'Orlaans, the higher they would be in his estimation, for whatever reason. Majesty flows from a fount, and those it trusts—or wishes to watch—are placed close to the source.

A ripple ran through them at the sight of Vianne. Not just of her straight slimness in blue and silver, but the fire on her chest. The Aryx glowed, its carved serpents shifting, and the ribbons of Court sorcery keeping the dust from us rose above her head, writhing as the Aryx did. Twas the sign of royalty, seen in many a tapestry and painting, those circle-twisting streams, and I suppressed a grim smile at the thought of d'Orlaans's fury as he watched her so neatly rob him of legitimacy.

He thought to have her wander to him as a beggar, instead of this.

As we drew closer, the shade of the Pavilion quaked. There was a weak shimmer from under the dome, and it was with no little satisfaction that I saw the gleam from Timrothe d'Orlaans's false Aryx stutter.

I halted Vianne's horse before the Pavilion. Inhaled deeply, and performed a herald's duty. *"Her Majesty Vianne di Rocancheil et Vintmorecy et Tirecian-Trimestin, Queen of Arquitaine!"* The charm was a simple one, to make a voice heard above a din or a multitude, and the words echoed as a cheer rose from the Guard both Old and New. It sounded thin in the hush, but the Aryx flashed, uttering a low hum, magnifying the cry until it fair threatened to shake the Pavilion. I felt it in every bone, the ache of our journey washing away under that welter of pure force.

The cupola ran with fierce golden light, tolling like a bell, and I do not know who was the first to kneel. What I *do* know is that the urge to bend knee caught like wildfire, and if enough in a crowd do so, it becomes well nigh impossible to halt the movement.

This will make him even more furious.

He stepped out of the Pavilion's shade, a tall figure in a fine blue doublet, a shade to match hers. A lean man—his brother had run to fat, but d'Orlaans had not yet. His hair was only touched with gray, instead of threaded heavily like Henri's; at his chest on a silver chain was a spot of brilliance.

Who could have mistaken that thing for the Aryx? The difference was obvious.

Had the death of Fairlaine's Queen broken whatever was necessary for its use? His grief had driven him mad, and he had the dubious distinction of being the only King of Arquitaine to die by his own hand.

If Vianne required me for the Aryx's use, or merely required *a* Consort, much hinged on whether the gods would bless whatever union she saw fit to make…It gave me much to think upon. And think upon it I had, during six days of hard riding.

D'Orlaans made a gesture. Limp white hands, rings flashing in the brilliant autumn sunshine. The season had changed overnight, as it sometimes does in the lowlands.

Perhaps we could hope for our fortunes to change for the better as well.

"Most beloved!" D'Orlaans used the same charm to make his voice echo. He now affected a pencil-thin mustache, and there were dark pouches under his sharp hazel eyes. "My dearest Consort!"

I remembered the hypnotic power of his heavy-lidded gaze, the softness with which he laid out the plot. *Do you merely remove the impediment, d'Arcenne, and you shall have all you wish. I am grateful to those who aid me.*

And he called my Queen "Consort," having proxy-wed her in the Citté's Ladytemple, the Grand Dama. My fist tightened on the palfrey's reins.

Had the Aryx still slumbered, had my *d'mselle*'s wits not been so sharp, had luck not run with us…he might well be calling her *Consort* in truth.

Vianne's chin raised. "Tristan," she said softly.

So easily, she slipped my leash. Unhooded the falcon, and now I only had to stoop to my prey. There is a certain relaxation in merely obeying.

I dropped the reins, my boots sounding on the stone as I strode forward. I had the pleasure of seeing d'Orlaans recognize me, whether from the set of my shoulders or the quality of my step I do not know. I reached the stairs as he stepped back a half-pace, and movement in the shadows behind him was his Guard, their blue sashes a lighter shade than his doublet.

I could not see if Garonne di Narborre was among them, but it did not matter. Nor did it matter who else he had in the Pavilion's shade. Those nobles he kept with him on the dais would feel the scourge soon enough.

The glove, borrowed from young Siguerre, left my hand. I'd weighted the fingers with small stones to make it fly true. It described a high arc, then landed with a soft sodden sound on the second of the four stairs. I had aimed at d'Orlaans's feet in their dainty half-boots, but this was far better.

"You accuse me of murder, Timrothe d'Orlaans." Each word clear and carrying, Court sorcery crackling as it spread the sound wide. *And it is true, but this is a theater of politics. Let us dance upon a stage, you and I.* "You accuse me of treason and treachery, and you further impugn the honor of my Queen. The insult you have offered calls for blood. *Sieur*, I challenge you."

Did I imagine the indrawn breath from those assembled?

No nobleman takes such a challenge lightly. D'Orlaans stepped forward, an ugly flush rising up his throat from the snow-white folds of his ruffled shirt-collar. Royal pride, and the pride of the viper that stings from behind because it feels its weakness keenly. He was ever a duelist at Court during Henri's life, imagining slights to remove those he took a dislike to. Or those who stood in the way of whatever he wished at the moment.

He mastered himself, the false Aryx on his chest shimmering a flat, unhealthy shine. How did he fuel such Court sorcery, for so long? Or did he merely use it for public occasions?

Does it matter? The curious comfort of being locked to a course of action deepened. There was naught for it, now, but to see how the dice landed. All else could wait.

D'Orlaans's rings glistened as he motioned. Stepping forth from the Pavilion's shadow came a familiar lean and hungry sight.

Garonne di Narborre bent, a trifle awkwardly, and scooped up the glove. We locked gazes, the Black Captain and I, as he straightened. He did not glance at Vianne.

I was unsurprised. Of course Timrothe d'Orlaans would not risk himself in a duel.

"Your challenge is accepted." The false King made another gesture. "Name your second."

I had considered the question. "*Chivalier* Jierre di Yspres."

A rustle behind me. Had Vianne glanced at her new Captain? Had she warned him of this?

Was he my replacement in other ways as well?

"Name yours," I said, the words ash in my mouth.

Garonne di Narborre's wolfish smile spread. "His Majesty the King of Arquitaine."

A ripple went through the assembled as they gained their feet. It was not *quite* meet for a man to stand second after his vassal had accepted a challenge on his behalf. Yet there was no iron-clad rule against it; if I made no objection, twas meet enough.

I did not object. To have both of them within reach of my blade was more than I had hoped for.

Chapter Twenty-Four

"Madness," one of the Duc's foppish followers crowding on my side of the circle said behind his hand, just loudly enough to be heard—but not loudly enough to carry across the expanse of blue-stone. "Should we not be fighting the Damarsene?"

"This will not take long," di Narborre sallied, and his words were passed back through the ranks on a rush of muttering.

Finer entertainment than a fête, I wager. And no doubt the wagering had begun in the rest of the army.

I loosened the laces on my doublet. The sun was high; the dueling-circle had been drawn with Court sorcery and chalk on the bluestone pavers. Vianne was still a-horse, a statue in the golden light, her back straight, her face set and white. The ribbons of Court sorcery weaving about her, veils of scarlet, gold, and pure white, moved with their own lazy rhythm.

"What are you about?" Jierre murmured. His fierce glare was turned on the pair across the circle, di Narborre and d'Orlaans conferring, master and lieutenant seemingly at ease.

Was he asking why I had called him as my second? "If they do not kill me, you may call me to account for the wrong I have done you." *I rather look forward to it. Perhaps afterward we might even return to some manner of friendship.* My tone dropped, became a half-whisper. "Do you still consider me a traitor?"

Jierre shot me a glance that could have broken a Polian shield. "Not truly. Twas necessary for all to believe I did, though."

My jaw threatened to drop. I did not look to Vianne, though I sorely wished to. My face kept itself in its pre-duel mask—interested, open, a faint line between my eyebrows deepening as I contemplated my opponents.

"I will ask an explanation," I murmured.

His reply was obdurate, and strangely comforting. "If *she* grants me leave, I shall give one."

My heart gave an oblique pang. Did she indeed prefer him? Who knew how a woman thought, or what she would choose? And for what I had done to her, there was no remedy.

I had, at last, decided as much during our ride through the underworld. The Queen of Arquitaine was lost to me. "I consign her to your care, then, if this—"

"Avert." He made the gesture against ill-luck. "Not before a duel, Tristan. Have you gone soft-wit?"

"Many years ago. When you arrived at Court with an introduction, and—"

"Saufe-tet." But there was no heat to it. "Di Narborre attacks with the *tierce*. But you know that."

"Yes." Did I feel better or worse, knowing he would watch d'Orlaans for foul play? Knowing that he had struck me, playing his part to a fare-thee-well, and I had not suspected? Or perhaps *she* had called upon him to dissemble, and…

I could not tell, and now twas useless to care.

This has gone long enough. I stepped into the circle, and the onlookers stilled. A furious ripple went through the back ranks as the oddsmakers noted I was eager to begin. Heralds cried, following the ancient formula of trial-by-combat. Did I fall here, I would be ajudged guilty. Did di Narborre, twould be a sign of my innocence—and once his vassal had fought, if I challenged again, d'Orlaans *must* step forth to answer.

Would Vianne watch? She was known to have a weak stomach at Court, always turning away after the first exchange of blows. Yet this iron-backed woman who had left me in a prison cell and was even now playing me against d'Orlaans for a besieged kingdom…she was not the Vianne di Rocancheil I had known. No, this woman surprised me. Intrigued me even more than her softhearted former self.

Even if I had lost her, I would still die for her.

But hopefully, not today.

Garonne di Narborre stepped into the circle. D'Orlaans, waited upon by a group of a half-dozen pages, took a glass goblet of something from one of them and quaffed it. Another, a slim honeyhaired youth in that same sky blue, fanned him with a perfumed paper contraption. But the false King's gaze never left me, hazel eyes cold and intent, and I braced myself as I drew and saluted, the ruby in the hilt of my sword—my grandfather's, passed to me at my Coming-of-Age ceremony, for we kept to the old ways in Arcenne—flashing a bloody dart.

Di Narborre swung his blade twice, whipping the unoffending air, and saluted perfunctorily. We both paced forward, drawing our daggers, and the Black Captain did not bother to hide his sneer.

A rapier is a fine-wrought weapon, and much depends on its temper. But a duel is not merely fought with steel.

D'Arquitaine rapiers are broader and heavier than the weapons the Sievillein in Navarrin sport with. A filigreed cage for the hand, a whisper-thin blade, Sievellein duels are more dance than deadly. There is a panel of *judges*, of all things, and the winner is not him left breathing but he whose score outweighs the other's.

Cowards.

A d'Arquitaine rapier also has a shield-cage for the hand, and flexes slightly as it cleaves air or flesh. A nobleman may request *l'petitte*, which is a duel fought rapier-only, to the first blooding. Most questions of honor are resolved thus.

But for the Black Captain and me, 'twas *cri di combat*. Rapier and dagger, no baffle over the arm, and no *cri mirci*. No judge but the gods, and no proof but blood admitted to this court.

"D'Arcenne." Di Narborre, no sneering now.

"Di Narborre." None on my part, either. We were both catspaws, after all. He was a Hand for his liege, and I for mine. Except he had never betrayed d'Orlaans.

At least, not where any could see.

He attacked *entierce*, of course, blade flashing as he tested my defense. Batted aside with contemptuous ease, I moved forward in an oblique line, all uncertainty falling away. First blood was mine, a stripe along his upper arm, he slashed low and wicked with the dagger and I leaned back. Court sorcery crackled as it wove between us, the Aryx singing like wine in my veins. The sorcery to fling light at an enemy's eyes swiftly opposed with my counterspell, breath coming hard and ribs tearing as sweat wrung from both our foreheads—true combat brings the saltwater much earlier than drill. No respite, blades slitherclashing, *quarto*, *ensiconde*, Signelli's defense and Caparete's gambit, an overhand cut and I had him against the circle…

…and I cut away, letting him regain his breath.

Di Narborre shook sweat from his brow and narrowed his eyes.

"That will not buy you quarter, d'Arcenne."

We were not merely dueling here. We were playing to the gallery of the army, and Vianne's Consort could not be seen to be less than honorable. My father would have approved—finally, we were in agreement about *appearances*. "I need no quarter from your kind," I spat. "Killing unarmed women has dulled your blade, *sieur*."

I sought to anger him, and half-succeeded. Court sorcery closed in earnest this time, spell and counterspell, savage bits of the Angoulême's inheritance meant to blind, to lame, to kill. Would he, that survivor of storm-wrack and conqueror of hedge-witch peasants, be shamed of what his noble children had wrought?

We closed again, and again di Narborre chose the *tierce*. Caparete's gambit again, then the reach of the rapier keeping his dagger at bay as he pressed me; we had watched each other duel too many times. Sorcery kindled, I averted the blow but my hip turned momentarily numb, my leg threatening to give as he surged forward with Antorieu's thrust. The dagger turned it, there was only one possible avenue to salvage my defense and I took it, a fast brutal jab-and-turn I had learned in alleyfighting where the quarters are close and the length of a rapier sometimes a hindrance. It restored the balance, and my hip returned to nor-malcy—that charm is short-lived, and can be used for a horse as well. If one does not mind killing an innocent animal.

Shuffling, grit under bootsoles providing traction, the smithy-ringing of a flurry of light, testing blows, both of us panting for breath. A cup of glassy silence descended over our dance. Warmed and loosened, blood dripping from my left arm and a smear of bright crimson on his face and dappling his sleeve, the steel whistling deadly-sweet courtsongs. Another jab for my eyes, a dart of sunlight harnessed and turned to ice, countered as the Aryx passed a thread of melody under my skin.

Is she watching?

The space inside the circle crackled and buzzed with stray sorcery. Normally a duel is done in four passes or less, inexperience or brutality forcing an opening. We may have been evenly matched, di Narborre and I—except for the breaking of the duel-circle, d'Orlaans shrieking as his false Aryx burned with unholy radiance. The poison killspell he flung was familiar—it reeked of apples, wet dog, and vileness. He had laid the same spell on Minister Simieri, the day the conspiracy broke loose and Henri met his death on my blade.

It was faint comfort to finally have the question of just who had sorcelled Simieri answered to my satisfaction.

The true Aryx matched his cry, a crystal-rimmed goblet singing as it is stroked by a damp fingertip, and the medallion on his chest cracked under the noise. My foot slipped, I lunged, di Narborre attacked again—

—but not with the *tierce*. No, he attacked *ensiconde*, and his blade slid past my guard, punching through muscle and lung, ramming out through the back of my shirt and doublet with a sound like the earth itself breaking in half.

Chapter Twenty-Five

Bubble of warmth on my lips. The blood ran down my chin. I stared at di Narborre, who wore a tight thin smile. My left arm extended, my dagger punching through muscle, slipping between ribs, and I had what seemed an eternity to think, *How strange, we are both dead*, before the pain began. It broke in my chest, a monstrous egg, and my legs sought to buckle.

No. Not yet.

Di Narborre folded, oddly boneless. For a moment I was in the Rose Room again, a King on my sword and the world about to fall to pieces. I twisted the dagger, but my hand was oddly weak.

The Black Captain's gaze dimmed. A candle, swiftly carried down a dark corridor. Fading to a spark, then vanishing.

I cannot die.

He perhaps thought the same.

The world tilted. The dagger tore free of my nerveless fingers, buried in his heart. *A pity that he had one. None would believe it.*

A high, retching cough spattered more bright blood from my lips. Silence, holding me in vast, feathery, cupped hands.

I cannot die.

It was too late.

I died.

Glare of white light. Bergaime and spice filling my mouth. Slick fabric against my tensed fists, handfuls of scratch-embroidered material. Copper-gummed blood dry on my lips, scabs coating my throat. I tasted blood with every breath of my salvation.

I was told afterward of Vianne's cry as di Narborre's rapier threaded my chest, a needle in the fingers of an enthusiastic sempstress. Of the Aryx's blaze, a crack of darkness in its heart as the serpents spun, their metal flowing like living scales. Of d'Orlaans's swift attack after he had called forth the poison killspell, his foul sorcery calling down a blight upon the stones, cracking and scoring them, a line of murderous intent swerving at the last moment, failing as my *d'mselle* opened herself to the Seal completely.

There was an orb of brilliance, hung in midair. Silver radiance outshining the harvest-season sunshine. Those who witnessed it—and every man afterward told roughly the same tale—found himself on his knees. A great silence, broken only by a rustling, as of a vast wheatfield brushed by the wind's caressing, invisible fingers. And somehow, every man of d'Orlaans's army saw Vianne, her arms about me, my head on her silk-draped lap as I choked my last, reaching with bloodstained fingers to touch her cheek.

Jiserah, some of them breathed, as if that queen among the Blessed had come to earth. Perhaps she had.

The brilliance shrank, a pinprick of white-scorch intensity, and the rattling whistle of tortured breath echoed amid the rustling. My foolish body jerked, striking out with fists and feet, but Vianne did not flinch.

A knife of ice through my chest. Bubbling clear fluid spuming from nose and mouth as she rolled me aside, the torrent fouling her skirts. I convulsed, and the force of that seizure cracked me open.

Mercifully, I remember little of it. Merely the pain, and even that fades. My cheek against cold cracked bluestone, Vianne's hands strengthless at my shoulders, plucking weakly at my doublet. She tilted back her head and screamed, a cry of utter negation.

And I...lived.

Chapter Twenty-Six

Weak as a newborn kitten. There was a cup at my lips—broth with bitter herbs; I drank. Sought to grimace at the foulness of whatever medicinal properties the draught had. Cursing, a lake of broth spilling over my face, a familiar voice answering my oath with an equally improper one.

"Do not *drown* him, lackwit!" Young di Siguerre grabbed at the cup, and a foreign voice cursed him roundly.

I found myself on a camp-cot, gracelessly sideways, my boots scraping at carpets as I recognized the fabric. Indigo, rich and expensive.

Vianne.

"Where—" My voice would not work properly. Burning invaded my cramped limbs. I coughed, harshly. A gobbet of something foul lodged in my throat, I retched, and the Pruzian cursed again, this time cheerfully, as a basin appeared to catch the blood-clot. Cold air stung all the way down, then, and I was suddenly exquisitely aware of the simple act of breathing in a way I never had been before.

"Son of a donkey-loving whore," he finished in Pruzian, spitting

each syllable disdainfully. *"I am playing nursemaid to a babbling* Hekzmeizten *so weak I could knife him with no trouble—"*

I jerked, twisting, and his harsh caw of amusement scraped my ears. *"I jest,"* he muttered. *"The* fralein, *she left thee in our care. Ease yourself, friend, the* Hekz *takes a toll even while it heals."*

A Pruzian Knife, calling me *friend*? I blinked crusted blood and other matter away.

Young Siguerre cursed as he lifted my legs, managing to slop me onto the cot in passing-fair fashion. "There. You weigh a dray-and-cart, d'Arcenne, and you smell none too fresh either. You are to rest, and the hedgewitch is fetching something for tisane—"

Hedgewitch? "Vianne..." I sought to raise myself. Managed it shakily, but the tearing in my chest forced me to cease. "What in the name of the Blessed—"

"You are to *rest*, she said. We follow her as soon as you may travel." Di Siguerre's young face was graven. "She rides for the relief of Reimelles with those who did not follow the Duc d'Orlaans. He escaped, and no few went with him. Methinks he goes to join the hounds of Damar, or some other such black treachery. Much joy may they have of him, too, wherever he lands. The Queen let him leave with his life." It was *awe* behind his gaze, I realized, uncomfortable but evident. "She says we will drive back the Damarsene. She says the gods have spoken."

Reimelles? The world had gone mad. I stared at him, forcing my wits to work through a cotton-fog. *Damn the woman. Will she never stay in one place?*

But Reimelles was one of the first defenses on the road to the Citté. If the Citté fell, Arquitaine was lost. Had Badeau, that ancient hedge against attack from the north and west, granted passage to Damarsene armies? If they had not, there was a faint chance—but Badeau could not hold out for long, and the Damar might simply march through their territory first and ask forgiveness later.

That had happened before, and tis said to be the reason why those of Badeau are ever nervous.

"Gods. What have they to do with Reimelles?" I tested each limb in turn. My chest was a cracked egg of tenderness and aching, but I could move.

"*I* do not know." Young Siguerre took the basin and blood clot from the Pruzian. "You were lung-pierced, Captain. She healed you. The Aryx broke d'Orlaans's…thing, whatever it was."

"He studied long on sorcery," I managed, gaining another deep breath. Lung-pierced. Such a wound was likely a death sentence unless one had a greatly skilled physicker immediately by, but I was merely tender all through. And strengthless, my limbs heavy and inert. *And he was never very careful of method. Only of results.*

Oh, twas possible, I supposed. The dark half of Court sorcery is fueled with blood and pain, and tis not meet for a nobleman. Nor is it quite safe—those who take the Rose Path, as it is known, risk the thorns and sores of sorcery-sickness, not to mention insanity.

I did not think d'Orlaans would cavil overmuch at the risk.

Di Siguerre shrugged. "Good riddance, whatever twas. Here's the hedgewitch now."

Twas Coele, one of the pair who had tended horse and Guard during our ride. His broad face was familiar, and his phlegmatic mien doubly so. He thrust a cup of something thick, foulsmelling, and sulfurous under my nose. "Drink, an it please you, *sieur*."

I had no choice, unless I wished to drown.

"He coughed this up. Should we worry?" Di Siguerre managed the impression of a fretting old maiden auntie tolerably well.

"Clears the lung." Coele nodded, one arm under my shoulders.

I sought not to splutter the contents of the cup. "See the charm, there? Fine work. A goodly scar to tell the *d'mselles* of."

The Pruzian glanced up at the tent's interior, then back to me. His quality of silence was the patience of a man who knew how to wait—perhaps the most dangerous sort there is.

When the hedgewitch finally took pity on me and removed the cup, I found myself breathing again with deep, disbelieving gratitude. "Reimelles," I croaked. "We must ride."

"Not yet." Coele immediately gainsaid me. "*M'dama* gave orders. Charm will tear if you ride now."

"How long?" I sought to rage, could only rasp. "Blessed curse you, *vilhain*, how long am I abed?"

"Longer you thrash, longer it takes." The man nodded to di Siguerre. "*Sieur*. I'm off to mix more tisane; back in an hour to charm him afresh."

"Very well." Siguerre was left holding the basin; he made a face at it and stamped out of eyeshot, the bowl clattering as he placed it somewhere.

The Pruzian leaned over me. "*Rest,*" he said, in his unlovely mother tongue. "*I shall be watchful,* m'Hier. *She suspects.*"

I would have inquired just what he meant, but Siguerre returned to my bedside. "Di Sarciere's half of the Guard went with Her Majesty, Captain."

"How many left with her? Who commands at Reimelles?"

"The Old Guard, half the New, more than half of d'Orlaans's forces gathered here. Of the command of Remeilles...I do not know."

Jierre would have known. I could have cursed at him. Instead, I merely closed my eyes. I had attempted what she asked of me—yet I had miscarried. D'Orlaans still lived. I had not gained the chance to challenge him afresh after di Narborre fell.

And here I was, lung-pierced, sedated by a peasant hedgewitch, and *useless*, while she rode with an army perhaps full of treachery. Much would depend on who commanded the forces at Reimelles, whether twas one of d'Orlaans's creatures or a noble who cared little for the erstwhile Duc. There would be much to do, and much she would not think to ask for or on. I racked my brains, but I could not think of who had been enseated at Reimelles during the last year.

It was perhaps not possible for her to turn back the Damarsene with a ragged army of possibly-treacherous men, and she must guard against d'Orlaans even more carefully now. Relieving him of the burden of ceremony and protocol meant that he could strike from the shadows at any moment—and she had none at her side capable of anticipating or turning aside such a blow.

At least she had her new Captain. Jierre, showing a depth of dissimulation I had scarce thought he possessed. Had he been pretending to think me a traitor, or was he pretending to think summat else now? Either way, he was showing subtlety.

Vianne could make a man into whatever she wished, did she but realize it.

She knew what I had done, and perhaps hated me for it. Yet she had spilled from her palfrey and come to me. She had *held* me. Had even cried aloud.

Because I could not stand the thought of your beheading, Captain, she had informed me, archly, once.

Could she still not stand the thought of my death? Twas another small mercy, one with thorns. But I took it, and fell into a drugged, twilit sleep.

The Field d'Or was deserted. Yellowed grass, stamped-bare dust, the charred remains of fires, the Pavilion standing lone and dark against a gray-clouded sky. Stray dogs nosed among the smoking midden-heaps d'Orlaans had left behind.

Packhorses and plenty of provisions were left for our small band. Perhaps Jierre had seen to it. Tents had been left as well for my nursemaids, and the large blue embroidered monstrosity as well. *I shall not need it,* Vianne had said to young Siguerre. *Let him rest in comfort, for once.*

Other than that, she had left no word for me. Nothing but the scar on my chest, angrily red and tender, and a matching scar on my back. Di Garonne had done his work well. The mark on my face did not count, for twas healed already. But still I felt it, plucking at my expression as I lay exhausted and fretting.

Coele did his level best to keep me down and drugged, but the second day after the duel I grimly hauled myself from the cot, barked at di Siguerre to fetch my shaving-kit, and cursed the hedgewitch roundly when he sought to dose me with a sedative draught again. The Pruzian found this amusing indeed, to judge by his sardonic grin.

At least he had not knifed me while I lay abed.

"No more sleep-herbs, by the Blessed," I snapped. "Dose me with aught else you will, hedgewitch, but do not blunt my wits. They are blunt enough."

"Aye to *that, sieur,*" he snapped in return, flushed and irritated, clutching the rejected cup in both hands. "The charm is fragile; it may tear and you will bleed out in a heartbeat. Or drown in your own claret. *M'dama* said you were to rest—"

"She is my Queen, not my nursemaid. I serve her better thus." I forced my legs to straighten, pushing myself up. To stand made my chest ache in a wholly different way, but twas bearable.

Just, but bearable.

"She said—"

"She is *not here*," I pointed out. "And I am determined, *sieur* physicker. Turn your attention to mixtures that will not send me to Kimyan's realm, and I shall take charge of aught else. And eat something," I called after him as he stamped away. "I shall need you hale!"

"*Idiot,*" the Pruzian commented, pleasantly.

"He keeps muttering in that foreign tongue of his." Siguerre, his thumbs in his belt, stood slim and dark and maddeningly young at the other doorflap. "What does he say?"

"Oh, he oft insults me. Mayhap he thinks I do not notice. *Son of a monkeyfaced dogsucking fishmonger's collop-rod.*" The little filth in Pruzian managed to vent some of my spleen.

The Knife actually laughed, a surprisingly merry sound. "*I begin to think you a worthy brother,* m'Hier."

"*Which does not explain why you are here, and she without your services.*"

He shrugged. "*She is remarkably persuasive.*"

"What does he say?" Young Siguerre looked uneasy. I had noted he did not turn his back to the Pruzian, which said well of him.

I did not give it much thought, being too occupied with keeping my unruly body from toppling. "He remarks that the Queen is marvelous persuasive when she makes requests of her subjects. So I have found, indeed." *Has she found it easy to outplay me? She was wasted as a lady-in-waiting.* "Did you bring my shaving-kit? Ah, good man. Tell the men to cache whatever we cannot carry; we leave for Reimelles at the nooning."

"Not another ride," he groaned, with feeling, and I was surprised into a grim laugh.

"We have a slow-moving army two days afoot of us. I *think* we are capable of catching such a beast without injuring your tender backside further."

"Dear Blessed"—he addressed the tent's indigo-dyed roof—"did our Captain unbend enough to jest with me? Surely the Riving of the Maelstrom is nigh."

He was young, after all—and he had earned some small right to jest at my expense. Jierre would have had harsher words for me—and he still might, did he survive Vianne's next adventure.

So I chose judicious severity, leavened with praise. "If the hounds of Damar break Reimelles, it may very well be. But with us in the field, Tieris, Arquitaine is safer. Your grandfather would be proud."

He all but flinched. "If he is, Captain, twould be the first time. We shall leave at the nooning." A nobleman's salute, and he ducked through the flap.

Well. That is interesting. I blew out a long, frustrated breath. When the body will not obey, despite all a man's cursing and will, tis almost as maddening as following a foolhardy woman across a war-torn country as she flings herself into every danger she can find.

Almost.

Fridrich van Harkke was suddenly at my side. He even *smelled* foreign, some odd combination of oil and tanned Pruzian leather, a bitter undertone as of young *dandille* greens. He braced me, and murmured something in his harsh tongue. Sorcery tingled along my fingers and toes. Twas merely a simple warming-charm, but its oily harshness scraped my skin.

"You will kill yourself." His Arquitaine had improved immeasurably. Even his accent was better.

"I cannot die." *I have too much to accomplish.* "The gods will not let me. Not as long as they wish Vianne to be Queen."

And should they change their Blessed minds about that, they shall see what a descendant of the Angoulême can do to gainsay even them.

"All men can die." Fridrich was pessimistic. "Here, I help you shave."

Chapter Twenty-Seven

Following an army's tracks is normally an education in misery. From the Field d'Or to Amielles, though, the Road was empty. Twas eerie—the fields were stripped, the Orlaanstrienne quiet and its game blinking in surprise at our passage. Smallholdings and tiny villages met us with blank doors and not a sign of life. Amielles itself was very quiet, and twas there we learned what was afoot.

Arquitaine had risen.

The peasants had stayed long enough to bring in the crops. Then they swelled the ranks of the Hedgewitch Queen's army, with whatever weapons were to hand. Scythes, flails, bows, a ferment of peasant unrest. D'Orlaans's tax-farmers and his invitation to the hounds of Damar were viewed as the reason for the plague, the scars of which could be seen in every village. The carrion had feasted well this year—crows sleek and glossy, young hawks circling hopefully, stray dogs and feral porcines avoiding the tramp of boots and shod hooves. Communal graves lurked on the outskirts of every *ville*, some marked with small shrines that would someday perhaps be expanded into Temples.

The Blessed ride with her, a few scarecrow-thin old women left in Amielles told us. The children who had survived the plague were big-eyed and fearful, peering at us around corners. *The plague flees as she approaches. May it strike Damar down instead.*

Indeed.

I clung to the saddle, my scarred chest fragile-sore. Coele cursed me steadily and roundly at each stop. We could not essay much more than a jogtrot, as if we were on promenade, and near it killed me with frustration. At least we were not far behind the Hedgewitch Queen's motley army, its ponderousness still moving at a clip that kept it just out of reach.

The Pruzian rode sometimes at the rear of our column, sometimes in the middle. Every night as we camped, he vanished; every morning I woke to find him standing guard at my sleeping-roll. I did not ever find him resting, and I wondered that I had grown so easy at the idea of such a man near me with a knife while I lay unconscious. Of course, he had been within reach of my shaving-razor and had not done me any ill. It was not as if I could gainsay him, weak as I was. I was mending, yes, charmed at every halt and filled to the back teeth with tisanes. Yet rage simmered in me. Helpless, just when I needed speed and strength most.

I had much time to think, and much time to curse myself for not expecting di Garonne's thrust. He had the habit of attacking *entierce*, true—but *ensiconde* was a child's ploy, and I had fallen foul of it. Wherever his shade was resting now, it was probably still having a hearty laugh at my expense.

At least he was among the shades, and I among the living. For now.

And while I was, there was much grist for the mill in my head. *She suspects*, the Pruzian had said, but I could not induce him to sally further. My father had a potential traitor in *his* sight as well, but I could not spare any worry for him. If Jierre could act the jilted soul so successfully with me, what could he not convince Vianne of? I knew enough of Timrothe d'Orlaans to suspect he had a plan, as well. What might it consist of—and how could I guard Vianne against its tentacles?

Early on the fourth day we passed through Nemourth. From there to Bleu-di-Font was a short day's ride, and my command to press on was almost gainsaid by a mutinous di Siguerre. *You will kill yourself*, he snarled.

I have already been dead once, I snarled in return, *but until tis a permanent state you are not free to treat me as your lackey.*

Nor are you *free to treat me as such*, was his sharp reply, but we left the matter there and continued riding. Evening rose in swathes of blue and orange, the sun dying over the westron horizon, and the shapes on the Road ahead resolved into creaking, brightly-painted wagons threading along single-file.

Twas a traveling band of R'mini. The wagons were drawn by horses instead of oxen, and a small flock of goats wandered on the hedge-side, tapped along by a slim youth with a slouching cloth cap. He touched the back of one goat with his crookstick, singing a wandering melody in a high piping voice.

"Tinkers." Di Siguerre glanced at me. "Come to strip corpses, no doubt. Shall we move them from the Road?"

A fresh pang went through me. "Merely pass by."

Some of the Guard made avert signs as we passed them. The R'mini did not call out a greeting, simply watched the band of crimson-sashed noblemen trot past. Their horses did not even seek to whicker at ours. The women were mostly inside the lumbering coaches; the men drove, some of the younger ones atop the wagons' carved roofs.

The head wagon's driving-seat held a R'mini headman and his

lean dark wife, both of them gazing straight ahead. The headman's proud nose jutted; his dark curly hair lay in sleek-oiled profusion. A red sash tied about his ample waist, a red kerchief about her luxurious fall of redblack hair, gold at her wrist and throat and ears swaying as the wheels turned.

My fingers tightened on Arran's reins. He merely flicked an ear, and we continued on into the twilight, the pinprick-lights of the Bleu in the distance a welcome beacon.

I remained passing thoughtful, and more than a little unsettled.

When last I had seen that R'mini headman, we had both been in Arcenne.

Some days later we found the war.

Merún is a day's ride from Citté Arquitaine. I had planned that we would swing north and east, taking the Road that strikes for Spire di Tierrcei; from there the Road was a river to Reimelles, and our chances were good of catching my Queen's army.

Or so I thought. We breasted a short broken rise; twas the last of the rolling ridges before the vast basin the Citté lay cupped like a pearl in—called *Paumelle d'Arquitaine*, after the hollow of a woman's hand—and halted, staring down.

Merún, the town of lacemakers, the royal seat of the White Kings before the Caprete line had failed and Tirecian-Trimestin became the next branch of the Angoulême's line to wear the Aryx, Merún of the narrow streets and the *Merúnaisse*, as its inhabitants are called for their lace ruffs, Merún one of the seven gateways to the Citté, was burning.

The hounds of Damar had not been held at Reimelles after all. Later I heard of the frantic retreat to Merún, of the shattered remnants of the defenders of Reimelles meeting the Hedgewitch

Queen's ragtag force and causing panic as they fled. I was told of Vianne's rallying them, riding forth on her white horse, the Aryx fiery on her chest—what had that fire cost her?—and the Guard, both old and new, behind her seeking to stem the tide of panicked retreat. Her Captain, di Yspres, commanded a rearguard action that gave enough lee for Merún to be hastily fortified and held.

I was grateful for that, though hearing him called *her Captain* sent a bolt of hot rage through me to match di Narborre's thrust.

If she was within Merún, I had finally caught pace with my Vianne. There was merely a Damarsene army, fortifications, and a few leagues of war-torn land between us. And if she required me for the Aryx to fully perform its function, how could I help her from *here*? Was she even *in* the city?

I could not know. The moment is one that still brings me to cold sweat. Uncertainty is almost worse against the nerves than disaster.

Arran stamped as we hastily backed down from the ridgeline. The Damarsene did not look to be setting patrols here; they were occupied with the town. A pillar of crimsonlit smoke hung over their efforts; their siege engines were busy. If the wind shifted, we would perhaps hear the rumble of battle.

"How did they break Remeilles? Or did they simply invest the town? Is that possible?" Tieris di Siguerre swore, his fist clenched, looking very much as if he wished to strike empty air in the absence of a better enemy.

"We cannot know at this juncture," I answered absently. "Peace, lieutenant. Hold a moment."

Sharp-faced Jaicler di Tierrce-Alpeis fidgeted. "If Merún falls, the Citté will too."

"Peace." I held up a hand. They were all so *young*. "Give me a moment to think, *chivalieri*. This is merely a riddle, and one we shall solve."

"The Damar." Thierre di Sanvreult shuddered. "Their god drinks blood."

They were at Arcenne's walls not so long ago, and handily dispatched. Of course, it had only been some few thousands, not this mass. Arran stamped again, catching the scent of nervousness among the men. "The time for faintheartedness was before we left Arcenne." My tone was harsher than I liked. "I asked for a moment, *chivalieri*."

There was no murmur of discontent, but I could sense their courage waning as evening filled the sky, Jiserah loosening her robe and Kimyan tightening hers. But tonight would be a night for Danshar the Warrior, sword flashing and shield lifted, or his bow drawn back to his ear.

No. Not Danshar. He is not subtle enough.

Cayrian, then. God of thieves, god of traders and the silver-tongued minstrels, of tightfisted merchantwives and those who live by the knife. He had married the Old Blessed goddess of justice, and oft made a mockery of her. Still, Elisara his wife—the blind boonsister of Alisaar, Elisara the goddess of honest measurement and swift retribution—always won out in the god-tales and teaching-rhymes. For Cayrian so loves her he cannot bear to truly cheat her. Besides, Alisaar's curse would descend upon him should he dare to do more than mock, and she is not merely the goddess of love, but of attendant pleasures most are loath to risk. Her wrath is to be feared.

Of such gods the d'Arquitaine are fond. Their weaknesses bring us easier sleep at night.

Had I been a more religious man, I would have offered to Cayrian once I was Henri's Left Hand. Of course, had I been more religious, I might have sought to win Vianne by another method. Who could tell what I would have done? I was faced with what to do *now*.

On his dun horse, under a spreading willum tree, the Pruzian's gaze met mine. He nodded slightly, and I cursed myself for being so slow and so transparent.

"*Sieur* van Harkke." I spoke as if I had my riddle ready, more decisive than I actually was. "Tell me you may enter yon city undetected."

A single shrug. *All things should be so easy*, that shrug said. *"I am a Knife."* The guttural Pruzian was far too harsh for a cool-turning-chill harvestwinter eve. Twas a night for cider and a bonfire, peasants dancing and nobles at a fête—possibly the Fête of Moonrising; twas the season for it.

Oh, there will be bonfire aplenty. Merún already burns.

"That you are," I murmured in Arquitaine. "Now, my Guards, I shall tell you what we will do."

They trusted me, those younger sons. Their faces, turning to shadow under hatbrim and dusk, turned to me as if I were their father. Perhaps I was; if the drillyard makes a soldier, the man who shouts and curses—who trains the muscle and sinew upon it—is a father of sorts.

Which made them all my sons. May the Blessed, old and new, forgive me for how harshly I led them.

Chapter Twenty-Eight

Dawn was merely a gray intimation on the horizon when Coele shook me awake. At least I had slept; some of the Guard were perhaps not so lucky. A cold night, for we could not risk a campfire's breath being remarked, did no wonders for anyone's mood.

I ignored the grumbling. And I did not ask where di Siguerre had procured the farglass he handed to me as I approached him behind a screen of hollisa bushes. Their berries were soft and fermenting now, a heady, sharp scent in the morning chill. In the lowlands they use such late berries to flavor their mead, if they can manage to collect them before the birds do.

I lifted the farglass, peered through. Merún lay dark, the fires extinguished and its walls featureless at this distance. The city's Keep was a pile of antique stone, defensible perhaps in the White Kings' time, but sadly ramshackle now. Outside the walls—at least they were strong, those sheer sorcery-carved graystone curves—the Damarsene swarmed. Blocks of their dark tents strung behind the inward-facing circles of their trenches and earthworks, marring the fields and network of holdings and hamlets lapping against Merún's walls. No few of those holdings had been torched and sent up their own thin threads of smoke to add to the haze.

Their owners must have resisted the quartering of Damarsene officers. The standard practice in such cases is to burn and level, even if it robs said officers of shelter for the night. Damar prefers obedience to comfort.

Perhaps that is why they ever seek to invade Arquitaine's fields and orchards, to steal what they do not think to make for themselves. Or perhaps they are drunk on war, craving it as the birds crave fermented berries or those with alesickness crave nothing but the next draught of oblivion.

Sourness filled my throat. Even the shacks of the city's poor had been cleared from their wall-hugging, the slum burning just as fiercely as the estates of petty nobles farther out. There must have been much butchery among those who could not gain the safety of the walls soon enough.

The Keep slumped dispirited under a pall of smoke. Was Vianne awake? Had the Knife managed to slip into her presence? Was I right in sending him?

Tieris could not contain himself. "Any sign?"

If there were a sign, I would have said so by now. "Not yet." I kept my tone light. "Break fast lightly, and acquaint them with their routes one more time. Every man to check his weapons. We are not armored enough for a full cavalry charge; speed and lightness must be our priority. Leave behind anything that will weigh us down."

"Aye." He paused. "Captain…"

I thought him merely nervous. "Ease yourself, di Siguerre. We have come this far."

"We have indeed. If I were to…"

Was Vianne inside that city? If they broke the walls, would she suffer a woman's danger at the hands of the Damarsene? Taken prisoner, she was a valuable playing-piece, and they might force her at swordpoint into all manner of things.

Politically, and otherwise.

I shook the idea away. It would not help. "If you were to *what*?" Irritation, sharp as a splintered bone lodged in my throat.

"Nothing, Captain." He stepped away smartly, to take my orders to the rest of them. I focused on the besieged city through the farglass and swore under my breath. As a method of relieving tension, it left much to be desired.

I watched for another hour as dawn strengthened, the sun bleeding as it threatened to rise. Red streaks clutched the horizon as if the Sun's chariot needed claws to heave itself free of night.

Perhaps it was an omen. We could not be lucky enough to avoid shedding blood ourselves, even if my plan succeeded.

I had just rested my eyes, rubbing at the bridge of my nose, and replaced the farglass, when it happened.

On the highest tower of the Keep, motion. I waited, unaware of holding my breath until the need for air grew dire and black spots danced before me. I sucked in a deep breath, twisted the farglass's largest lens slightly, and my heart rose inside my bruised, aching chest as the flag unfurled.

Twas red. Red as the dawn, red as the sash of her Guard, red as the blood in my veins.

Vianne was in Merún. The Knife had reached her, and she had agreed to my plan.

I snapped the farglass into its leather case. My jaw set, and the sudden calm of a course of action descended on me. Now I did not need to worry; I needed only to *do*.

Tis amazing, how such a small distinction eases a man's nerves.

Horses stamped nervously. I gave Coele the purse. It should take him home handily, plenty of coin for his comfort and his trouble, and a request for my father to settle an annuity on him and the other hedgewitch, should *that* man return alive. The Blessed knew they had earned it. "Stay off the Roads."

He gave me a withering glance as he handed the small bit of crumbling earth to me. "I ent stupid, *sieur* d'Arcenne. Mind they have a hedgewitch physicker reinforce that charm, now."

The dirt-clod reeked of hedgewitchery, and I held it carefully. "If we gain the city safely, I am certain I shall have no trouble with that." I clapped him on the shoulder. "Blessed guard you. I shall miss your tisanes."

He snorted, and clicked his tongue to the packhorse. They disappeared into morning mist on the other side of our camp-clearing. The young Guard, muffled in layers of cloak and great-coat, sparked with stray sorcery. Each layer of cloth would hold its own particular turn-aside or defensive measure, to be shed as it was expended or as need dictated. They were all at least acquainted with the basics of Court sorcery—I had made certain of that—but they were by and large lamentably unpracticed.

"Hold up the hilt thus." Jaicler di Tierrce-Alpeis flicked his fingers, and a complicated webbing of pale blue sorcery descended down chased metal, gathering in the steel, coming to a crackling point at the tip. "Then, *thus*—" A swift flicker, and the blade was sheathed. "And when you draw it, *so*. A burst of air, capable of knocking a man down. My brother and I used to surprise each other with this." A soft, remembering tone. "How *m'Mère* would scream."

"Watch the man before you, and ware your feet," Tieris di Siguerre repeated. "They will seek to cut your horse from under you, do you break your sorcering."

"We know, Mother," someone chanted in a singsong, and there was a muted ripple of laughter. A group of men bracing themselves for battle are apt to laugh at anything—or nothing. Tis a different manner of armor than the plate a *chivalier* used to be required to maintain.

"*Chivalieri.*" They straightened at my tone, hounds hearing the keeper's silent whistle. "Dawn strengthens. Let us begin. You know your routes?"

Grave nods from every quarter. They were haggard, some unshaven, and in their dark eyes blazed the flame of the Angoulême. A nobleman's fire, kindled in the face of impossible odds. A *d'mselle* to rescue, a Queen to be of service to, such things were courtsong-worthy and proud honors to be worn. They were young enough to still believe such things ended with a blaze of glory and renown.

I had fostered that idea on the drillyard, seeking to give them a reason to fight—at least, a reason beyond pettiness and jealousy.

I succeeded all too well.

"Then let us begin." Creak of leather, jingle of tack, we pulled ourselves into the saddle once more. I gained Arran's back a trifle gingerly, my chest aching from the damp chill. The dirtclod, cupped in my free hand, crumbled a bit more. "Separately or in pairs, *chivalieri*, and mind you do not speak once I have laid the illusion." I paused. "In the Queen's name."

"For the Queen's honor," they answered as one, softly but with great force.

I tossed the dirtclod, hard enough to shatter it. The hedgewitchery inside flashed green, and from its pieces thin traceries of vapor rose. Then I closed my eyes and invoked Court sorcery.

Twas easier than ever to pull at light and air, shaping it to my will. Did Vianne feel it, as I felt it in every nerve when she used the Seal? I was perhaps too far away. In any case, the illusion rose in fine threads, spinning about each rider.

One cannot build multiple perfect illusions. What one Court sorcerer *can* do, however, is blur the outline of multiple forms, a subtle shifting and shading so that a casual observer sees only what he *expects* to—for example, fellow Damarsene in their distinctive high-collared dark tunics and blackened half-armor with its high-curved shoulders. The hats became low-sloping, unfeathered things, ugly and shapeless.

Each of them murmured the word that would take the illusion from my control. I felt the snap like a crystal wineglass breaking inside a muffling cloth, and opened my eyes to find that Coele had wrought true. The hedgewitch's charm poured mist from the ground like a fountain, and di Tierrce-Alpeis let out a long sharp breath, not quite a whistle. Hedgewitchery and Court sorcery blurred together, and the fog thickened. It washed past us, a heavy autumnal mist gathering strength as it drew from the fields and trees and open sky. The breath of wind di Siguerre's Court sorcery provided sent it down the hill toward Merún. The sun would burn through the covering vapor by midmorn, but while it lasted we were even more heavily shrouded.

Like ghosts, we vanished into the fog, indistinct shapes. By ones and twos we threaded our way toward the Damarsene, hoofbeats muffled and our horses—appearing dun nags by now, since their ugly cobs bear no resemblance to the grace and beauty of even the humblest d'Arquitaine horseflesh—wearily plodding inside the woolfog their world had become.

Chapter Twenty-Nine

The north face of Merún's walls was not quite as high as the others, but still sheer. A culvert and a water-gate pierced it, with archers poised to make the culvert's valley a ride to the underworld for any attackers. Fine thin threads of Court sorcery refracted through hanging water-droplets—the fog had surpassed my expectations. Of course, morning cloud-along-the-ground is common in the lowlands, so the sorcery did not have to work against the grain. It merely had to help things along, like Mithin the Physicker in the old limericks.

Arran stood, stolid and patient, at the edge of the culvert. The Damarsene suspected something was afoot—their call-challenges as the guards went about their rounds were increasingly sharp. I was not the first to arrive here—a dozen indistinct shadows ranged in front of me. The defenders above had not opened fire, though I knew they were there. One had coughed not too long ago, and the scrape of a crossbow-stand as the weapon atop it swiveled had fallen like an iron ingot into the silence below.

They came singly or in pairs, and as soon as I deemed it safe I extended one gloved hand. A small gesture, and the shell of illusion on me folded aside, bursting like a soap bubble. A tiny thread of Court sorcery touched the web of triplines stretched across the water-gate. They flushed, shivering, and the sudden silence was ominous.

A throatless, chill whisper from above. "The Fête of Flowers." *Why did you dance with me? I've often wondered.*

I found my mouth was dry. "No. The Festival of Sunreturn." She had been in dove-gray velvet, the oversleeves and overskirt slashed to show crimson and orange silk, as a sunset on the shores of the Mare Mari, where *demianges* sing amid the waves. I should not have danced with her—by that time, it was suspected that I had a weakness in her direction. But she had been rosy, flushed with cider and laughter, giggling behind her carved sandwood fan as the Princesse sallied a remark or two, and I had not been able to stop myself. When she spun, the skirts belled, and she became a flame.

"Hurry," the voice overhead whispered. The filaments of Court sorcery drew aside, and the water-gate had been eased open.

"Go," I said softly. Hooves rang against stone and I winced. Splashing, the indistinct shapes rode down the slope and into the water, loud as cannonfire to my straining ears. I counted—*one, two, three.*

Eight. Nine. Where were the rest of my men?

Twelve. Thirteen.

Fifteen. Here came another through the fog, the set of his shoulders reminding me of soft-faced Sarquis di Pothefeil. I could not be certain…but I thought twas he.

A pair looming through the grayness. Seventeen, one without a protective shell of illusion. Twas di Tierrce-Alpeis, grimacing as he held his shoulder, and my chest constricted. The scar twinged sharply, as if remembering the touch of steel.

"Go," I whispered fiercely.

He nodded, and they vanished into the culvert's dark mouth. The sound of their steps vanished too, cut off cleanly as if with a knife.

Nineteen, twenty. Four more of them threading through the Damarsene, with only their wits and such a thin protection of airy cloud and illusion.

Dawn had come and left, and the Sun, false friend, was strong. Twould be a perfect late-harvest day, mild enough for the ladies of a Court to accompany a hunt. Picnicking in the royal woods outside the Citté, easy riding sidesaddle for them, the Guard in their finest accompanying. A vision of pretty grace and easy laughter, and suddenly I realized I would give up anything I could call my own, even my nobleman's name, to see Vianne di Rocancheil et Vintmorecy smile during a picnic again.

But the fog was already thinning, and it was discernibly warmer.

A cry went up. Another of my Guard loomed out of the vapor, a hoarse whisper-cry as his illusion-shell breached. Twas Antolan di Margues, his hat gone and his dark curls draggled. "Ware! They come!"

Twenty-one. I motioned him for the dark mouth, and his horse slid down the stone gully with a clatter.

Alarums began, muffled by the fog—but not nearly enough. I breathed a curse, since my shell was already broken. The Damarsene roused themselves, a roiling anthill. A breath of sulfurous sorcery—Graecan fire, simmering or newly ignited.

The Sun would not have to burn the rest of the fog off. Another fire would do just as well. Cracks of green like morning-vine tendrils curled through the warp of the fog, and the stink increased.

Four more. Where are they? "Come," I muttered, without

meaning to. "Come, my boys, do not dawdle."

The green vines flushed with red. I smelled charcoal, and salt.

Clashing steel. Cries. Hoofbeats, and a roar as of some gigantic creature prodded rudely from its dreaming.

"Tristan!" The voice from above, a thin thread of sorcery used to disguise it, but it could not hide the frantic hiss in the middle of my name. "*Tristan*, for the love of the Blessed, come inside!"

An exquisite stroke along every nerve I owned. The Aryx, close. Delicate living green fought the harsh red for control of the fog, which thinned and tore, unable to serve both masters. More clashing steel, ringing hoofbeats.

One more, his horse bloody and foaming; his illusion-shell was breached as well. I flung out a hand, pointing, as Sieris di Montalban clattered down into the culvert and splashed through the darkness. He was a fine horseman, controlling even a pain-maddened animal so.

Steel ringing like a smithy. Another hoarse cry. Chill touched my nape. I dismounted, caught Arran's bridle, and gave him to understand what I wished.

When I let loose of him with a *"Ha!"* he shot down the slope, into the culvert's mouth. They would do well by him inside.

I drew my rapier. Settled my dagger along my other forearm, ignored the repeated plea from above. "*D'Arcenne!* Do not be a fool! Come!"

Jierre di Yspres had held the survivors of the Old Guard on the slopes of Mont di Cienne, waiting for me to appear, those many months ago. I could not do less for the men under my care now.

Never too late to begin becoming the man she once thought you were. Ware now, they come.

Great gaps tore in the fog. Through the thinning screen, an absurd three-headed shape. Twas d'Embrail and di Haseault, on foot, with Tieris di Siguerre slumped between them. Blood dripped, and he hung in a sodden mass. Their illusion-shells were gone, and they had all shed layers of protective cloth. Tieris was all over mud and missing his hat.

And behind them, the Damarsene. Just four pursuers for now, and gaining on the men carrying their wounded lieutenant.

"Move!" I barked, and the echo of the drillyard acted as a tonic. Their heads rose—except Tieris's. They hastened, and I lengthened my stride, ignoring the cry from the tower above. Was it Vianne, watching this?

All the more reason to do what I must, then. I set myself, ignored the aching in my chest, and broke into a run.

Chapter Thirty

In Damar, those who fight afoot are largely peasants, and trained for it. The officers are a-horseback, and noble, since only a nobleman can afford a horse. It used to be a crime for any of the lower orders to own horseflesh. Oxen for plowing and pulling carts, horses for war and pleasure, is still their custom. Their peasants fight with pike and sword, and had I been facing four pikes twould have been a much different battle.

But these were officers, one could tell by the quality of their swords and by the half-armor they had been laced into. The extra weight would tell on them—or so I hoped. One let out a watch-cry, and the fog about us roiled afresh.

Behind me, Tieris and his helpers struggled down the stone slope, boots clattering. A short cry of pain before they began splashing, damnably slow, and I closed with their pursuers in a furious spatter of chiming steel and a short-snapped word of Court sorcery.

When you are faced with one-against-many, speed and maneuverability are your watchwords. My chest flamed with tearing pain, but it did not matter. The battle-madness was upon me, and in that fiery glow it did not matter that the wound might reopen, or that my limbs were leaden and weak, or that the fog had shredded and the Damarsene had realized what we were about.

Inquatorce, half-thrust, my rapier darting for the throat and I faded aside, shuffling, as two of the attackers tangled with each other. They are not normally bumbling idiots, but awakened roughly and forced to battle afoot in the heart of their own camp does tend to maze men used to discipline and a-horseback charges. Even the hounds of Damar trained from childhood to the martial.

My dagger left my hand, buried itself in the throat of another—he was not quick enough, and fell a-gurgling. The next I took *intierce*, his blade slid aside just slightly as I turned, inside his reach and thrusting, the rapier ramming into his lower belly where the half-armor was cut away for freedom of movement while horsed. Pulling it free with a twist, my hand searching for another knife and finding it behind my hip—not dagger but poniard, more suitable for throwing, but I had already tossed one knife and been luckier than I deserved. More choking, more cries and running feet. The fog lifted, flushed with red, the green tendrils shrinking as they folded into the earth's embrace. More splashing behind me, grunts of effort.

A crossbow quarrel bloomed in the chest of my third opponent just as I slashed at his arm. His sword fell with a clatter, but the fourth had recovered his wits and I was almost lung-pierced again. I saved myself by lunging aside, chest tearing afresh and sick liquid heat in my throat. A line of tents before me blocked us from view, but that would not last. Already I saw motion, the fog retreating in rivulets as the crimson *Hekz* ate at it. There was no longer truly "fog," merely patches of thin vapor as if a cloud with mange had fallen to earth.

Coele deserved far more than a purse; twas a charm well-

wrought. I had no time for the thought, twas there and gone in a blink. I braced myself, moved forward, the intended strike countered in a flicker, and now I was faced with just one man to kill as two of his companions gurgled their last and the one with the bolt to his chest lay drumming his heels in futile nerve-death, the body not knowing quite what had befallen it.

The fourth was a stocky Damarsene youth, his dark hair cut in the bowl-shape their *chivalieri* fancy, ghosts of the skinspoil still on his cheeks. He had not even achieved a respectable beard, such a thing being a mark of virility among them. Wisp-fuzz touched his cheeks, but for all that, he was strong and quick, well-trained. And he had perhaps shaken off his amazement, his wits fully engaged in the fight before him.

Which meant he had to be killed quickly, before he thought to raise another cry and bring more of his fellows a-running.

The splashing behind me cut off. They were through the culvert. His eyes narrowed, and he lunged *inprimier*, a textbook-perfect move.

That is the trouble with the young. They still think "correct" in a book is always correct in a fight.

I flung myself forward, my blade-tip circling and the edges grating. Sparks spat as he flung sorcery at me—but the Damarsene *Hekzen* is inelegant and ineffective on a personal level, and he did not have the Aryx singing in his veins and bones and breath. I batted it aside with a countercharm, reflexively tilting forward as my blade-tip caught the shieldcage around his hand and stung him. But twas the poniard, flickering forward and burying itself in his throat, that did the murder. I wrenched it back and forth, the sudden gush from the artery bedewing my face and hand. I wrenched back as my chest cracked afresh, glanced at the battlefield, and turned to flee.

Smoking with blood, slipping, stumbling, I splashed through cold thigh-high water. Shouts behind me, and a cry from above. The crossbows hummed, quarrels streaking overhead. 'Twas cover, and I was grateful for it, even though my feet shot out from under me and I fell into the water. Floundering, desperate, clumsy as a newborn colt, I plunged into darkness and safety.

The hedgewitch—a heavily pregnant peasant woman with a wide face and grave dark eyes—shoved my shirt aside. Her blunt callused fingers tested the charmed wound.

I jerked as the scar twinged sharply. "What are you *doing*, whittling it deeper?"

"You have breath to complain," Jierre retorted. "Count yourself lucky, *sieur*. That was a fool's job, d'Arcenne."

"He'll live," the other hedgewitch—a man with a heavily bandaged foot and a crutch—said, straightening from the side of Tieris di Siguerre's cot. "'Tis merely bloody, and that arm will pain him in the winter. I've put him asleep. He needs boneset and charming; I shall return with both."

"Very well." Jierre nodded. He was even leaner than he had been, gaunt and worn, but his face had changed little. Set and imperturbable, his hair haphazard and dark with soot, he was much the worse for wear. "Thank you. Find some food too, Aranth."

"Too much to do," the limping peasant said cheerfully, and stumped away. Jierre sighed.

The woman nodded and mumbled to herself, burying her chin in her dirty lace-ruff. This time the charming was a mass of razor spikes, twisting at my heart and lungs. I choked, hot water rising to my eyes, and was glad my face was a-filth with blood and muck to disguise the tears.

"Serves you right," she finished, and took her hand away, flicking her fingers as if to rid them of foulness. "Am'mist tore the charm clear through. Are you *mad*?"

The *Merúnaisse* are known for speaking their minds. And a woman bearing may speak as she pleases, rank and station be damned. They are sacred to Jiserah, those heavy with new life, and that gentle Blessed's only curse is reserved for those who injure them.

"Not mad," I countered, when I had gained enough breath to speak. "Merely stubborn, *m'dama*. My thanks."

She heaved herself to her feet, cupping her belly with one hand and ignoring Jierre's proffered hand. "There are other wounded to tend to. I canna answer for'im, *sieur*; it could take a bleed any moment."

"I shall tie him to his bed and set a guard, Heloese." He rubbed at the bridge of his nose, a familiar movement when he was restraining himself. "My thanks. Go to your rest."

"Canna. Others to tend to." And with that she was gone, with the peculiar gait of a pregnant woman, sailing with skirts swishing and one hand clasped to the lower back.

The temporary infirmary was in a warehouse, bales of wool and spun linen pushed aside and piled to make walls. Groans and sometimes screams punctuated the morning hush. I met Jierre's gaze. "The men?"

"Hale enough. The worst is the youngling there; he showed a fair measure of steel." From di Yspres, this was a high compliment, and I hoped di Siguerre knew it. "What news do you bring?"

News? "Vianne? Is she well?"

"Well enough." But his jaw set. "Why are you here? You were left with—"

"Nursemaids and tents, while you came to have a war without me. I cannot let you have all the maying about. I was fit to ride, and so I came. What ails Vianne, Jierre? Have I not some small right to know?"

He sighed. Ran stiff fingers back through his dark hair, disarranging it, and for a moment I saw age settle on him. Soon we would be my father and Siguerre, old warhorses, with a common bond, whether we were quite *friends* or not. And would Vianne be my mother, safe in the Palais with a harp and her garden, and a library of Tiberian philosophy and history stuffed to the brim?

I could only hope. "And we have unfinished business," I reminded him. "There is the little matter of you believing—or unbelieving—me a traitor."

"You do not know what I believe." Yet he merely sounded weary unto death. "We cannot hold this city, Tristan. The walls will crumble before long. *She* says help is coming; she says the gods have spoken. But she is…you do not know. You cannot understand."

I watched him. This was summat new, practical hardheaded Jierre speaking so oddly. "You try my patience. Pray try my comprehension with this riddle, too." Dried blood and drying mud cracked as I grimaced. My chest was a tender egg, the scar deepaching. Once the fever of battle is over, one feels the weariness, and the muscles one has misused.

"*At least Tristan is safe*, she said. *At least I have accomplished that much.* Now you are here, where it is *not* safe, and she is fretting herself dry worrying on what dire tidings could have brought you to risk your life so."

I almost winced. "No tidings I can give you, Captain." Perhaps there was a slight emphasis on the title.

Perhaps it was ill-natured of me.

He shrugged. "She required it of me."

I could not help myself. "And what else does she *require* of you?"

Did he turn pale, eyeing me? It seemed so. "That," he said stiffly, "is between myself and Her Majesty. *Sieur.*" A half-bow, and he whisked himself forth as I cursed internally.

He did not tie me to the cot after all, or set a guard. But he did not need to. My body finally rebelled at the demands placed upon it, and after seeking to haul myself upright and failing twice, I lay there and waited, listening to the screams of the wounded and Tieris di Siguerre's labored breathing.

Chapter Thirty-One

Confused motion. My fist came up, my hand caught and wrist deftly locked, and I opened my eyes to see Fridrich van Harkke grinning like a madman. He was unshaven, his cloth sadly the worse for wear, and looked *very* pleased with himself. *"Son of a potbellied sow,"* he greeted me. *"Thou sleeps as one dead."*

"Can you blame me?" I muttered in Arquitaine, twisting my wrist free of his grasp. "What is it?" My head was clear, at least, and I felt...not exactly strong, but wonderfully rested.

"The fralein *calls, my friend."* His grin broadened a trifle. *"I trust this is welcome news."*

I had fallen asleep covered in filth, and now I felt it as the Pruzian helped lever me up. This time my legs held me. "I do not suppose there is time for a bath."

"If you like." This time he spoke in Arquitaine, though he could not handle the vowels as gently as they require. "She will not be leaving us behind again."

I glanced at Tieris's bed, but twas rumpled and empty. "How does the rest of the Guard fare?"

"Attending to the city's defense." He shrugged. "Tis only a matter of time." The fey smile widened. "Then we shall see what it is to die like men."

I have no intention of dying, sieur. "Very well." I am certain my expression spoke more loudly than my courtesy.

His laugh, for all his grinning, was mirthless, and we sallied forth into dimness reeking of blood, sickness, and wool. The infirmary was abuzz—hedgewitches working grimly, the quiet eerie. They had the set gaunt look of those who understood that there would soon be more wounded to attend to, and the faraway, closed gazes of those who must shut away their compassion if they are to provide aid effectively.

I gripped van Harkke's arm. "No bath, *sieur*. But I do need the privy. Then take me to her."

The small round room was full to overcrowding, tapestries doing little to soften the harsh stone walls. Messengers came and went, a table littered with dispatches and other paper, and Adersahl di Parmecy seeking to retain some sort of order among the press of those seeking entrance or audience.

"The west wall. Take this to the archers; they will see to it," Jierre was saying as he strode from the door toward the crowd at the back of the room. A stolid, soot-covered Messenger next to him wrung his hands, seemingly unaware he was doing so, but he took the message with a half-bow and spun, shoving for the door.

The din was overwhelming, candleflames in sconces along the wall adding to the oppressive heat. The Keep slouched above; this small audience chamber was reached easily by means of the large, drafty greathall, full of other supplicants and men awaiting orders.

Twas chaos, and my chest gave a flare of twisting scorch-pain. The scar on my face twitched as well.

She stood behind the table, listening and nodding as another hedgewitch spoke rapidly, shaking her finger for emphasis. It appeared the woman was taking my Queen to task, and Vianne…

She looked even frailer, her plain gray dress lacking any ornamentation, the Aryx humming against her chest. But it was not the smudges under her eyes or the hollowing of her cheeks that sent such a hideous shock through me.

Her gaze had ever been soft, before, even in the midst of her anger. Even when she took the tone of chill brittle royalty, a man could see the weeping in her. If he knew how to look.

The softness was gone.

The Hedgewitch Queen's gaze *burned*. Her eyes were just as dark as ever, but they pierced swiftly and seared all they lighted on. Something had changed, and the woman inside her slender frame was no longer merely Vianne. Something inside her had unfurled, something bright and honed as the rapier at my side.

Was this what I had fallen in love with, so many years ago? Or was this a new woman? It did not matter. Every nerve in me sang like a harp at a skilled minstrel's touch at the mere sight of her.

She leaned forward, touched the angry hedgewitch's elbow. A few words, and the woman, her head wrapped in a scarlet kerchief, appeared satisfied. She nodded, her shoulders easing. Vianne bent to a stack of fresh paper, dipped a quill, and wrote a few swift words. The Aryx sparked, the serpents writhing about each other lazily, and Vianne folded the paper, gave it to the woman, and beckoned the next supplicant forward.

The Pruzian pressed through the throng. Twas hot as the Torkaic underworld here, and there were short tempers in every corner. A messenger burst in.

"More fire in the *Quartier* Sothian!" he yelled, and Adersahl collared him neatly, beckoned to a waiting soldier, and sent them both out the door to collect aid from the throng outside.

Vianne's glance passed over me, with no sign of recognition. No, she looked *past* me, to see the result of the commotion at the door. The next man, his arm in a sling, began shouting over the din—something about the workers given over to making crossbow quarrels and their materials.

Jierre stepped around the table to Vianne's side. He listened, gave a crisp order, Vianne nodded, and the man turned on his bootheel and began forcing his way out with alacrity.

I saw di Yspres lean toward Vianne, whose dark head bent. Her braids were disarranged, curls springing free, and no ear-drops swung glittering to tap at her cheeks. She tucked a strand of her hair back, listening, and made a quiet remark to him. There was no heat between them, no indication that he had taken on any role but that of adviser.

Fridrich shoved past a knot of merchants in soot-stained doublets. "*Ach*, prettybit, look what I bring you!" he announced, his gravelly rasp cutting the din. "What more do you need?"

Vianne looked up. Her face did not change. She merely nodded absently. "My thanks, Fridrich. Tell me, have you supped?"

He shook his head, his clubbed braid swinging. "Had enough. Where am I needed?"

"Luc di Chatillon is above the gates; he may need relief. If he does not, bring me word of how he fares and how long he thinks we may hold." A slight smile, she offered her hand; I saw ink had splattered her sleeve and a fine crystal dewing of sweat on her wrist. "I do not know how I should fare without you."

"Flattery, *fralein*. I serve." He bent over her hand, nodded to Jierre, cast me a single still-amused glance, and was gone.

Her hand fell, and she regarded me. "*Sieur.*"

The world threatened to fall away and leave merely us, my Queen and me. I met her gaze and found that the relief of knowing she possessed my secret, that I had precious little to hide from her, was as sharp as it had been before.

Whoever this woman was, whatever had lit inside her like a maying fire, she was still Vianne. The idiot stubbornness in me knew only one thing: she was still *mine*.

I bowed—a trifle stiffly, to be sure. My chest twinged, the Aryx sparked again, and she winced slightly. The Seal's power stroked along my body, and I wondered that every Arquitaine in the room did not shiver in response. "At your service, *d'mselle*. Command me."

"I require merely your presence. Captain, fetch him a chair—yes, my thanks."

I had twitched at the *Captain*, but twas Jierre who dragged a chair from the end of the table and settled it beside her.

"There." Vianne pointed.

"It is not meet that you should stand while I take my ease. Your Majesty."

"Tristan." Irritation, sharp as a rapier point. "I do not have *time* to argue with you."

I navigated past Jierre, my back to the stone wall, and lowered myself gingerly onto the uncomfortable horsehair cushion. It fair killed me, but I kept my mouth firmly closed. She nodded briskly, and I set myself to listening.

Merún was holding, but only just. Some supplies were reaching the city, for the Airenne's cousin-river, the Marrenne, flowed past and the wharves were out of siege-engine range. The Damarsene had enough troops to choke the Marrenne to the east, and the river was low as usual before winter storms swelled it. All supplies had to come laboriously against the current from the Citté, which had its own troubles, between the panic of the Damarsene and the added panic of the false King's disappearance. Word of the trial-by-combat and the breaking of the false Aryx had spread swiftly, helped no doubt by messengers dispatched by my Queen, but that would not stop the ferment while she was trapped in Merún.

"We must only hold a short while. Have faith." She said it many times, in many ways, and those who sought her command or decision welcomed the certainty. They went on their way heartened. Twas impossible not to believe, when she turned that burning gaze upon you.

Yet I did not hear what relief she expected. Was she merely heartening them to stave off the inevitable?

Then we shall see what it is to die like men. How very Pruzian of him. Would he dare say such a thing to her?

The Harbormaster, broad-shouldered and weathered, stinking of tar, appeared. Not quite peasant, but definitely not noble, his unease in the face of her quality was marked. Vianne actually smiled—a tight, thin grimace, but still lovely. "What news?"

"Two days. Then, Your Majesty, you must consider—"

"What of the wounded? Can more ships be brought upriver from the Citté? I do not know much of the Marrenne and the ways of ships, nor do my counselors."

I know some little, but I have not been here to ask. I kept the words behind my teeth. I did not know enough to be helpful, though I suspected the Citté would not send ships upriver. Twas too much of a risk, and why should they if they might need them soon to flee down the Airenne, away from Damar's advance? The Maelstrom itself might be preferable to the pillage the Damarsene would wreak.

The Harbormaster spread his hands, a gesture of helplessness. Unshaven and red-eyed, the deep weathering of his skin and his squint marking him as a riverman of long standing, he looked surpassingly ill-at-ease. His city was sieged and his ships in danger;

twas enough to make any man blanch.

"The Marrenne is low. Which is good to bring the ships back—less current. But bad, because they must hold to the bank opposite. Not much room to maneuver, and upriver…well. The Damar could send rafts down, I suppose. So we've a watch, but…"

"Yes." She considered this. Jierre handed her a paper, she glanced at it. "Here is a list of hedgewitches among the wounded. Two on each ship, for greater safety. Damar does not like our hedgewitchery; they are the best protection we can offer. The Cité will do what seems fit to them as far as more ships, no doubt. Your captains are brave, *sieur*, and you set them a fine example." She paused. "Continue evacuating the children and elderly. Make certain the younglings have their mothers, should they be *too* young. Should there be…difficulty, with men who doubt our strength, notify *Chivalieri* di Sarciere and di Montfort *immediately*."

In other words, should there be a panic and men seek to storm the ships, Antolan and Jai are to restore order. Di Sarciere is too young to do such things, but he may hold if di Montfort does. And di Montfort is not a man who forgives cowardice easily. Very canny of you, my Queen.

The man nodded. "Yes, Your Majesty. Please listen. Consider a ship for yourself. The Cité is better guarded; we may have you safe in less than—"

He halted in confusion, for her face changed. Twas not the almost-pained expression she had been using for a smile, but an honest smile like sunrise. It shone through the weariness and dishevelment on her. "Here is where I am needed, *sieur* Kaeth."

The man mumbled, his fingers working at the brim of his hat—lacking a *chivalier*'s feather, an imitation of a nobleman's like so many of the trading classes—and his weathered cheeks suddenly stained with red. "Arquitaine will need you at the Citté, Your Majesty. If I may be so bold."

You may not, sieur. *But I happen to agree with you.* "He has a point," I offered mildly.

Jierre shot me a glance I found I could read with little difficulty. Twas profoundly grateful, and without meaning to, I found my mouth stretching in the half-smile that would mean rueful acceptance of the responsibility of an unpleasant truth spoken to royalty.

I had never asked what di Yspres thought of Henri. Perhaps I should have.

"He does," Jierre agreed.

"Here is where I am needed, *sieurs*." Her smile did not falter. "Thank you, *sieur* Harbormaster. Go now, and waste no time."

He did.

So she was determined to stay. I caught Jierre's glance again, and found with some relief that he and I were in accord on one question, at least. She should not be allowed to persist in this folly.

The trouble would lie in convincing her so.

Chapter Thirty-Two

"There is nothing more to do at the moment." Jierre took the quill from her fingers. "Should there be an emergency, I will send for you."

Her mouth turned down, doleful and weary at once. "Tis *all* an emergency. The walls are—"

"They have held so far, they shall continue to do so for a short while. Di Chatillon and di Vidancourt are working wonders in your name, *d'mselle*. Go and rest, so you may be ready for the dawn serenade."

Another face, her nose wrinkling. She swayed, and I was up from the chair in a heartbeat, my hand around her arm. Jierre had caught her too, from the other side.

"I am well *enough*." She sought to free herself of Jierre's clasp first, and that sent a flush through me. The reclaiming of her arm from my hand was just as decided. "Cap—ah, d'Arcenne." She did not flush, nor did she glance directly at me. "My thanks for your company. I shall send for you anon."

"Vianne." I could not help myself. "I shall go with you." Twas difficult to strike the right tone—firm but not commanding, asking but not pleading. I wondered too late if outright begging, perhaps on my knees, would be more likely to secure me a measure of forgiveness.

"I require you for the Aryx, *sieur*. That is all." Coolly, as she might address an overbearing swain at Court. Jierre had averted his gaze, studying the mess of paper on the table. The room was not quite quiet—Adersahl was at the door, and beyond that barrier there was much shuffling and murmuring. I could not tell what hour it was. Late, I suspected, and the Damarsene gathering their strength for tomorrow. Should they send scaling-parties, twould be knifework and grapple-sorcery on the walls. Dark work, requiring much nerve and wit.

My temper all but broke. "Do you plan to reduce me to begging? I wish to be at your side; do you not *understand*?"

"I suppose if I sent you away I would merely wake to find you looming over me again." More trembled on her lips, but she pulled the words back with a visible effort. "I do not have the strength for this, d'Arcenne."

"Then use mine." Memory threatened to choke me. I had told her this before.

"Yours carries too high a price, *chivalier*." She slid past Jierre, her skirts brushing his knees. He did not move. "Do as you please. You will in any event; I cannot gainsay you. Jierre, my thanks."

"*D'mselle.*" His cheeks were red, too. But he offered nothing more as I made it to my feet and followed her. The pain in my chest was not merely the wound.

Still, I followed as she brushed past Adersahl. He fell into step behind her, and the swelling whispers through the crowd outside her door mocked me. She looked neither right nor left, her hands at her skirts to keep them free of her feet, and such was her air of royalty that even those desperate for audience gave way.

* * *

The Keep was drafty and ramshackle; Merún's liege was di Roubelon, and he had spent most of his time at Court. He was perhaps in the Citté, either writhing at the thought of the damage to his rents and tithes, or glad he was not enduring the discomforts of war. Either was equally likely. He would no doubt present a bill to the Crown if the miraculous occurred and Arquitaine freed herself of the Damarsene. Otherwise, he would turn himself to being agreeable to the conquerors.

The quarters given to Vianne's use were…adequate. This had perhaps once been a queen of the Caprete's line's bedroom, its window-casement looking onto a sadly bedraggled garden of roses gone to rot and wither. It must have hurt her to see it so neglected; any hedgewitch would feel a pang to see such disrepair.

The bed was wide but its curtains were stiff-dusty, its linens threadbare, and dust also lay on heavy graceful antiques last fashionable in King Archimvault's time. The watercloset worked, however, and fresh clothing arrived for me. At least, I think twas intended for my use, and I took the stack from a young wide-eyed pageboy who attempted to peer past me into the room. Vianne was safely in the watercloset, the sound of splashing and an occasional rushing spatter as the ancient fallwater inside choked on fluid spilling through uncertain pipes. Twas lucky water was not rationed; the Marrenne had not fallen very far this summer.

Merely far enough.

When she emerged, re-laced into her dress and her hair merely damp, her eyes were red-rimmed. She gave precious little evidence of weeping, merely crossed to the bed and dropped down with a sigh. I was left, still filthy with blood and ditch-muck, holding a stack of linen and doublet that might have been intended for another man, pointedly ignored by the woman who turned her back to the room and pretended immediate slumber.

My throat had gone dry. Again. I was hungry, but that was of little account. The scar on my chest burrowed deeper, green traceries of hedgewitch charming almost visible to Sight as my strength waned.

"Vianne." Hoarsely. "Please." *Forgive me. If you will. If you can.* She did not respond.

It strikes at a man, that brand of a woman's silence. Not quite as a mailed fist to the gut, but close enough—and a little lower, as well.

"I could not stay away." As an explanation, it left much to be desired. "I still cannot."

Did she move? No, twas merely a flicker from the dim glow-globes in their wall sconces. She retired still-gowned, so she could be dressed when fresh crisis arose. Ever practical, my Vianne. But she should not have to be, not in this manner.

"Merún will fall," I continued, quietly. "They cannot hold. You must be a-ship and away before that happens. Must I drag you?" Would her temper rise?

It did not. The silence stretched. Her breathing evened itself. She could perhaps be truly asleep. Exhaustion is a wondrous aid when one seeks to ignore a man, I suppose.

Finally, I stamped into the watercloset. Most of the filth had fallen from my boots; twas a joy to have a real fallwater again, even if it did choke with alarming regularity. The clothes could have been meant for me—the breeches a trifle loose, the shirt and doublet a trifle too large, both plain and dark.

And there, folded into the middle of the shirt, a red sash. Which did not solve the riddle of quite whose clothes these were.

I cannot gainsay you.

How right she was. I could stride into the bedroom, shake her awake. Strike her. *Make* her respond. She was only a woman, despite the Aryx.

And what was I?

The slice of looking-glass over the sink was ancient and cracked. I touched it, fingertips scratching and still faintly stained with grime. Hard riding does not wash out so easily. I turned away, not wishing to see the dusty ghost of my reflection. Stopped in the watercloset door, gazing at the bed's stiff brocaded draperies.

Only a woman. I could do what I liked. Truly, who was there to halt me or say me nay? She needed me, by all appearances far too much to do more than leave me behind with nursemaids. I had won her once; I could win her again. Patience and time—but my patience was sorely lacking, and there was no time.

Was it not just this morn I had resolved to make myself into a man she could be proud of? And now, simply look at what I contemplated. There was a word for it, and it was not noble.

I stood in the ashes of my dreams, in the midst of a city that would suffer the sword in a short while. I had betrayed my King and my family, brought unimaginable suffering to my land, and drove the woman I loved into a Damarsene hell.

I had done this, and none other. I had even died for it. Were I more religious, I could consider everything before that moment a stain washed away.

But I was not, and there was no water for the stain on me. There was not enough even in the wide salt seas to cleanse the first layer of dirt smirching my self, and I had applied every inch of it myself.

Did I even truly love her, if I would use her thus? And yet she had not let me die, and had believed in my innocence until

226

I had riven that belief with the truth.

I am not fine enough for you, Vianne. I have not ever been.

The gnawing suspicion that I would not ever be was familiar. That emptiness had always been within me, and it had led me to do the unthinkable and unspeakable, thinking it would earn me what I coveted.

The room was dim and quiet. You could almost imagine no battle outside, a *d'mselle* from a courtsong sleeping as her *chivalier* stood, loath to wake her. I had sworn her my service not once but twice, she had touched my rapier-hilt and accepted both times. I prided myself on being her Left Hand—and yet, look at the pass I had brought Arquitaine to.

If I had left Henri alive, what would have happened?

Such a question is useless. Think on what must be done now.

Well, what was to be done? I could hope not to make aught worse. And most likely fail in *that*, too.

There was one chair in the room—a rickety ironwood thing, carved with ancient spikefruit and possessing a mouse-eaten cushion. It looked decidedly uncomfortable, and I cast another longing glance at the dusty bed. The tapestries hung rotting on the walls, hanging in a stasis that would continue until their threads frayed and they folded to the floor in puffs of dust. By that year, would there be songs of how I betrayed my King? Would I be a footnote in the secret archives, my name blackened?

She would be buried in the chapel of royalty, and I…in a nameless hole, perhaps, my bones crying out for hers as they moldered.

What would the man she could love do at this moment, Tristan d'Arcenne?

When I opened the door, a familiar face met mine. Jierre paused, crouching, caught in the act of unrolling a sleeping-pad on the opposite side of the hall. He gazed at me dully, exhaustion plainly written on his gaunt face. "Robierre di Atyaint-Sierre and Adersahl have the reins." He turned back to the pad, smoothing it down. "They shall send for us, if there is need."

Us. Does he mean "Vianne and me"? Or does he mean all three of us? Or, even, "Captain, you and me"? There was no way of knowing save to ask, and I did not feel like asking.

I closed her door softly. Leaned the chair against the wall, dropped into it, my sword to the side. The ache in my chest would not cease. Was the charm holding? It had held through a short vicious fight, but that was no indication.

"You have done well, *chivalier*." I leaned back, propped my head against the wall. "I owe you my thanks."

Sound of cloth moving as he settled himself. The witchlight torches hissed slightly—no glowglobes here in the hall, too expensive for merely a passageway. "Merún will not fall tonight." Flat, monotone. "She should take ship for the Citté. She has some plan; she keeps its particulars close. Tinan di Rocham was sent, to do I know not what. She says we shall not leave Merún, that relief is nigh. I fear she may have gone mad."

"Not mad." *At least, not yet.* "Now you see the steel in her."

"I could wish she had less steel and more sense." He sighed, and perhaps twas exhaustion that made him so unwary. "Tristan?"

Are you about to tell me I should hang myself to spare her pain? I might. I settled myself, seeking any comfort I could in the chair. There was none to be found. I had slept in worse, though, and though I had done nothing but sit and watch through that long afternoon, I was fair worn through. "Aye?"

"I do not think you a traitor. I never did." His tone was harsh, but the lie—if twas such—was kind.

My eyes squeezed shut. *Do not break her confidence.* I sighed. "It matters little now." *And I cannot tell if you are misleading me.*

"It matters." He paused. "If we die here, I wish for you to know."

"We will not die here." I sounded as certain as *she* did. Had I not just been standing in her bedroom, thinking of the lies I had told to bring us to this place? And yet, if Jierre's faith were shaken, he would not be half as effective in her defense. "I promise you that, di Yspres. We are simply too marvelous to die."

His weary laugh rewarded me. "What was his name? Arkaeon dev Kadat. A petty *chivalier* of Badeau."

"Only outnumbered eight to one, we were." The memory brought me a grimace too pained to be a smile but too cheerful to be a frown. When one has survived such a thing as the Battle of Lithielle, tis the only possible expression to wear.

"You sent back the herald to say you would wait, and he should bring back another four hundred of his kin to make the battle even." Jierre moved again. "Adersahl was near to killing you himself."

"He *enjoyed* it. And the reception from the town afterward left little to be desired." In fact, that had been the only time I had allowed every member of the Guard to become blind-sotted at once. They had deserved it, after all. Arkaeon dev Kadat had never troubled the north-and-west of Arquitaine again. And Badeau had taken quite a more reasonable tone with Henri afterward, parrying Damar's requests for trade concessions that would sting Arquitaine's merchants.

Jierre's weary laugh was balm and a fresh scoring all at once. "Di Montfort and the *m'dama* of the pleasure-house on Rieu di Chier. *I am a hero, woman!* And her reply."

"You are a sot and a base rogue, and a boylover beside." I could still remember the woman's very tone and the stained kerchief knotted about her head, her broad fist raised.

His tone dropped, an imitation of di Montfort's broad north-coast accent. *"I care little what I bugger at this moment,* m'dama, *and you look fine enough."*

A laugh startled me. Thin and inexpressibly weary, my chest gripping and aching as the pale shadow of merriment took voice, answered by his. "And the sourhead afterward. Twas lucky Badeau did not think to field an attack while you were all recovering."

"Aye to that." The old comfortable silence fell between us. Jierre's breathing took on the rhythm of sleep, and I rested my left hand on my rapier-hilt. I longed for slumber, but Kimyan's gift was long in coming.

Honest men were faithful, and Jierre even more so. *I never did.* He had played his part well, for Vianne's sake.

I was not honest. Perhaps twas too late to become so, as well.

Chapter Thirty-Three

I woke to shouting, and my rapier cleared the sheath before I blinked and found myself spilling out of an uncomfortable chair, while Jierre pounded on Vianne's door. *"Wake!"* he yelled, and twisted the knob, striding through. His hair stood up in spikes and his eyes blazed, and fair blond Luc di Chatillon had just skidded to a stop, out of breath and pale as a woodchopper faced with *demieri di sorce.*

"The Gate!" he choked. "All that could be spared! Damarsene—"

I needed to hear no more, spun on my heel and followed Jierre.

Vianne was already upright, her hair a tangled glory. "The dawn serenade," she said, and laughed bitterly. "At least it interrupts my dreaming. Quickly, now!" She brushed past me in a breath of skirts and the smell of her, hedgewitch-green and spicy, filled my head. "Come along!" And, wonder of wonders, her hand closed about my wrist.

I remember little of the stumbling behind her, still mazed with sleep, the tearing in my chest familiar and so, pushed aside. I remember even less of the wild ride a-horseback through Merún's burning streets. A predawn attack, and it blurs together in my dreams with Arcenne and the Graecan fire. At least I had resheathed my sword, and someone had saddled Arran for me.

Hooves sparking on paving-stones, flames and the *stink*, Vianne's tangled head bobbing as the white palfrey bestirred herself to a gallop she had rarely been called on for in Arcenne. The slope of the ramparts behind the gate, switching back and doubling on itself to provide the horses with enough footing. Silvery witchfire crackling around the Hedgewitch Queen as she rode, a globe of protection forming even as she pulled her horse to a halt atop Merún's eastron gate and flung out both hands, the Aryx's singing reverberating through my body like the tramp of boots on a stone bridge, a harmony that could crumble granite.

A shattering rumble, hedgewitchery burning like a green flame and the witchfire surrounding her brightening. Arcs of Graecan fire halting, spinning, smashed aside, Merún's walls shuddering as sorcery plucked at them.

Behind us, the cup of the city smoked and fumed, alive with screams. Massive orbs of Graecan fire, smears of deadly orange-yellow on the hush of the darkest portion of night—the long dark shoal of fourth watch, when the old die and the living feel their blood slow if they are unlucky enough to be waking—poured up in high arcs from the siege engines massed below the walls. The white horse standing frozen as a statue, and the high whistling sound is coming. I cannot stop it; I *know* what comes next, as dream and reality twist together in a fevered braid.

For I *was* fevered. The weakness in me was infection, always a risk with hurts newly mended. The charm holding my chest together had not frayed much, but perhaps the ditchwater had done the work d'Orlaans could not finish. I fell from Arran's back, the tearing in my lungs becoming a river of hot acid in my throat. I spat blood, stumbled as the whistling became a scream—

—and the crossbow bolt pierced the still-building shell of witchfire, shrieking like a mountain-spirit, burying itself in Vianne's shoulder.

The Aryx, bell-like, tolled, almost throwing me to my knees. I skidded, caught her as she spilled from the horse in a gray blur. Her cry was lost under the noise of the Seal screaming its distress and the howls of Graecan fire, now rising unchecked and falling in long slow liquid streams into the city.

Knees hit the stone flooring of the walkway, jarring through me. She was paper-white, her mouth moving slightly, perhaps praying. My hand closed around the shaft of the bolt. *Get it free, then staunch the blood. And hope tis not poisoned.*

Twas a fine time to wish I were a hedgewitch. The bolt was an ugly thing; she would be lucky to escape a shoulder-halt. My lips moved as another bubble of warmth broke on my lips, Court sorcery flaming against my fingers, the bolt shivering. It had not gone all through, the barbed tip grated on bone, and I *twisted*, wood suddenly flexible in my hands and the metal of its head giving out a low note of distress unheard in the cacophony.

Jierre was suddenly *there*, ashen, his hand under her shoulder as she thrashed. Her skirts tangled, her hair curtaining her face as she sought to breathe, a double shock of pain and sorcery she should never have had to bear. More warmth ran down my chin. I let out my own frantic cry, Jierre's Court sorcery stinging my fingers as I pulled the suddenly-drooping bolt free. Weakened by sorcery, it bent instead of breaking, and did not tear muscle and skin overmuch.

I clapped my hand over the wound. *"Hedgewitch!"* I screamed, blood spraying from my lips and dripping down my chin. *"Fetch a physicker!"*

Vianne's head tipped back. The Aryx boiled with light, silver blazing from its writhing curves. Shadows leapt, there was a breathless moment of stasis as they reloaded the siege machines below. Archers from our walls let loose, and the flaming city behind us convulsed.

Her hand came up, clamped over mine at her shoulder. Her blood, slippery and hot against my fingers, sent a flare of nausea and weakness through me.

Merely a nightmare. I will wake and find this a dream.

But there was no waking. Her hair brushed the ground; I bent over her as her fingers bit with surprising strength. The Aryx spoke again, and her entire frame stiffened, the heels of her familiar pair of garden-boots digging into stone.

The body will seek to escape mending from such a blow, if possible. It will thrash with surprising strength, thinking the charming is a fresh assault. I held her, and Jierre shouted something over my head. I turned my face to the side, coughed out a mouthful of hot copper, seeking not to foul her hair.

She sagged, and the moment of breathlessness ended. The Aryx twinged sharply, power shaking me as a trained farrat will shake a caught mouse. I folded over, her only shield my aching, wound-racked mess of bones and meat, the scar on my face shivering madly as if I had the falling-sickness.

Hands on me, seeking to draw me aside. I denied them until she twitched, her hair finally falling back as she shook her head as if to clear it. White as flour, two spots of hectic color high on her gaunt cheeks, blood spattering her face. Was it mine or hers? Mine, I hoped. The thought of her bleeding would unman even Danshar himself.

She struggled against my grasp. I let her go and slumped aside into someone's embrace—twas a hedgewitch, I caught a blur of green and a shocked face under a glaring, bloody head bandage. My chest was afire, and I coughed yet more blood.

Vianne surged to her feet. Jierre lunged upward and caught her elbow, bracing her. She shouted something, pointing at me, and stumbled for her horse. Her dress flapped at her left shoulder, pale skin underneath.

She had charmed the wound closed, and even now caught up her skirts. The horse sidled nervously, but Jierre laid hold of its reins and Vianne had the saddle-horn. She mounted with more determination than grace, wincing as she pulled herself into the saddle, cinders raining from the dark sky.

The charm on my chest gave a burst of spiked agony. I coughed more blood and fluid; the hedgewitch rolled me aside. I cared little—I could still see Vianne, twas all that mattered. The Aryx flamed, and the globe of silver witchlight shimmered into being around her again. This time twas stronger, and her chin rose. The siege engines below released their cargoes of fiery death—and Vianne's hands lifted.

In the east, the first faint gray of dawn was rising, along with white veils of fog.

Chapter Thirty-Four

Dawn came up red as blood, again, through a screen of ground-cloud. The white horse stood braced, her head hanging, and Vianne looked at least as weary. Quiet had fallen, only a few whistling bolts from below, answered occasionally from one of our crossbows. Jierre conferred quietly with a haggard blond Luc di Chatillon—there had been another attack on the southron side while we had been occupied here. Ladders and grapples, and a swarm of men. They had been thrown from the walls with a vengeance, but di Chatillon was not sanguine about success on our side should another night such as this one pass.

Tieris di Siguerre crouched easily at my side. He had come to bring word of the fires—still raging in a third of the city, there simply were not enough hedgewitches to corral them. Also crouching over me was a young peasant boy—a hedgewitch with a bandaged head and a torn, much-mended lace ruff, his hand glued to my chest as he repaired the torn charming. Every so often, coughing and shuddering would rack me. At least I had ceased spitting blood, and the fever was receding.

Vianne, atop the white palfrey, clutched at her right shoulder.

Morning breeze played with her dark curls, and she gazed down at the fogbound Damarsene army, expressionless. The silver protection-globe was pale in the morning light, drops of water vapor scintillating as it shifted. At least they had ceased to shoot at her.

She dismounted, awkwardly and unremarked. I ached to help, but my limbs would not obey me. "Tieris," I croaked, my throat slick and foul. "Attend her."

He rose in a rush and was at her side in a moment. "Your Majesty?"

She handed over the palfrey's reins. "My thanks." Hoarse and weary. "Find someone to take her to stable, an it please you, and Tris and Jierre's horses as well. Treat them well; they have endured much this dawning."

"Aye, Your Majesty." Was it worship on his young face? No doubt. "Is there aught else I can do?"

"No, *sieur*. I thank you for your pains." She still clutched at her shoulder, and Jierre broke away from di Chatillon as she swayed.

"*D'mselle—*" Jierre was pale, too.

"The city?" She did not look at him. Instead, her dark gaze lit upon me. Twas welcome, even if I was filthy with soot and blood, not to mention struck to the ground and unable to rise.

"Fully third of it burning. We shall not last another such serenade. There is a ship prepared to bear you to the Citté. Please, *d'mselle*—Vianne. *Please.*"

A slight, weary smile. She was still looking at me. "There is no need, Captain. I shall remain here until we are relieved. Continue evacuating the children, the old, and the wounded."

"There is no relief," he pressed. "Were there hope of one, we would know by now. The Citté—"

"The Citté is safe enough for the moment. Here is where I am needed, else this collection of wolves will descend upon the heart of Arquitaine. We must merely hold a little longer."

"*D'mselle.*" Luc di Chatillon approached. Bloody, singed, but unbowed, his golden hair grimed until twas near as dark as Jierre's, he made as if to bow and she waved the courtesy away. "Jierre has the right of it. We will not hold another night, and their strength has not diminished. If anything, they have received reinforcement from their fellows in the *Dispuriee.* I am loath to flee as any noble-man, but—"

"Here is where I stay, *chivalieri.* Do you wish to seek refuge downriver, I release you." She dredged up a smile, and it took the sting from her tone. "If you do not, there is much work to be done to ease the suffering of those under our care."

Di Chatillon was no match for her, but he still tried. "*D'mselle.* I would beg you to take more care with yourself."

"And take my ease?" She shook her head. Even now, her hair loose and tangled, drying blood a river down the right side of her dove-gray dress, she was, in a word, magnificent. "Or flee when I have asked them to hold? No, Luc. The gods have spoken. If you would be of use, find some breakfast and return to your tasks."

He accepted the rebuke and the command with equal grace, swept her a bow, and was on his way.

Jierre sighed. "I suppose if I were to ask…"

I waited to hear what he would ask of her.

Her weary smile broadened. "I would tell you that *I* know, and it is enough." She winced, peeling her fingers away from her shoul-der. The hedgewitch next to me muttered, and a fresh wave of coolness slid through my body from head to toe. "Mauris, is it?"

The boy nodded, his attention all on my chest. "Aye, tis. The fever's down, but the charm here unravels 'lessits refreshed. Fine work, but he's torn it to shreds."

"He is most enthusiastic, yes." She approached, slowly. Jierre offered his arm, and she accepted with a grateful glance. Then she was beside me, looking down, a ghost of amusement in her worn, beautiful voice. "I begin to think I should lock him in a donjon cell to force him to rest, but I have proof twill not work. Here, *sieur*, let me help." She bent to touch his shoulder. "Take what you need."

I opened my mouth to protest—she was well-nigh dead on her feet, as were we all—but the flood of sorcery roared into me, the spiked mace in my chest receding. The unhealthy heat of fever faded, and I shivered, suddenly aware I had been lying on damp stone for hours.

If I survive this, I shall not stir from a comfortable bed for a month. Twas a comforting thought—I had it at least once each time I found myself exhausted and in danger.

Her knees buckled. Jierre braced her. She opened her eyes and lifted a hand, touching her forehead as if unable to quite credit her head was still on her shoulders. "Jierre?"

"Here, *d'mselle*." Hushed and respectful.

"See to his comfort." She gained her balance and stepped away. "I will be here."

"But surely, breakfast and—"

"You may send breakfast up with Adersahl; I would speak to him. Something to drink would not be amiss either, I am parched."

"Vianne," I croaked. "If you stay, I stay."

She looked about to command me to close my mouth, then visibly checked. Our gazes locked, and the hedgewitch next to me muttered something about a tisane. He seemed supremely unconcerned otherwise.

We eyed each other, my Queen and I. Flat on my back was not

a position to bargain from, but I would not be carried hence without some protest.

Finally, she nodded. "Very well. Send something more comfortable for him to rest upon, Jierre. And, Mauris, tell *sieur* di Yspres what you require for tisane." And she turned away, making her way to the edge of the wall. She took care that her head did not show above the parapet, though, and I held my peace.

The fog was a living thing. Muffled clanks from the Damarsene below, closed in its thick white curtains, billows of ground-cloud snaking through the city. The walls were patrolled, the river-harbor under heavy guard, and Vianne leaned with her back against the parapet, safely hidden behind stone. The witchfire shield had drained away, and she closed her eyes. Did I not catch her peering out from under her lashes, I would think she slept afoot like a weary horse.

In a little while, braced on a stack of sleeping-rolls, I swallowed mouthful after mouthful of foul tisane. The hedgewitch boy, Mauris, spoke little, and moved with amazing precision for one half-asleep himself. There is a certain point of exhaustion at which a man will simply *act*, doing what is needful and no more, slack-faced and absent. The youngling in his torn Merúnaisse ruff had passed that point and was grimly hanging to consciousness, determined not to miss a single event.

Adersahl had brought mince pies, hot broth, and waterskins. Vianne had gratefully drained a skin, and I had attempted the other. Now twas used to dilute the tisane, and I was glad of it—except dilute meant more to swallow, and I was *not* glad of that. It tasted of donkey byre and burning pathweed.

Adersahl paced, well back from the parapet in the event of odd bolts from below. Midmorn came and went, the fog thinning slightly. The guards patrolling this section of the wall gave us a wide berth.

"Unnatural," I finally rasped.

Adersahl halted, glanced at Vianne. "The fog?"

"Aye. And I should know." My voice evened as I used it, though my throat still tasted foul. Mauris blinked sleepily, pouring out a fresh measure of tisane.

Adersahl stroked his mustache. He looked remarkably fresh, having had a chance to clean himself before bringing breakfast. Still, his eyes were red, and another decade's worth of lines had graven themselves onto his countenance. "Mayhap they shall attack the harborage. Tis what I would do."

And I. "Except they would pay for it in blood, and they have the rest of Arquitaine to subdue afterward. Easier simply to starve us, perhaps?"

"Your optimism fills me with hope." He glanced at Vianne again. "The *Dispuriee* is ravaged, of course. There could be another army marching through."

I settled myself a touch less uncomfortably. "Their banners are not just from the border provinces, as those in Arcenne were. Most are from Thuringe and Hessanord. Which means…"

"What does it mean?"

I spoke not merely for his benefit, but for Vianne's. "Which means the royal House did not send any of *its* provincial units. We may be viewing a way to cause havoc and clear some of the troublesome nobles from Damar. Which will give us leverage, do we find some means of defeating *this* army."

"Which will be just as easy as setting cats at cream?" A bitter snort of laughter. Adersahl resumed his pacing. "I am all agog to hear how we will set about doing so."

My friend, I have no idea. Perhaps Vianne will hear reason in this, though. "Not here. The Citté, perhaps. If we can hold there long enough for my father to bring an army…perhaps. I do not know."

Vianne stirred slightly. Her hand still cupped her right shoulder, though she had shown she could move her right arm and hand with little discomfort. Perhaps she was thinking of how close the bolt had been to piercing something else—her chest, perhaps. Her head. Was she trembling at the thought?

Good. She is not made for this. She should listen to Jierre and Luc, and take ship. "The Citté is a far better place to hold them, though. And did we leave, they will still have to invest Merún. Twill bleed their strength."

The boy next to me said nothing, but his jaw tightened. Of course, a *Merúnaisse* would not take kindly to the thought of their city left so.

Vianne pushed herself away from the parapet. She approached, dangling the empty waterskin in her right hand. Flakes of ash clung in her hair, and two of her side-laces had broken. The neckline slid aside, showing a slice of her shoulder; more flesh was visible through the rent made by the bolt. "Take heart, Mauris." Her tone was gentle, and she halted before me. "These fine gentlemen may take ship to the Citté, but I'll not leave until we are relieved. Just a little longer."

He made no answer, swishing the tisane in the heavy wooden goblet that had been found for his use.

"The Queen speaks, boy." I sought to sound menacing.

"Leave him *be*, Tristan." She winced. The Aryx, still glowing, writhed on her chest. "When I wish for you to bludgeon younglings in my honor, I shall inform you of the event."

The Blessed know I have done much more in your honor. But to say such would not do well. "My apologies, Your Majesty." Quiet and brittle. *You are being a fool*, my tone said.

No more than you, she replied silently, with a fractional lift of her eyebrows and a slight movement of her mouth. She might have been tempted to say more, but she halted, her head tilted slightly.

"Vianne?" I cursed my weakness. The hedgewitch boy proffered the goblet. I pushed it aside, and, irritated, he slapped my hand down and put the cup to my mouth.

Vianne turned. Her shoulders came up. The fog flushed gold, the Sun showing his face with a vengeance. Adersahl's pacing ceased. I gagged on the foulness of tisane.

"What is that?" di Parmecy asked, his hand to his rapier-hilt. My fingers sought my own, but I was half-drowned, swallowing as fast as I was able, thin trickles of the brackish concoction sliding against my stubbled chin.

Vianne straightened. Her hands fell to her sides, and she dropped the empty waterskin. It made a slight sound against the paving, and there was a different noise intruding on the morning hush.

A rumble and a clashing, as the fog steamed and thinned, pulling aside.

"What?" Adersahl asked again, and she turned to him with a smile of such utter radiance I choked.

"'Tis aid, my Guard." Her eyes lit from within, and in that instant every echo of the lovely girl she had been and the beautiful woman she had become was left in the dust. Now she was purely splendor itself—ashen and bloodied, disheveled and draggled as she was, still the most glorious thing I have ever witnessed.

Thus it was that I was gagging on tisane when she looked to me, joyous and half-disbelieving. "'Tis aid," she repeated. "We are relieved."

Chapter Thirty-Five

They fell upon the backs of the Damarsene like ravening wolves. Instead of one thin screen of fog to mask them, they had a whole contingent of hedgewitches reinforcing several charms to hold the morning's vapor and thicken it. They had marched long and ridden hard; they were not so large as the besieging force, but they had the advantage of complete surprise.

The hounds of Damar are well-trained, and they fought well. Yet by the time the fog vanished completely, showing the dimensions of the battle, twas too late. They struggled to move the siege engines, struggled to form and re-form their shattered lines. The Pruzians struggled as well, for they do not retreat easily—if at all.

Yet the fourth charge broke even the horsehair-crested Pruzians, and though much is sung of the Battle of Merún, none of the songs speak of the cries of the dying. Or the smell of the field after twas soaked in blood and fouler matter. There was precious little difference between the screams of the city under siege and the cries of the Damarsene and their fellows falling beneath the blades of the army flying the devices of Arcenne, Siguerre,

Timchaine, Markui, and other provinces that had declared for the Hedgewitch Queen. Peasants with pikes and scythes were also much in evidence—but the measure that tipped the balance was the detachments of ragged Shirlstrienne bandits and less-ragged Navarrin under a strange device, a simple red flag.

And who should be riding at their head but Adrien di Cinfiliet?

Adersahl and Mauris held me up, the boy openly weeping, Adersahl's cheeks wet as well. The walls were full of cheering men, the crossbows hummed, bolts laden with death-sorcery crackling into the mass pinned close to the walls. When the Damarsene broke into full flight, harried away from their trenches and the walls, abandoning their siege engines and supplies, another massive cheer went up. Even a fool could have seen the battle was over. The Temple bells of Merún rang wildly, peal after peal, and I was told later that the scenes of joy at the quays were almost as dangerous as the melee outside the walls.

Vianne did not weep. For some while she stood on the battlements, motionless, watching, her face colorless and her hands fists in her skirts. She sent for Jierre, left orders that I was to be taken to the infirmary, and retreated to the Keep to begin preparations to welcome the relieving army.

Thus it was that I did not see the scene at the battered Gates of Merún, where the old Conte di Siguerre, in armor that was older than his grandson Tieris, swept the Queen a bow and greeted her with fine flowing oratory. I also did not see when Adrien di Cinfiliet rode to the Gates, dismounted, and my Vianne ran to his arms. Their embrace caused a round of fresh cheering, and the bandit and the old Conte were the heroes of the day.

No, I was in the infirmary. It was there that Bryony, sunburnt and dusty, found me. The hedgewitch, my childhood friend, sent the *Merúnaisse* boy from the room with its walls of wool-bale, and examined the charm on my chest.

"*You* are a right welcome sight!" I had actually been laid atop a couch made of wool-bales, and I must say, twas more comfortable than any bed I had been possessed of lately. "How does Arcenne fare? How did you come to be here?"

"Arcenne still stands." He looked grave, but I thought twas because he was peering at the scar on my chest. "You have been seeking to kill yourself, as usual. Dear gods."

"How did you—"

"I bring word. One message from your mother—she says to take care and sends her regard. One from…your father. Divris di Tatancourt was found on Rieu di Heifors. He had been set upon and stabbed several times. Your father thought it best to ride with what army we had gathered."

"I last saw di Tatancourt in the *Quartier Gieron*." I thought on this. "Stabbed?"

"Aye. Your father…Tristan." He ceased poking at my chest and looked up at me. "I bring news."

Outside the wool warehouse, the entire city was still pealing and cheering with joy. Even the wounded and burned packed among the bales sought to cheer instead of moan with pain. "Well, out with it, Bry!"

He stepped back, spread his feet, and clasped his hands together. "There is no easy way to say this…"

"Bry, for the love of the Blessed, simply spit it forth. I must be fit to ride in short order, and have little time to waste."

"You will not be riding soon, *sieur*, with that charming on you. I bethought myself to find you first. You will be seeing Siguerre soon."

For a moment I thought he spoke of Tieris, and I made an impatient movement. "Of course, but what…"

I suppose twas then that I knew. The words halted. I lay, near to witless with shock, and stared at him.

"Conte di Siguerre has your father's signet." Bryony took a deep breath, visibly bracing himself. "He…*Sieur*, your father has fallen. He fell at Bleu-di-Font. D'Orlaans was there, with some Damarsene from the *Dispuriee*. The false king was riding for the Citté; we gainsaid him. Your father…" The hedgewitch swallowed hard, his dark eyes suddenly full. "Your pardon, Tris. I was not able to…there was no…He fell against d'Orlaans."

I stared, unable to quite credit what my ears heard. Surely there was a mistake. This was a dream brought on by fever and foul tisane. It could not be true.

"D'Orlaans." My mouth shaped the word.

"In a tumbril, kept under guard. Siguerre wished to kill him outright, but the Conte di Dienjuste said twas the Queen's pleasure he was remanded to. Di Dienjuste was left to guard him; he follows our army within a day or so. I am…I am sorry, Tris."

"Tis not your fault," I said, woodenly. "I thank you for your pains, Bry."

"We sought to save him. Twas…there was *nothing—*"

A nobleman does not strike an underling for bringing ill news. My father had oft quoted the proverb, usually with a grim smile and his hand to his rapier. "I understand. Ease your mind, my friend. If he could have been saved, I know you would have done so. Please, withdraw a little." *I would not unman myself with an audience.*

He nodded. Unwilling pity and relief warred on his countenance. "You are Baron now. We have not sent word to your mother. Siguerre did not think it wise."

"He was right," I said through the numbness descending on me. "She has enough to bear. My thanks, Bry. Leave me."

He did.

My father. I tried the words inside my head. They refused to form. *Is dead. Someone is dead. It cannot be him.*

He had told me to take care as I left him in Arcenne. Had even granted me his *blessing*, and now…

Now what?

I did not know.

My eyes were dry, and burned fiercely. I could not even weep. I lay on the bales, looking at the ceiling beams, smelling wool and foulness and my own unwashed illness, as around me a city celebrated deliverance.

Twas a day and a night before Conte di Siguerre appeared. At least I had lee to stand, and could wash myself. I was moved from the infirmary to a drafty but more comfortable room in Merún's Keep, and attended by Tieris and a new hedgewitch physicker, a wide-hipped dame with the sharp face and blue eyes of Arcenne, a newly arrived and most welcome addition to the physickers. Beadris was her name, and rarely have I had a more grueling commander. I would mend, she announced, and *she* would see to it, for she had been commanded to do so by the Queen herself.

Tieris found this highly amusing.

The Conte tapped lightly at the door, on one of the rare occasions *m'dama* Beadris was off mixing ever-fouler concoctions to pour down my throat. Tieris opened the door and stepped back quickly as if discovering a coiled serpent. "Enter, an it please you."

His left thigh was bandaged, but his gaze was still keen, and Conte di Siguerre did not hobble overmuch. He merely moved stiffly, showing his age. His hair had whitened considerably, and the Sun had touched him with bronze. His doublet was blazoned with Siguerre's device—the crag-ram, with its curling horns and stubborn hooves, rearing in defiance.

He nodded shortly at Tieris. *"P'tifils."*

Tieris bowed. He had gone pale. *"Granpère."*

"D'Arcenne." The Conte's gaze turned to me. At least I was clean, and shaven, and had the benefit of fresh cloth. Including a new red sash. I was still of the Queen's Guard, perhaps only until she could find enough time and attention to formally deny me the honor.

Or perhaps she did not mean to. Hope is a drug, and I could not give up the habit of its use. If I had proven myself unfit to be called noble or honest, at least I had also proven a protection against Graecan fire. How many times would I shield her with my own body, or my own lies?

And yet, I had failed to shield her where it mattered. And now, here was my father's friend, and my father...dead.

I still could not fathom it. "Conte," I greeted him. "Pray forgive me that I do not rise. Your arrival is most welcome."

He waved the pleasantry aside. "Wait until you hear my news."

"I have been told of my father's demise." I had practiced the sentence. There was no betraying hitch in the rope of words, no indication of the rock in my throat. If a man can stand, he can weep in the privacy of a fallwater, or in the dark. I must have been hardened beyond measure by my sins, for I could not weep even in that safety. The tears refused to come.

I had no *acquavit* to render me insensible, and my physicker could not be induced to bring any. Tieris di Siguerre could not be so induced, either.

I gather he thought I might harm myself.

"It does not surprise me." The old turtle hunched his shoulders. "I know twas not my grandson, for I did not inform him."

"Your grandson is a fine Guard." I shifted a little, seeking to ease an ache in my hip. Bed rest wears on the body almost as much as battle.

He waved the question of Tieris's fineness aside, irritably. A glitter in his hand resolved itself into a fine silver chain, threaded through a heavy ring. Twas a *siang*-stone signet, the mountain-pard of Arcenne clawing, its jaws wide in a silent roar. My carnelian signet was the Heir's, and grime had settled into its fine carving. Many times over the years I had been possessed of mad thoughts of returning it to my father with a curse.

Now I would never have the chance. Nor would I have a chance to…what?

What would I have said to my father, had I known? Was he watching as his son continued in a manner to blacken his proud name? Did he curse me from the golden halls of the gods?

Oh, tis very likely. No more than I curse myself, though.

Old Siguerre was not to be deterred from giving his tidings, fully and completely. "Twas d'Orlaans. Di Dienjuste denied me the killing of that parasite. Yet do you cry for vengeance, I do not think any will gainsay you." Flung like a challenge. One I deserved, no doubt.

"How did it happen?" I sounded strange even to myself. Throatsore, and oddly breathless.

"They were both unhorsed. Twas a confusion. There was sorcery…" The Conte made a restless movement, staring at the signet. Was there still blood on its shining, or had he washed it? "Perseval was never a fine Court sorcerer. He preferred steel. I…"

Incredibly, the stone-hard face cracked a trifle. The Conte's mouth turned down, bitterly. Was that water against his lashes?

Truly the age of the Angoulême's miracles had returned.

The old man coughed, and I caught Tieris's gaze. Young Siguerre read my silent dispatch and murmured a courtesy, slipping out into the hall. The door closed with a quiet click.

"I thank you for bringing the news." Twas a mannerly thing to say, but it seemed…bloodless. I sought for more. "My father prized your friendship, Conte. He oft remarked that you were one of the few honest men in Arquitaine."

"Did he, now."

I meant to ease di Siguerre's sorrow, and suspected I had not. For his face crumpled and smoothed itself silently, and I found myself facing not the terrifying gravel-voiced Siguerre of my childhood, but an old man, almost frail despite his breadth of shoulder and small, hard gut. His hair was thinner, and the map of veins on the back of his knotted hands was of a country I might reach one day.

If I did not die before my time, of knife or poison or sheer mischance. What did it matter? I was already dead. And so was my father now.

Dead. I could not…There was no way I could think on it that would convince me of the truth of it. He could not be. My father and his disapproval were eternal. A world without either was…

Terrifying. That is the only word that applies. "He did." The man using my voice was not Tristan d'Arcenne. For d'Arcenne, Captain and Left Hand, would not have to swallow a hot weight of unspilled grief. Even if he was now beginning to realize the truth of the words he mouthed. "He thought very highly of you."

"And I of him." The Conte's chin rose, and he gazed at me with disconcerting directness, ignoring—or perhaps daring me to mention—the tear-track glistening on his weathered cheek. "His thoughts were much on you, Tristan. He was very proud. You were a joy to him."

I doubt that very much, sieur. But it was a kind lie, one I suspected di Siguerre half believed himself now. The dead do not misbehave; they become a mirror we may safely gaze into and see what we will.

What would I see, now that I was gazing? "My thanks." Whose was that quiet, steely tone? Who was using my voice as his own?

Whoever he was, he sounded so like Perseval d'Arcenne that my father could not be gone to the West, the realm of the Blessed. Surely he was still here.

Di Siguerre approached my bedside. The signet was heavy, dropped into my reluctant hand with a rattle like chains. "A man reaches a certain age, and he loses the habit of showing anything but harshness. What he feels and what he may express are not…they are seldom one and the same. He was proud of his son, *sieur.* Every day I spent in Perseval d'Arcenne's company, he spoke of his Tristan. His boy. The only person higher in his regard was *m'dama* the Baroness. I tell you this because sons do not understand their fathers."

I understand enough. "Nor their grandfathers." It escaped me before I could think on the likely consequences of such an observation.

"Hm. Even so." He nodded slowly. "Even so."

"Di Dienjuste has d'Orlaans? In a tumbril?" I turned the signet up, the mountain-pard's roar forever caught and held. Arcenne was an old province, and held by our family since the Angoulême's time. Our device has ever been the cat—a fierce, stealthy hunter, an animal who does not flee from man.

And now I was an animal who could not even flee from himself.

"Aye." Now Siguerre's tone held no softness. "Cyriot di Dien-juste cried me nay when I would have taken that *saufe-tet*'s head off. They follow from Font-di-Bleu. The Queen is to have the judging of d'Orlaans." He seemed very absorbed in studying the wall over my head. "Will she do what is necessary?"

She will not need to. I folded my fingers over the signet. Closed in my palm, it clicked against the Heir's ring. "She is the Queen. She will do as she must."

"Very good." Gruff and uncomfortable now. "Indeed."

"My thanks, Conte di Siguerre. It is an honor to know you." Very formally. "I hope our Houses remain friends."

"Until the Angoulême returns, *sieur*." Equally formal, and much more comfortable now. "I take my leave, an it please you. I am sorry to bear you such news."

"And I am sorry to receive it." Formulaic, the security of etiquette easing the sharp edges. "Blessed guard you, *sieur*."

"And you." Old Siguerre made his way to the door. He halted. "Tristan?"

"Halis." Twas the first time I had used his given name.

"His last words were of you and your mother. He regretted not seeing your face again. *My son*, he said. *Tell him he has my blessing, and that I have always been proud of him*."

Was it a mercy, that I found no trace of falsehood in his voice? Or a fresh knife to my heart? I could not decide.

The Conte stepped forth into the hall. He spoke, low and passing gentle, to Tieris. I could not hear what passed between them, for old Siguerre pulled the door closed. I was left to my thoughts for a short while.

I was glad of it. I do not like being seen to, finally and completely, weep like a child.

Beadris shook her head. "You are fit for *gentle* riding," she said, hands to her wide hips and dark strands threaded with gray falling into her sharp face. "None of this Arcenne-to-d'Or-in-a-week nonsense. And no duels."

I checked my dagger—still easy in its sheath. "I shall seek to avoid dueling if at all possible, *m'dama* Physicker. I do not wish your wrath."

"Ha!" She turned away to the small table littered with herbs and a syph-æther lamp, glass tubes and other implements for making the terrible brews she forced down my throat. I was not sad to see the last of *those*. "Tis not my wrath. Tis the Queen's, and she is most concerned. Every day it's a visit to Her Majesty, and her asking, *How does your patient fare?* I'll be locked in the Bastillion do you take an ailing and die, young *sieur*, and where will that leave my Consort and family?"

"Left in the cold and the rain, and winter coming on," I chanted. "I shall save you from such a fate, *m'dama*, by taking excessive care of my person. Tell me, the Queen asks every day?"

"Oh, aye!" She grinned, blue eyes twinkling. In the old days, those with light eyes were not precisely feared, but not welcomed overmuch, either. *An Arquitaine eye is a dark eye*, as the proverb runs—*and a dark eye knows its place*. "She did ask me not to tell you, thinking you'd worry if you heard her inquiring so closely. *I told her, Your Majesty, said I, tis no shame to inquire after one's Consort!* But she sought to ease your recovery, *sieur*."

Did she? Or are you giving me a gentle lie? Would I even recognize a truth, were it spoken plainly to me?

There was a tap at the door. Tieris di Siguerre appeared. Fatigue and dirt had both been sluiced from him, and he was carrying himself more lightly these past two weeks. Which irritated me to no end—but being trammeled in this windowless room would have made a curmudgeon out of the sweetest temper. Add to that the fact that I received no visitors, that Tieris imparted precious little in the way of gossip or information, and Beadris's clucking and fussing, and my temper was none too sweet.

"Ah, my jailer!" I greeted him. "Am I on furlough?"

"You must be recovered. You are ill-spoken as *Granpère*." He hissed and jabbed an obscene gesture at me. "Avert, *demieri di sorce*!"

I found a laugh in that, though his tone was sharper than I liked. Of course, the prospect at being set at liberty was enough to make me merry as a maying. "*You* lie abed for two weeks under the care of *m'dama* Henpeck there, then we shall see who is ill-spoken."

"*Sieur!*" Beadris was shocked.

"Forgive me, dearest physicker." I half-turned, caught her work-roughened hands, and lifted as if I would kiss them. She shrieked and pulled away, and Tieris's laughter joined mine. The Arcenne hedgewitch scolded, blushing and delivering a tongue-lashing I would have quavered at as a stripling, but she offered her cheek for a peck afterward, and the fire in her cheeks was not merely embarrassment but secret pleasure. She had labored long over my care, and my chest did not pain me now. The scar was pink instead of angry crimson, and the cut down my cheek near to white. 'Twas interesting to shave around, and the sliver of glass in the water-closet showed me new lines on my face. The gray streak in my hair had widened as well.

Merún, like me, had not recovered fully. The Damarsene were routed, harried for the border by Irion di Markui and an army of disparate parts—angry peasants, the troops of the mountain province, and those of d'Orlaans's host who took advantage of the amnesty granted to them did they serve the Hedgewitch Queen.

So much I had been told, and some little I could guess—the Conte di Siguerre tarried with the Queen, as did Adrien di Cinfiliet, to begin the work of rebuilding. Why she stayed in Merún was a small mystery, until I hit upon the thought that a victorious entry into the Citté took some little time to prepare. Such an entry would be necessary, both for the theater of the gesture and to put paid to d'Orlaans's claims.

Of d'Orlaans there was no word uttered to me. Tieris merely looked pained and said he did not know, and he would not ask for fear his grandfather would give him a lashing. Tieris was called into the Queen's presence once a day, like Beadris, to offer a report on me. He was not given lee to ask questions, and Vianne made no reply to any question I sent with him to beg an answer.

I did not like that.

Rivertraffic had resumed; there were refugees to care for and the evacuated to return to their families and homes—if such homes were left standing, that is, for almost half of Merún had barely ceased smoking. And yet there was an air of festival in the city. Though the *Dispuriee* had been ravaged, the harvest in other places had been generous. And the plague? The sickness of fever and boiling, vomiting blood?

Vanished overnight. No new sickness was reported, and deaths from its touch had ceased in the Citté, at least. Every province that had declared for Vianne had been free of its depredations, and it appeared those offering fealty to d'Orlaans were chastened.

Temples were full of those offering in thanksgiving and those seeking news of lost loved ones. The weather was fine, an *estivallefaus*, as such an after-harvest lull was named, and this was attributed to the Hedgewitch Queen's intercession with the Blessed.

I did not think Vianne likely to be amused by such rumors.

Instead of the small circular room, she was now ensconced in the Keep's high, drafty main hall. Some attempt had been made to freshen the room, to clean the cobwebs and free the ancient tapestries of dust. The dais had been hung with crimson, and the Guard, both Old and New, were much in evidence, red-sashed and sober with their hands to their rapiers. The huge fireplace had been unblocked and a blaze set in it took much of the damp chill from the air, though the massive doors to the entry-hall stood open and the Keep's front was thrown wide to welcome suppliants and those who had business with or reports to give the Queen.

Tieris accompanied me up the middle of the main hall, hurrying as my stride lengthened. I had exercised myself as much as Beadris had allowed, and some little bit more. At least I had not been chained while I did so.

A great chair had been found and wrapped with scarlet cloth, and Vianne was upon it, her head tilted as she listened to the Harbormaster, who looked far more at ease now. Jierre was in attendance next to her, standing precisely where the Captain of her Guard should. To one side, behind a table stacked with paper, Conte di Siguerre questioned a bedraggled nobleman with a doffed hat. The man looked damp and wary; I stored up his features and forgot him, for on Vianne's other side Adrien di Cinfiliet was deep in discussion with Adersahl di Parmecy and a group of Shirlstrienne bandits and hard-faced young Navarrin bloods in their dark, high-collared doublets, the X-shaped device of their High God blazoned in white on their chests. Their thin rapiers hung easy at their sides, their hats held wide-sweeping feathers, and their foreign tones rose and fell in a murmur of easy power. Theirs is a rolling language, at odds with their harsh land. Some scholars hold tis related to d'Arquitaine, but I do not know. Tis an easy enough language to learn.

Not like Pruzian.

Fridrich van Harkke lurked behind Vianne's chair. He seemed ill at ease, though I doubted anyone else could tell. He kept to the shadows under the hangings, and his gaze flickered through the hall. The Knife did not look overjoyed to see me, though he reserved most of his attention for di Cinfiliet.

My palms were damp. My throat was dry. My father's signet was a chill lump, tucked under my doublet on its thin fine chain.

I could not bring myself to take the Heir's signet from my finger.

The Aryx rang softly with light, and I felt it. My steps slowed. I approached her throne—for such it was; she made it so—and allowed myself to look at her.

Wine-red velvet laced over silk, the oversleeves cut away and the undersleeves coming to points on the backs of her hands. Her hair, braided in the style of di Rocancheil, glowing in the mellow glowstone light. Globes of witchlight hung lazily above the crowd—twas a Court in miniature, again, and she its beating heart. Her ear-drops were rubies and beaten silver, and a gleam on her left hand was the copper marriage-ring.

Why does she still wear it?

My heart twisted on itself. Perhaps Beadris was wrong and it would wrench itself free through the scar. If it did, who would mourn my passing?

Would *she*?

The dark circles under her eyes had lessened. She was not so gaunt. The burning of her gaze was unabated, but her mouth was not set in a grim line. Instead, she smiled as Jierre made a point, touching his finger to his palm as he listed something for her. The Harbormaster nodded, his gaze fixed on her face. She considered for a few moments after Jierre finished, then softly spoke. The

Harbormaster bowed, begged leave to withdraw, and she granted it with a nod. He hurried away, brushing past me, and the Queen of Arquitaine looked upon me coolly, lifting her chin slightly.

"Consort," she greeted me, and a roaring filled my head.

She had not renounced me yet.

Chapter Thirty-Six

I went to one knee, slowly, and rose. "Your Majesty." At least I sounded steady. The noise inside my skull receded as I concentrated, fiercely, on not toppling and making a fool of myself. "I am gladdened to be in your presence again."

She did not smile. Instead, she watched me gravely, and did not invite me to approach. "I am gladdened that you are recovered. I…feared for you."

What use could there be in sweetening me so? Or had she truly feared for me? "I am sorry to have caused you grief." *In any way. Will you believe that?*

The weight of gazes upon us was familiar. At Court, I would never have spoken to her even this much. An uneasiness touched the space between my shoulder blades.

"I was also grieved to learn of your father's passing." Had she paled?

"I thank you for your pains." Meaningless words. *Why here, Vianne? Why before everyone? Is it because you do not trust me, were we to speak privately? Is it that you think I will force my way into your chambers again?*

Would I blame her for such a fear? No. I had richly proven myself a *vilhain* many times over. I had little idea of how to even *begin* to be a man she might not fear.

Adrien di Cinfiliet was watching, his pale eyes narrowed. He was still weathered, and the arrogance of a nobleman was still evident even as he merely *stood* there. It grated on me, and I sought not to look upon him.

Vianne shifted slightly, her hands resting prettily-clasped upon her knee. Her spine was absolutely straight. "I am to enter the Citté soon." Clear and low, and a hush had fallen over the hall. "There will be a coronation in the Ladytemple. It would please me, were you to attend."

A Temple. Did she think to renounce me before she was crowned? Publicly, and in no uncertain terms?

"If it would please you, I will attend." *Here is my throat, Vianne. Drive the knife in, should you wish it.* "Command me, my Queen, and it will be done."

A flush rose in her cheeks, died away. Left her even paler, and the shape of her lashes against her cheekbones as she blinked sent a thin Sievillein rapier through me, as if one of the Navarrin had plunged his blade through my freshly healed scar.

"We go forth at tomorrow's nooning, then." A small, private smile, and she glanced up and to her left.

Adrien di Cinfiliet's gaze met hers. His expression did not change, but he did straighten slightly. Vianne quickly looked away, and the smile vanished as if it had never been born.

"Rest well, *chivalier*," she told me, and I was dismissed. I did not even beg leave to go. Nor did I bow. I turned on my heel and Tieris di Siguerre followed in my wake until I gained the wretched, ruined rose garden I remembered from my second night in this accursed heap of stone. And when I snarled at him to *leave me be, for the sake of the Blessed,* he did.

That night I was to pass in quarters more befitting the Consort—dusty and ancient, to be sure, but at least there was a sitting room. And a high narrow window. It looked down upon a disused bailey, weeds forcing their way up between cracking paving-stones. Tieris led me to it after a dinner I observed a stony silence through, taken in a dining-hall full of draughts and faint sour smells. He stiffly bade me a restful sleep.

I considered running him through.

I had no more than glanced out the window and thought of the drop to the stones below when a knock sounded at the sitting-room door. I thought it Tieris come back and said not a word, for the curses that rose to my lips were fit to scorch the air itself.

The knob turned, and I strode for the door, ready to flay the intruder with a cutting remark or two.

Vianne closed the door and sighed, rubbing delicately at the bridge of her nose. She turned to face me; I had halted near an ancient, tumbledown, brocaded sopha that had perhaps last seen use before the turn of the centuriad.

"I crave your pardon, *sieur,*" she said softly. As if she *needed* to, from me. "I—"

"Are you well?" My hands knotted themselves into fists. "Are you safe? Who guards your door? Your food, is it tested for poison? What of d'Orlaans?"

She winced, clasped her hands before her. It had taken on the quality of a habitual movement, and I do not know if anyone else would have remarked how tightly her fingers clenched one another. The Aryx, glowing, gave a softer light to her face. The rest of us seemed to have aged, lines graving themselves through our faces—but she did not. Or perhaps I did not see any brushing of

Time's feathers upon her, because I looked so closely.

"I am well enough. Relieved, in more ways than one. There is summat I would speak on, Captain, and I—"

"*Captain*. For how much longer? By the Blessed, Vianne. Call me *Tristan* or nothing at all. I will not have this distance."

"Oh, you will not have it?" Her chin lifted slightly. "And what Tristan d'Arcenne will not have should be my northneedle, aye? I shall address you as I see fit, *sieur*. You will grant me that, at least, for the remainder of the time we must endure each other."

"Endure?" So she did mean to cast me off. I did not blame her, and yet...

No. Please. Vianne, no.

"You are the Baron d'Arcenne now." Her fingers tensed, tighter and tighter. She seemed fair to bruise herself. "And...*sieur*, I crave your pardon. I came to tell you Timrothe d'Orlaans has disappeared."

I froze. My wits raced.

Di Dienjuste, half-drawing his rapier as I burst in the door. Overplaying his sympathy for me, and paying her every attention. Of course. Of course.

What had d'Orlaans promised him? Perhaps Vianne herself, though I could not see d'Orlaans dangling the prize he had reserved for himself before a mere *chivalier*. Most likely the reward was some tidbit or two to repair the family Dienjuste's noble poverty. How had we not seen?

How had *I* not sensed the danger?

The urge to swear vilely passed through me in a scorching tide. "Di Dienjuste." My rapier-hilt was cold as ice under my fingertips. "He was too nervous. I would lay odds he sought to kidnap you. And likely twas he who found di Tatancourt and—"

"Di Tatancourt?" One eyebrow raised. The look she wore

would make a man spill every secret he owned, merely for the joy of feeling her undivided attention for a few moments longer. "I see."

"The Messenger was alive when I left him, Vianne." The words were ash in my mouth. "I do not expect you to believe me."

"I find I may believe much of what you tell me, at least now." Was it resignation in her tone? "And it would not have served your purposes to kill him, Captain." Yet her slim shoulders came up, the familiar movement of a burden laid upon them. The velvet and silk rustled. Bergaime and spice and green hedgewitchery, a breath of her scent reaching me over the dust and sharpish rot of the Keep. "I do not lay Divris di Tatancourt at your door."

"What *do* you lay at my door, *m'chri*?" *Tell me. I must know. If it is to be the worst, at least let it be from your hand. Please.*

"You won the trial of combat. In the eyes of the law, in the eyes of Arquitaine and the Blessed, you are innocent of the King's murder."

I do not care. "What of your eyes? They are all that concern me, Vianne. What you would have of me is all that concerns me."

She unclasped her hands, finger by finger. Shook them out delicately, a pretty Court-trained mannerism. "It matters little what I think, Captain. Soon we will be free of each other, and no doubt you will be relieved at the event."

Ice in my vitals. What would she do if I laid hands upon her? If she struggled, if she screamed…

"Vianne." Hoarsely, now.

"I brought you this news myself, privately, because I do not wish you hunting d'Orlaans. He will be attended to. I wish you to return to Arcenne." She turned away.

A cry rose within me. Was suppressed. The ice was all through me.

Her hand on the knob. "Do you hear me?" She addressed the door as if it were my face, earnestly. Softly. "Do you?"

"I hear," I croaked.

A slight turn of her head, as if she wished to glance over her shoulder. Dry-eyed, pale, and utterly lost to me. "Tristan." Her lips, shaping my name. "Believe me when I say this: I wish you to *live*."

A rustling, a quiet step, a brush of her skirts, a click...and she was gone.

She wished me to *live*. Oh, aye. I'd no doubt she did.

After all, there could be no greater revenge.

Chapter Thirty-Seven

The Citté is the heart of Arquitaine. Under the slopes of Mont di Cienne the Palais gleams, white and gold and sprawling, the mark of each reign stamped in its corridors and passages. Below it, in the cup that the River Airenne threads a long silver ribbon through, the Citté throbs and pulses. Biscuit-colored stone, roofs of slate and red tile and wood, the Ladytemple's dome and the twisting streets that can confuse even a lifelong inhabitant; the *Quartier Montarmête* and the Pleasure District, the quays and the bridges, the glitter of Court and the ragged poverty of the beggars. The Citté, built where the Blessed demanded, the city of our gods and our hope. The plague had run rife through it, and those who lined its streets to welcome their Queen no doubt were too happy to be spared to think of the chaos hosting an army would cause.

She wore white, and rode my mother's well-traveled white palfrey. The gentle mare looked near to expiring with satisfaction, glossy-brushed and oiled, red silk ribbons tied in her mane and tail, tiny silver bells jingling on her reins and decking the saddle, so that the Hedgewitch Queen rode on a wave of music. You could not hear the sweet sound, though, for the crowds roared fit to drown even the thinking inside a man's skull.

Adrien di Cinfiliet rode beside her, tall on a nasty-tempered white stallion, also in spotless white. Without a hat, the blue-black sheen to his hair threw back the sun, and they made a pretty picture indeed.

Arran stepped high and proud; I rode with the Conte di Siguerre and Jierre di Yspres at the head of the Guard. The survivors of the Old Guard, worn and wounded but grinning hugely and in fresh uniforms, were given pride-of-place. The New Guard caught the thrown flowers—where the blooms were found that showered our path, I do not know.

After us in procession rode the Navarrin and the bandits of the Shirlstrienne, and then the d'Arquitaine army itself. The peasants had begun to trickle away home; d'Orlaans's pardoned troops marched behind the Mountain Army, as twas called. The amnestied marched under the black banner of penitence. After the coronation they would be granted the right to bear a device again. The long snake of humanity took a day to file into the Citté, and the cheering never abated.

The Ladytemple greeted us the morning after our entrance, while the dregs of the procession were still winding into the city. I do not know if Vianne slept—we were quartered not in the Palais, for she would not enter it until crowned, but at the edge of the Pleasure District in the *P'tipalais d'Orlaans*, the vast, traditional house Timrothe the Accursed—for so they had named him now, with characteristic desire to bite the author of their suffering—had inhabited while the brother of King Henri.

She is old, the Ladytemple, built when places of worship were full of sharp spires instead of the softer shapes later generations fancied. Her stone is dark, and the vast round window over her wide, never-closed doors is named the *Rosaille*. A great sorcery is contained within it, and the glass shifts color according to its own whims. During the quiet observance at dawn or dusk, when all in the vicinity of *l'Dama* hold their tongue and breath, you may hear the tiny bits of glass shifting and clicking, a dry song of power.

The inside was packed with nobility of the sword and the robe. Songs have been written of the Hedgewitch Queen, how she paused in the courtyard and knelt, silent, for twelve long peals of the Ladytemple's great bell. How she rose gracefully, a silver-eyed man at her side. How she climbed the steps into the Ladytemple and was greeted with absolute silence.

The Consort strode behind her. One woman, two men, treading with the measured ceremonial gait observed for the most solemn of Court occasions. Step, pause; step, pause. The Aryx sang, the *Rosaille* answering and the Great Bell overhead trembling with reverberations. The crowd elbow-to-elbow, the heat of massed bodies causing sweat; twas crowded too tight within to draw a poniard. Those of the sword, the descendants of the Angoulême's noble companions, removed their hats as she drew abreast of them. Those of the robe were already hatless, and breathless beside. Later they would begin to play the games of privilege and position at Court. Later they would jostle, and she would need a shield. Later, those who still owed d'Orlaans some loyalty might prove troublesome, and I? Would I be admitted into her presence? Would I be able to guard her from afar?

Arcenne was a long way from Court. And hither she wished me to take myself.

I wish you to live.

But for today, they watched her approach the Great Altar, her head high and her hair pulled back into a simple half-braid, the remainder of its curling mass alive with golden highlights. The white she wore, subtly brocaded, glowed as the Aryx rippled with light. Witchlights spun and wove overhead, hissing and crackling in the charged hush. Her fingers rested on Adrien di Cinfiliet's arm, and his shoulders were tense.

He was armed. So was I, though no other in the Ladytemple was to carry a weapon. The Guard were outside, waiting in the crisp harvest sun. The morning had been etched with frost.

Winter was coming.

The Great Altar is an empty block of bluestone, the same stuff as the Pavilion of the Field d'Or. It is roughly squared, and it is dedicated to Jiserah the Gentle first and the rest of the Blessed afterward. Offerings laid upon it vanish, taken straight to the Blessed.

Or so tis said. It is one thing the Left Hand does not know the truth of.

There are others. Too many for my comfort. And chief among them was exactly what my *d'mselle* thought as she paced that processional way.

Step, by step, by step. Once she reached the altar and the Aryx spoke, she would be crowned. Irion di Markui was in place, holding the iron casket. Inside it, the confection of spun lightmetal— *platiere*, more precious and rare than gold—and sapphires would rest on gray velvet. She would take it from the casket, settle it on her brow, and be crowned Queen of Arquitaine.

Would she renounce me at that moment, or afterward? Would she take a new Consort? They were cousins, but closer marriages have been made in the name of power. And as the hero who had brought the Navarrin and his bandits to the relief of Merún, and Henri's son, no matter how bastard, he was a fine choice.

And he was not a murderer. At least, not as her Consort was. He would not be able to keep her from the knives of intrigue half so well.

But perhaps he would also not wound her. Perhaps he would not bring her world down in flames about her with his unthinking desire. Perhaps he would not shame her, or make her weep.

Perhaps, just perhaps, Adrien di Cinfiliet was a better choice. If I were to be honest—and aye, starting now was too late, as always—I could admit as much.

And yet.

She reached the Three Stairs, and she halted. She glanced up at di Cinfiliet, and they shared a moment of silent accord. My heart writhed inside my chest. My place was next to di Markui, hands loose though they longed to clutch a rapier-hilt, my face set and composed.

The years of not even daring to glance at her at Court were nothing compared to this.

She stepped forward. So did di Markui. A long pause. She took the next step. Di Markui approached the bottom of the Stairs. Di Cinfiliet glanced at di Markui, whose craggy face was unreadable. *Do your part*, that glance seemed to say, and my pulse raced. Treachery? Here?

No. I was merely too practiced in the art to credit truth when I saw it.

She took the last step, and turned. The Aryx glowed. She beckoned, and a gasp went through the assembled.

Di Cinfiliet took the first Stair. A pause, and the second. Would she declare him Heir? What was this?

He took the third, and Vianne's hand came up to her chest. She cupped the Aryx in her fingers, lovingly, and her lips moved. None could hear, but with the ease of training and habit I deciphered the words she spoke.

I have done what you asked. Let me free. Let me go.

And the Great Seal...*sang*.

The Ladytemple shook, the *Rosaille* echoing and blazing, and a fierce silver light burst free. Twas not witchlight or any other earthly radiance. The only time I had witnessed its like was in Arcenne's Temple, on my wedding day, when the statue of Jiserah kindled and my Queen had stared unblinking into that light.

The blaze did not dim, but it became easier to pierce. Blinking furiously, tears rising to every eye, Arquitaine witnessed the Aryx pass from the Hedgewitch Queen's hands. She folded Adrien di Cinfiliet's fingers about the Seal's glow, and the picture they made…

I cannot describe it. The courtsongs will tell you. They will not be able to express a quarter of its fineness.

The cry that rose was Vianne's, and it carried a deep authority. Had I not known every shade and tone of her, I might have mistaken it, as every other present did, for the voice of Jiserah herself.

"Arquitaine!" she cried. *"Behold your King!"*

And the Hedgewitch Queen, before the Great Altar, knelt to Adrien di Cinfiliet. A rippling wind went through the Ladytemple, its walls groaning, and the assembled nobility fell to their knees. Heralds posted on the steps cried out the news.

The silvery radiance intensified, flushed with gold as if the Sun and Moon had come together atop the Great Altar. A roaring cheer rose, every bell the Ladytemple owned tolling at once, and wild jubilation roared over the Citté.

When the light faded, Adrien di Cinfiliet was crowned. The Hedgewitch Queen had brought the Bandit King to power. She had never wished the burden of rule; she had only appeared, twas said, to turn back the tide of invasion and civil war. She was blessed of Jiserah, or Jiserah's hand on earth, but the important thing, the critical thing, was this:

Vianne di Rocancheil et Vintmorecy had vanished.

271

Chapter Thirty-Eight

I took advantage of the ensuing confusion to vanish of my own account. For one who had been Left Hand, twas child's play. The Cité enfolded me as Arcenne's Keep would; I took further advantage of confusion and celebration outside to steal a cloak and shed my fine hat. I stole a not-so-fine drover's headgear, and made my way to the Palais's shimmer.

My apartments in the Guard barracks had been ransacked and sealed. Dust lay thick over every surface, and the brazier I had burned the incriminating papers in still had ash in its depths. My clothing had been shredded, my narrow bed torn apart, my cabinets hacked open. For all that, they had not found everything, and only a fool has merely *one* hiding place.

Life returned to the Palais that evening. Twas midnight before a certain quiet descended. An hour passed, and another.

I waited.

The traditional resting place of a new monarch after crowning is the Angoulême's Cell in the west wing of the Palais. Tis a narrow room, with a narrow bed and only one tapestry—a *fleurs-di-lisse*, white thread upon deep blue. The narrow window casement looks only upon bricks, for the Cell has been enclosed by other parts of the Palais, accreting around the most ancient bits in layers, as a pearl. Or a gallstone.

The blank window is shrouded with deep blue velvet curtains, stiff with age and dust even when hastily beaten clean. Twas there I waited, and I knew my prey was close when a servant bustled in to light the fire in the tiny fireplace with a coal from a Ladytemple brazier and the flick of a hedgewitch charm. The servant—no doubt he had performed the same office for d'Orlaans—shuffled away. I relaxed into dimness, breathing softly.

They approached. Several, the tramp of booted feet. I rested a hand on my rapier, my boots glove-supple from hard use and not creaking as I shifted my weight to keep muscles ready for action. Did he suspect? If he did, he might well order the Cell searched, though I had waited until they had already performed such a search before secreting myself here.

Some low conversation. But only two men entered the Cell, and I closed my eyes. Reopened them in the stiff, dusty darkness behind the curtain.

"At the end of the hall," Adrien di Cinfiliet said. "Tis enough."

Jierre di Yspres sighed. "A foolish risk. You know he will at least wish to pass words with you."

"He is more likely to seek *your* company, Captain. What am I, to him? Nothing."

"I hope he will pause to hear your argument before seeking to run you through." Jierre, ever pessimistic, heaved another sigh. "Should I search the room, Your Majesty?"

"For the love of the Blessed, address me as Adrien. If he is here...then perhaps he *will* listen to my argument. Perhaps he will listen when I say I do not know where she has vanished to, and that I wish I could have gainsaid her. And that, does he wish any aid at all, he has merely to ask it of me."

I blinked, but not in surprise. No, it was merely to keep myself in readiness. Or so I told myself.

Jierre's sardonic tone, well-known to me. "I hope you are correct. Arquitaine cannot stand to lose more royalty."

"And there is *this*." A touch of loathing in the bandit's tone, now. "Cursed thing. What would *you* say to him, were he here?"

Jierre was silent for a long moment. I shut my eyes.

Yes, what would you say, Lieutenant? You played your part to perfection, and I can credit it was at her bidding. Would to the gods I had seen enough to know.

But a guilty conscience makes a man blinder than a clear one ever shall.

When Jierre spoke, it was softly, and for my ears alone, for all that the new King was the only man he could see. "I would tell him," he said softly, "that I regret playing my part so well. And, should he ever wish to have a blade at his bidding, that we are too marvelous to die."

My jaw set, hard enough to crack my teeth. Loyal to the end, Jierre. In his own fashion.

Adrien di Cinfiliet's laugh was a bitter bark. "You are passing strange, *sieur*. Off with you. I am certain that Pruzian will be about as well; he is a tick upon a deer's leg. Why she left him to nursemaid me, I have no—"

"She is thorough, our *d'mselle*. Safe dreaming, Adrien."

A low bitter laugh. "Gods be praised, you have finally unbent. Safe dreaming yourself, Jierre. Tomorrow we begin our thankless task."

"We? My only task is to keep your skin whole. To you lies the rest." Jierre's step, light and familiar, and the door swept creaking shut behind him.

I waited. The bed groaned as he settled upon it. The fire crackled.

"You may as well come out," Adrien di Cinfiliet said quietly.

So I did, cautiously pushing the curtain aside, my poniard ready. My boots touched the floor, and I braced myself—but the newly-crowned King merely sat on the edge of the bed, still in his white finery, and regarded me with his storm-gray gaze.

I faced the bastard son of the man I had killed. Lifted the poniard slightly, firelight playing along its freshly honed blade. "I should kill you." The truth was ash against my tongue. "Were I the man you think I am, I would."

I was that man, but I wish not to be.

He nodded slowly, his dark hair falling over his forehead. "No doubt. But a certain dark-eyed *d'mselle* would not look kindly upon such a deed."

The knife was too tempting. I sheathed it. "Are you satisfied?" I merely sounded curious. Perhaps twas the tightness in my chest that robbed my words of the weight I wished them to carry.

The Bandit King gave another sharp, bitter bark of a laugh. "You think I wished for this? I knew she was up to mischief, d'Arcenne. I did not expect to be snapped into traces and neatly put to plow. She laid her plans well, and outwitted us both."

I could almost believe you. "Where has she gone?"

"Were you not listening? *I do not know.* Amid the feasting and every man who can lay claim to being a soldier drunk and celebrating, who could find her?" He sagged, and I saw his exhaustion. "She said that had I need, I should send her this. But where to send it, she did not tell me. A riddle from *m'cousine* Riddlesharp, and one I cannot solve." A green gleam in his hand, carefully lifted. Twas an ear-drop, and I finally recognized it as hers. She had been wearing them the day the conspiracy was loosed.

Much became clear to me at once. *I shall send the other half as proof.*

If this was a message from my *d'mselle*, how could it be deciphered?

We regarded each other for a long while, the fire crackling and shifting. Sweat gathered on my back, dewed my brow.

Finally, some of the tension left me. I stalked across the Cell. He did not move, and when I took the ear-drop from his fingers I was surprised to find I did not wish to murder him.

At least, not at this moment. Perhaps not ever. Leaving him with a crown to wear and the Pruzian to nursemaid him was a far better revenge.

I backed up with a shuffle, a swordsman's move. The scar on my chest ached. I had not put it to much of a test. Perhaps twas the heart underneath that pained me so. My face twitched, its scar plucking at itself. "Someday, you may think she is a threat to you." Each word carefully enunciated, slow and quiet. "If that day should come to pass, remember only that I will be watching. As long as you do not seek to harm her, you are safe from me."

"I would not harm *her.*" He cocked his head, and the mocking expression was Henri's, down to the last line and quirk. "There is one thing, d'Arcenne. She left me a letter."

I waited.

"Tis burned now. But in it, she warned me that I would need a Left Hand."

Where in the Shirlstrienne could he have learned that delicate insinuation? The right note of velvet threat and dangling bait. A lure, perhaps, to make a hawk rise—and even in the forest, perhaps he had known something of hawking.

I swallowed dryly. "My thanks, Your Majesty. But I already serve." I paused on my way out the door. "The Pruzian isn't fit for it, and neither is Jierre. Try di Siguerre. His grandfather has already prepared him nicely."

And with that, I slid into the corridor, turned away from the guard posted at the end of the hall—they were inattentive, conversing with each other in hushed whispers—and slipped into darkness. I passed Fridrich van Harkke, hidden in a pool of deep shadow behind a moldering cupboard that had perhaps once held rapiers for the dueling-hall just past the next archway. He did not breathe as I ghosted by, and I did not turn or speed my step, though my back roughened with gooseflesh.

The Knife did not strike. I left the Palais an hour later, and by dawn I was outside the Citté.

Twas time to find my Queen.

Chapter Thirty-Nine

They gathered at their fires, bright-eyed and dark-haired, and the throbbing beat of their music rose as they finished their dinner. Bubbling, fragrant meat stew, different spices than an Arquitaine cook would use, woodsmoke, and the odor of difference and green hedgewitchery.

It had taken me weeks to track them.

After the feasting, the dishes were cleaned. Laughter rose among them, bright ribbons of their odd liquid language. Gold twinkled at ear and throat and wrist, thin golden rings and some of the dark women sporting thread-thin noserings. Splashing and jests, merriment and the cries of joyful younglings, then the central fire was carefully tended and the children soothed.

The instruments came forth. Gittern and tambour, pipes like wailing *demieri di sorce*, the rhythm driving and odd, burrowing into breath and bones and blood. Two lines of dancers, male and female like some of the maying dances, and the women's voices lifted.

Their dancing is strange, too. Flicker of hips, stamping sandals working into the dusty earth, arms held stiffly and eyes mostly lowered. There is no word for the grace, but the sway of their hips and the hitched-up skirts showing their ankles, their bare brown arms gleaming with gold and effort…it makes a man think of other dances.

The men, straight and tall, took up the challenge and danced forward. Pairs were formed, older married women calling from the sidelines. The older women are held to be experts, and their judgments accepted without question. Pairs retired, breathing quickly and taking swigs of their fiery clear *rhuma*, joining the on-lookers and adding their voices to the song. I touched the lump of my father's signet under my doublet and watched.

When one pair is left the music intensifies, and they are called upon to perform. They must provide a spectacle, and should they be judged insipid or unworthy of the honor, the mockery, while good-natured, is intense.

She stood at the edges, a shawl wrapped about her shoulders. The headman's wife, dark and lean, stood next to her, calling out advice and clapping her narrow brown hands. They conferred together like myrmyra birds, the way a Princesse and her lady-in-waiting might.

My chest ached, ached.

When next I peered out the tiny window, she was walking, head down and barefoot, her sandals swinging from one hand. She climbed the steps, lightly, and opened the wagon's cunningly designed door. Painted in red and gold, the small house-on-wheels was neat, and trim, and pulled by a pair of good-natured roans who were at the pickets, munching contentedly.

She hummed, a wandering melody threading through the thumping beat outside. Opened a tiny cabinet, standing on tiptoe, feeling for something in the darkness. She cursed under her breath, not finding what she sought, and swung the cabinet closed.

Court sorcery flashed. A candle guttered into life, and she swallowed her scream, clapping a hand over her mouth and staring at me.

I was, perhaps, not a comforting sight.

We regarded each other, Vianne and I. My back was to the hedgewitch-armoire built into one whole wall of the wagon, the bed at the far end, the scarves and skirts hung on pegs on the other wall. She had traded the Palais for these cramped quarters, and there was a book tangled in her bedclothes. A treatise by a Tiberian philosopher, a man who had given up the rule of his city and retreated to a farm, only to be slain when the king following him grew suspicious.

Was she reading for her future, then?

Finally, she dropped her hand. Her sandals dropped as well. Her hair, braided in loops over her ears as the R'mini women do, had pulled free and framed her face with curling tendrils. She had gained some little weight, and there were no shadows under her eyes.

Her throat worked as she swallowed. "Captain," she whispered.

"Vianne." I could not speak any louder.

She visibly gathered herself. I waited. "Is it…is it time?"

I realized what she was asking, and cursed myself for being lackwitted clear through. "'Tis time, Vianne, but not for what you think. I would not harm you."

She shook her head. "I…"

"How can you even *think* I would harm you?" Quietly, but with great force.

Her chin lifted a fraction. "I had…I must be sure. How did you…"

"I am a fool *for* you, *m'chri*. Not an idiot." I spread my hands slowly, so she could see what I held.

The ear-drop glowed in my palm. She inhaled sharply, and her gaze fluttered to my face, seeking to read whatever it could.

I wished her luck. I wished to be an open book to her. But would she ever know what language to read upon my features? "He is well, Vianne. You would have heard by now, were he not. We have come to an agreement, your bandit cousin and I."

"And I am unnecessary, now?" Her chin tilted up slightly, brave to the last.

"Not to me." I searched for the right thing to say. "I am not his Left Hand."

The breath left her in a rush. She had paled alarmingly. "Tristan…" A mere ghost of a word.

Finally. Not "Captain" or "sieur." I throttled the hope rising in me. "Do your R'mini pass near Arcenne, Vianne?"

"What?" She struggled to understand. Or perhaps to throttle the hope plainly visible on her features.

Finer than I deserved, as always. She hoped for my redemption, my Vianne. She had played her hand well, and freed us both. Except she could not unlock the chains of what I had been, and what I had done.

Not even the Blessed held that key. But if I could, if she let me, I would do my best to be the man I should have.

Unless it was too late. I cast my dice. "I would see my mother again. She would no doubt be glad to see your face as well. We may not stay in Arcenne. It could be…misconstrued. But over the mountains, to Navarrin…or, Tiberia. There is a house in *Citté Immortale*, ready to be filled with books."

"And if I do not wish to?" A swift, abortive movement, as if she wished to flee.

I pointed to her left hand. The copper marriage-band glittered as the music throbbed outside, yells rising as the pair dancing performed some sorcery that earned the approval of their audience.

"It seems I cannot rid myself of…" She lifted her hand slightly, gazed ruefully at the band. "Tris."

"You do not have to forgive me." The consciousness of lying struck me, quick and hard as a mailed fist. My pulse pounded in my ears. "I will not ask it of you." *That* was the truth. "If you tell me to go, I will. I will pass the remainder of the life the Blessed see fit to grant me in Arcenne, waiting for your call. I will even, do you require it of me, return to your *cousin* and safeguard his life with my own. I will trouble you no more. I am…sorry. It does not erase the ill, Vianne. I am worse than you can imagine. But I would be…better, if I could."

She hesitated. Did she wish to, she could scream. They would come running, her traveling-companions.

Her shoulders lifted. She stepped back, her hand searching for the door. I forced myself to stand mute, frozen, every scar I had gained in my life a map of fire and failure, the blackness in me rising as my hope drew back from me. I closed my eyes. Why were my cheeks wet? The scar on my face gathered a tear, hot salt water tracing a runnel down its seam.

There was a click. Slight creaking as her weight shifted.

Her fingertips touched my damp face. Slid down the scar she had gifted me, and twas a balm. Mercy for the desperate, hope for the hopeless.

She had locked the wagon's door.

"Tristan."

"Vianne." A whisper. I could not speak louder.

"If I am to trust you, there are things you must *do*."

"Anything." The word was merely a croaking prayer. *Please. If there is any mercy, let it be spent here.*

"No politics." Her voice caught. Was there summat caught in her throat, as there was a rock in mine? "No Queen, no Left Hand. No Court. No power, or position, or games of loyalty. No betrayal, no assassination, none of it. I will not have it. I cannot bear it. I have given up *everything*." She touched my lips. "Are you willing to be simply Tristan, as I am simply Vianne?"

I nodded, helpless. "That was all I ever wanted," I admitted. *D'Orlaans may show himself again, though. If he does, he will strike at you.* "Vianne—"

She covered my mouth, standing on tiptoe, her slender weight pressed against me and her soft palm a brand against my skin. "Hush."

I did. I found the courage to look at her again. No more burning in her gaze. Nothing but sadness and terrible knowledge. A burden I would ease, would share—if she would let me.

If she would *allow* it.

She bit her lower lip, and I longed to erase her uncertainty.

Finally, she reached yet another decision, and her face eased. She nodded, once, as if I had spoken. Perhaps she thought I had; perhaps my longing was a cry she could hear.

"Douse the candle," my hedgewitch said. "I will think of something to tell them in the morning."

A small golden flame winked out as the music crashed to its finish outside, and the cheers and laughter of the R'mini echoed, rising to the cold stars. She took me in her arms once more. And here I will cease, for what else that night held is not to be told to strangers, and the Left Hand is dead.

For now.

Glossary

Ansinthe: A venomous green liquor distilled from wyrmrithe

Aufsbar: (Prz.) Client

Blessed, the: (Arq.) The Twelve Gods of Arquitaine, six Old (indigenous) and six New (brought by the conqueror Angoulême)

Demiange: (Arq.) Sorcerous or half-divine spirit; many of them wait upon the gods in the Westron Halls

Demieri di sorce: (Arq.) Sorcerous spirits of night and mischief

D'mselle: (Arq.) Honorific, for a young woman

Festival of Sunreturn: One of the great cross-quarter festivals

G'ji g'jai: (R'm.) Foreign (lit. *Other*) whore

Hedgewitch: (Arq.) One who practices peasant sorcery

M'chri, m'cher: (Arq.) Beloved, dear one

M'dama: (Arq.) Honorific, for an older woman

Rhuma: A fiery clear liquor distilled from sucre

Sieur: (Arq.) Honorific, for a man

Valadka: A clear, very potent liquor

Vilhain: (Arq.) Bastard

extras

orbit

meet the author

Daron Gildow

Lilith Saintcrow was born in New Mexico, bounced around the world as an Air Force brat, and fell in love with writing when she was ten years old. She currently lives in Vancouver, Washington. Find her on the web at www.lilithsaintcrow.com.

introducing

If you enjoyed THE BANDIT KING,
look out for

THE IRON WYRM

Banon and Clare: Book One

by Lilith Saintcrow

Emma Bannon, Prime sorceress in the service of the Empire, has a mission: to protect Archibald Clare, a newly unregistered mentath. His skills of deduction are legendary, and her own sorcery is not inconsiderable. Yet it doesn't help much that they barely tolerate each other, or that Bannon's Shield, Mikal, might just be a traitor himself. Or that the conspiracy killing registered mentaths and sorcerers alike will just as likely kill them as seduce them into treachery toward their Queen.

In an alternate London where illogical magic has turned the Industrial Revolution on its head, Bannon and Clare now face hostility, treason, cannon fire, black sorcery, and the problem of reliably finding hansom cabs.

Chapter 1
A Pleasant Evening Ride

Emma Bannon, Sorceress Prime and servant to Britannia's current incarnation, mentally ran through every foul word that would never cross the lips of a lady. She timed them to the clockhorse's steady jogtrot, and her awareness dilated. The simmering cauldron of the streets was just as it always was; there was no breath of ill intent.

Of course, there had not been earlier, either, when she had been a quarter-hour too late to save the *other* unregistered mentath. It was only one of the many things about this situation seemingly designed to try her often considerable patience.

Mikal would be taking the rooftop road, running while she sat at ease in a hired carriage. It was the knowledge that while he did so he could forget some things that eased her conscience, though not completely.

Still, he was a Shield. He would not consent to share a carriage with her unless he was certain of her safety. And there was not room enough to manoeuvre in a two-person conveyance, should he require it.

She was heartily sick of hired carts. Her own carriages were *far* more comfortable, but this matter required discretion. Having it shouted to the heavens that she was alert to the pattern under these occurrences might not precisely frighten her opponents, but it would become more difficult to attack them from an unexpected quarter. Which was, she had to admit, her preferred method.

Even a Prime can benefit from guile, Llew had often remarked. And of course, she would think of him. She seemed constitutionally incapable of leaving well enough alone, and *that* irritated her as well.

Beside her, Clare dozed. He was a very thin man, with a long, mournful face; his gloves were darned but his waistcoat was of fine cloth, though it had seen better days. His eyes were blue, and they glittered feverishly under half-closed lids. An unregistered mentath would find it difficult to secure proper employment, and by the looks of his quarters, Clare had been suffering from boredom for several weeks, desperately seeking a series of experiments to exercise his active brain.

Mentath was like sorcerous talent. If not trained, and *used*, it turned on its bearer.

At least he had found time to shave, and he had brought two bags. One, no doubt, held linens. God alone knew what was in the second. Perhaps she should apply deduction to the problem, as if she did not have several others crowding her attention at the moment.

Chief among said problems were the murderers, who had so far eluded her efforts. Queen Victrix was young, and just recently freed from the confines of her domineering mother's sway. Her new Consort, Alberich, was a moderating influence–but he did not have enough power at Court just yet to be an effective shield for Britannia's incarnation.

The ruling spirit was old, and wise, but Her vessels…well, they were not indestructible.

And that, Emma told herself sternly, *is as far as we shall go with such a train of thought.* She found herself rubbing the sardonyx on her left middle finger, polishing it with her opposite thumb. Even through her thin gloves, the stone prickled hotly. Her posture did not change, but her awareness contracted. She felt for the source of the disturbance, flashing through and discarding a number of fine invisible threads.

Blast and bother. Other words, less polite, rose as well. Her pulse and respiration did not change, but she tasted a faint tang of adrenalin before sorcerous training clamped tight on such functions to free her from some of flesh's more…distracting…reactions.

"I say, whatever is the matter?" Archibald Clare's blue eyes were wide open now, and he looked interested. Almost, dare she think it, intrigued. It did nothing for his long, almost ugly features. His cloth was serviceable, though hardly elegant—one could infer that a mentath had other priorities than fashion, even if he had an eye for quality and the means to purchase such. But at least he was cleaner than he had been, and had arrived in the hansom in nine and a half minutes precisely. Now they were on Sarpesson Street, threading through amusement-seekers and those whom a little rain would not deter from their nightly appointments.

The disturbance peaked, and a not-quite-seen starburst of gunpowder igniting flashed through the ordered lattices of her consciousness.

The clockhorse screamed as his reins were jerked, and the hansom yawed alarmingly. Archibald Clare's hand dashed for the door handle, but Emma was already moving. Her arms closed around the tall, fragile man, and she shouted a Word that exploded the cab away from them both. Shards and splinters, driven outwards, peppered the street surface. The glass of the cab's tiny windows broke with a high, sweet tinkle, grinding into crystalline dust.

Shouts. Screams. Pounding footsteps. Emma struggled upright, shaking her skirts with numb hands. The horse had gone avast, rearing and plunging, throwing tiny metal slivers and dribs of oil as well as stray crackling sparks of sorcery, but the traces were tangled and it stood little chance of running loose. The driver was gone, and she snapped a quick glance at the overhanging rooftops before the unhealthy canine shapes resolved out of thinning rain, slinking low as gaslamp gleam painted their slick, heaving sides.

Sootdogs. Oh, how unpleasant. The one that had leapt on the hansom's roof had most likely taken the driver, and Emma cursed aloud now as it landed with a thump, its shining hide running with vapour.

"*Most* unusual!" Archibald Clare yelled. He had gained his feet as well, and his eyes were alight now. The mournfulness had vanished. He had also produced a queerly barrelled pistol, which would be of *no* use against the dog-shaped sorcerous things now gathering. "*Quite* diverting!"

The star sapphire on her right third finger warmed. A globe-shield shimmered into being, and to the roil of smouldering wood, gunpowder and fear was added another scent: the smoke-gloss of sorcery. One of the sootdogs leapt, crashing into the shield, and the shock sent Emma to her knees, holding grimly. Both her hands were outstretched now, and her tongue occupied in chanting.

Sarpesson Street was neither deserted nor crowded at this late hour. The people gathering to watch the outcome of a hansom crash pushed against those onlookers alert enough to note that something entirely different was occurring, and the resultant chaos was merely noise to be shunted aside as her concentration narrowed.

Where is Mikal?

She had no time to wonder further. The sootdogs hunched and wove closer, snarling. Their packed-cinder sides heaved and black tongues lolled between obsidian-chip teeth; they could strip a large adult male to bone in under a minute. There were the on-lookers to think of as well, and Clare behind and to her right, laughing as he sighted down the odd little pistol's chunky nose. Only he was not pointing it at the dogs, thank God. He was aiming for the rooftop.

You idiot. The chant filled her mouth. She could spare no words to tell him not to fire, that Mikal was—

The lead dog crashed against the shield. Emma's body jerked as the impact tore through her, but she held steady, the sapphire now a ringing blue flame. Her voice rose, a clear contralto, and she assayed the difficult rill of notes that would split her focus and make another Major Work possible.

That was part of what made a Prime–the ability to concentrate completely on multiple channellings of ætheric force. One's capacity could not be infinite, just like the charge of force carried and renewed every Tideturn.

But one did not need infinite capacity. *One needs only slightly more capacity than the problem at hand calls for*, as her third-form Sophological Studies professor had often intoned.

Mikal arrived.

His dark green coat fluttered as he landed in the midst of the dogs, a Shield's fury glimmering to Sight, bright spatters and spangles invisible to normal vision. The sorcery-made things cringed, snapping; his blades tore through their insubstantial hides. The charmsilver laid along the knives' flats, as well as the will to strike, would be of far more use than Mr Clare's pistol.

Which spoke, behind her, the ball tearing through the shield from a direction the protection wasn't meant to hold. The fabric of the shield collapsed, and Emma had just enough time to deflect the backlash, tearing a hole in the brick-faced fabric of the street and exploding the clockhorse into gobbets of metal and rags of flesh, before one of the dogs turned with stomach-churning speed and launched itself at her—and the man she had been charged to protect.

She shrieked another Word through the chant's descant, her hand snapping out again, fingers contorted in a gesture definitely *not* acceptable in polite company. The ray of ætheric force smashed through brick dust, destroying even more of the road's surface, and crunched into the sootdog.

Emma bolted to her feet, snapping her hand back, and the line of force followed as the dog crumpled, whining and shattering into fragments. She could not hold the forcewhip for very long, but if more of the dogs came—

The last one died under Mikal's flashing knives. He muttered something in his native tongue, whirled on his heel, and stalked toward his Prima. That normally meant the battle was finished.

Yet Emma's mind was not eased. She half turned, chant dying on her lips and her gaze roving, searching. Heard the mutter of the crowd, dangerously frightened. Sorcerous force pulsed and bled from her fingers, a fountain of crimson sparks popping against the rainy air. For a moment the mood of the crowd threatened to distract her, but she closed it away and concentrated, seeking the source of the disturbance.

Sorcerous traces glowed, faint and fading, as the man who had fired the initial shot—most likely to mark them for the dogs—fled. He had some sort of defence laid on him, meant to keep him from a sorcerer's notice.

Perhaps from a sorcerer, but not from a Prime. Not from me, oh no. The dead see all. Her Discipline was of the Black, and it was moments like these when she would be glad of its practicality–if she could spare the attention.

Time spun outwards, dilating, as she followed him over rooftops and down into a stinking alley, refuse piled high on each side, running with the taste of fear and blood in his mouth. Something had injured him.

Mikal? But then why did he not kill the man—

The world jolted underneath her, a stunning blow to her shoulder, a great spiked roil of pain through her chest. Mikal screamed, but she was breathless. Sorcerous force spilled free, uncontained, and other screams rose.

She could possibly injure someone.

Emma came back to herself, clutching at her shoulder. Hot blood welled between her fingers, and the green silk would be ruined. Not to mention her gloves.

At least they had shot her, and not the mentath.

Oh, damn. The pain crested again, became a giant animal with its teeth in her flesh.

Mikal caught her. His mouth moved soundlessly, and Emma sought with desperate fury to contain the force thundering through her. Backlash could cause yet more damage, to the street and to onlookers, if she let it loose.

A Prime's uncontrolled force was nothing to be trifled with.

It was the traditional function of a Shield to handle such overflow, but if he had only wounded the fellow on the roof she could not trust that he was not part of—

"*Let it GO!*" Mikal roared, and the ætheric bonds between them flamed into painful life. She fought it, seeking to contain what she could, and her skull exploded with pain.

She knew no more.

Chapter 2
Dreadful Aesthetics

This part of Whitehall was full of heavy graceless furniture, all the more shocking for the quality of its materials. Clare was no great arbiter of taste–fashion was largely useless frippery, unless it fuelled the deductions he could make about his fellow man–but he thought Miss Bannon would wince internally at the clutter here. One did not have to follow fashion to have a decent set of aesthetics.

So much of aesthetics was merely pain avoidance for those with any sensibilities.

Lord Cedric Grayson, the current Chancellor of the Exchequer, let out a heavy sigh, lowering his wide bulk into an overstuffed leather chair, perhaps custom-commissioned for his size. He had always been large and ruddy, and good dinners at his clubs had long ago begun to blur his outlines. Clare lifted his glass goblet, carefully. He did not like sherry even at the best of times.

Still, this was…*intriguing*.

"So far, you are the only mentath we've recovered." Grayson's great grizzled head dropped a trifle, as if he did not believe it himself. "Miss Bannon is extraordinary."

"She is also severely wounded." Clare sniffed slightly. And *cheap* sherry, as well, when Cedric could afford far better. It was obscene. But then, Grayson had always been a false economiser, even at Yton. *Penny wise, pound foolish*, as Mrs Ginn would sniff. "So. Someone is killing mentaths."

"Yes. Mostly registered ones, so far." The Chancellor's wide horseface was pale, and his greying hair slightly mussed from the pressure of a wig. It was late for them to be in Chambers, but if someone was stalking and killing registered mentaths, the entire Cabinet would be having a royal fit.

In more ways than one. Her Majesty's mentaths, rigorously trained and schooled at public expense, were extraordinarily useful in many areas of the Empire. *Britannia rests on the backs of sorcery and genius*, the saying went, and it was largely true. From calculating interest and odds to deducing and anticipating economic fluctuations, not to mention the ability to see the patterns behind military tactics, a mentath's work was varied and quite useful.

A *registered* mentath could take his pick of clients and cases. One unstable enough to be unregistered was less lucky. "Since I am not one of that august company at this date, perhaps I was not meant to be assassinated." Clare set the glass down and steepled his fingers. "I am not altogether certain I was the target of *this* attempt, either."

"Dear God, man." Grayson was wise enough not to ask what Clare based his statement on. This, in Clare's opinion, raised him above average intelligence. Of course, Grayson had not achieved his present position by being *completely* thickheaded, even if he was at heart a penny-pinching little pettifogger. "You're not suggesting Miss Bannon was the target?"

Clare's fingers moved, tapping against each other restlessly, precisely once. "I am *uncertain*. The attack was sorcerous *and* physical." For a moment his faculties strained at the corners of his memory of events.

He supposed he was lucky. Another mentath, confronted with the illogic of sorcery, might retreat into a comforting abstract structure, a dream of rationality meant to keep irrationality out. Fortunately, Archibald Clare was willing to admit to illogic–if only so far as the oddities of a complex structure he did not understand *yet*.

A mentath could not, strictly speaking, go mad. But he could *retreat*, and that retreat would make him unstable, rob him of experiential data and send him careening down a path of irrelevance and increasing isolation. The end of that road was a comfortable room in a well-appointed madhouse, if one was registered–and the poorhouse if one was not.

"If war is declared on sorcerers too…" Grayson shook his heavy, sweating head. Clear drops stood out on his forehead, and he gazed at Clare's sherry glass. His bloodshot blue eyes blinked once, sadly. "Her Majesty is most vexed."

Another pair of extraordinarily interesting statements. "Perhaps you should start at the beginning. We have some time while Miss Bannon is treated."

"It is exceedingly difficult to keep Miss Bannon down for any length of time." Grayson rubbed at his face with one meaty paw. "At any moment she will come stalking through that door in high dudgeon. Suffice to say there have been four of Her Majesty's registered geniuses recently lost to foul play."

"Four? How interesting." Clare settled more deeply into his chair, steepling his fingers before his long nose.

Grayson took a bracing gulp of sherry. "Interesting? *Disturbing* is the proper word. Tomlinson was the first to come to Miss Bannon's attention, found dead without a scratch in his parlour. Apoplexy was suspected; the attending forensic sorcerer had all but declared it. Miss Bannon had been summoned, as Crown representative, since Tomlinson had some rather ticklish matters to do research for, cryptography or the like. Well, Miss Bannon arrived, took one look at the mess, and accused the original sorcerer of incompetence, saying he had smeared traces and she could not rule out a bit of nastiness instead of disease. There was a scene."

"Indeed," Clare murmured. He found that exceedingly easy to believe. Miss Bannon did not seem the manner of woman to forgive incompetence of any stripe.

"Then there was Masters the Elder, and Peter Smythe on Rockway—Smythe had just arrived from Indus, a rather ticklish situation resolved there, I'm told. The most current is Throckmorton. Masters was shot on Picksadowne, Smythe stabbed in an alley off Nightmarket, and Throckmorton, poor chap, burned to death at his Grace Street address."

"And…?" Clare controlled his impatience. Why did they give him information so *slowly*?

"Miss Bannon found the fire at Throckmorton's sorcerous in origin. She is convinced the cases are connected. After Masters's misfortune, at Miss Bannon's insistence sorcerers were hastily sent to stand guard over every registered mentath. Smythe's sorcerer has disappeared. Throckmorton's…well, you'll see."

This was proving more and more diverting. Clare's eyebrow rose. "I will?"

"He's in Bedlam. No doubt you will wish to examine him."

"No doubt." The obvious question, however, was one he was interested in Grayson answering. "Why was I brought here? There must be other unregistereds eager for the chance to work."

"Well, you have been quite useful in Her Majesty's service. There's no doubt of that." Grayson paused, delicately. "There *is* the little matter of your registration. Not that I blamed you for it, quite a rum deal, that. Bring this matter to a satisfactory close, and…who can say?"

Ah. There was the sweet in the poison. Clare considered this.

"I gather Miss Bannon is just as insubordinate and intransigent as myself. And just as expendable in this current situation." He did not think Miss Bannon would be *expendable*, precisely.

But he did wish to see Cedric's reaction.

Grayson actually had the grace to flush. And cough. He kept glancing at Clare's sherry as if he longed to take a draught himself.

I thought he was more enamoured of port. Perhaps his tastes have changed. Clare shelved the idea, warmed to his theme. "Furthermore, the *registered* mentaths have been whisked to safety or are presumably at great risk, so time is of the essence and the need desperate—otherwise I would *still* be rotting at home, given the nature of my…mistakes. I further gather there have been corresponding deaths among those, like myself, so unfortunate as to be *unregistered* for one reason or another."

Grayson's flush deepened. Clare admitted he was enjoying himself. No, that was not quite correct. He was enjoying himself *immensely*. "How many?" he enquired.

"Well. That is, ahem." Grayson cleared his throat. "Let me be frank, Archibald."

Now the game truly begins. Clare brought all his faculties to bear, his concentration narrowing. "Please do be, Cedric."

"You are the only remaining unregistered mentath-class genius remaining alive in Londinium. The others…their bodies were savaged. Certain parts are…missing."

Archibald's fingers tightened, pressing against each other. "Ah." *Most interesting indeed.*

CPSIA information can be obtained at www.ICGtesting.com
Printed in the USA
LVOW081214100113

315168LV00001B/2/P